THE HEYDAY OF EMPIRE

In *Pebble in the Sky*, Trantor has long since established its supreme Empire and rules all the worlds of the Galaxy. The Galactic Empire is at the height of its power. But all is not peace. Neglected and despised, the Ancients of Earth have found a way to bring death to every other world in the Galaxy.

THE GALACTIC EMPIRE NOVELS

These three novels by Isaac Asimov show the development of the Galactic Empire, whose decay gave rise to the Foundation. They span the time from the first star kingdoms to the full flowering of the Empire that ruled all the Galaxy. Each is a complete, independent novel. Together they provide facts, history, and human developments that are often only hinted at in the Foundation Series. Much of the material in the bestselling *Foundation's Edge* derives directly from background material to be found in these marvelous precursor novels.

ISAAC ASIMOV

PEBBLE IN THE SKY

A Galactic Empire Novel

A DEL REY BOOK

BALLANTINE BOOKS • NEW YORK

CONTENTS

1. BETWEEN ONE FOOTSTEP AND THE NEXT

Two minutes before he disappeared forever from the face of the Earth he knew, Joseph Schwartz strolled along the pleasant streets of suburban Chicago quoting Browning to himself.

In a sense this was strange, since Schwartz would scarcely have impressed any casual passer-by as the Browning-quoting type. He looked exactly what he was: a retired tailor, thoroughly lacking in what the sophisticates of today call a "formal education." Yet he had expended much of an inquisitive nature upon random reading. By the sheer force of indiscriminate voracity, he had gleaned a smattering of practically everything, and by means of a trick memory had managed to keep it all straight.

For instance, he had read Robert Browning's *Rabbi Ben Ezra* twice when he was younger, so, of course, knew it by heart. Most of it was obscure to him, but those first three lines had become one with the beating of his heart these last few years. He intoned them to himself, deep within the silent fortress of his mind, that very sunny and very bright early summer day of 1949:

> "Grow old along with me!
> The best is yet to be,
> The last of life, for which the first was made..."

Schwartz felt that to its fullness. After the struggles of youth in Europe and those of his early manhood in the United States, the serenity of a comfortable old age was pleasant. With a house of his own and money of his own, he could, and did, retire. With a wife in good health, two daughters safely married, a grandson to soothe these last best years, what had he to worry about?

There was the atom bomb, of course, but Schwartz was a believer in the goodness of human nature. He didn't think there would be another war. He didn't think Earth would ever see again the sunlike hell of an atom exploded in anger. So he smiled tolerantly at the children he passed and silently wished them a speedy and not too difficult ride through youth to the peace of the best that was yet to be.

He lifted his foot to step over a Raggedy Ann doll smiling through its neglect as it lay there in the middle of the walk, a foundling not yet missed. He had not quite put his foot down again...

In another part of Chicago stood the Institute for Nuclear Research, in which men may have had theories upon the essential worth of human nature but were half ashamed of them, since no quantitative instrument had yet been designed to measure it. When they thought about it, it was often enough to wish that some stroke from heaven would prevent human nature (and damned human ingenuity) from turning every innocent and interesting discovery into a deadly weapon.

Yet, in a pinch, the same man who could not find it in his conscience to curb his curiosity into the nuclear studies that might someday kill half of Earth would risk his life to save that of an unimportant fellow man.

It was the blue glow behind the chemist's back that first attracted the attention of Dr. Smith.

He peered at it as he passed the half-open door. The chemist, a cheerful youngster, was whistling as he tipped up a volumetric flask, in which the solution had already been made up to volume. A white powder tumbled lazily through the liquid, dissolving in its own good time. For a moment that was all, and then Dr. Smith's instinct, which had stopped him in the first place, stirred him to action.

He dashed inside, snatched up a yardstick, and swept the contents of the desk top to the floor. There was the deadly hiss of molten metal. Dr. Smith felt a drop of perspiration slip to the end of his nose.

The youngster stared blankly at the concrete floor along which the silvery metal had already frozen in thin splash marks. They still radiated heat strongly.

He said faintly, "What happened?"

Dr. Smith shrugged. He wasn't quite himself either. "I don't know. You tell me.... What's been doing here?"

"Nothing's been doing here," the chemist yammered. "That was just a sample of crude uranium. I'm making an electrolytic copper determination.... I don't know what could have happened."

"Whatever happened, young man, I can tell you what I saw. That platinum crucible was showing a corona. Heavy radiation was taking place. Uranium, you say?"

"Yes, but *crude* uranium, and that isn't dangerous. I mean, extreme purity is one of the most important qualifications for fission, isn't it?" He touched his tongue to his lips quickly. "Do you think it was fission, sir? It's not plutonium, and it wasn't being bombarded."

"And," said Dr. Smith thoughtfully, "it was below the critical mass even if it were pure." He stared at the soapstone desk, at the burned and blistered paint of the cabinets and the silvery streaks along the concrete floor. "Yet uranium melts at about 1800 degrees Centigrade, and nuclear phenomena are not so well known that we can afford to talk too glibly. After all, this place must be fairly saturated with stray radiations. When the metal cools, young man, it had better be chipped up, collected, and thoroughly analyzed."

He gazed thoughtfully about him, then stepped to the opposite wall and felt uneasily at a spot about shoulder height.

"What's this?" he said to the chemist. "Has this always been here?"

"What, sir?" The young man stepped up nervously and glanced at the spot the older man indicated. It was a tiny hole, one that might have been made by a thin nail driven into the wall and withdrawn—but driven through plaster and brick for the full thickness of the building's wall, since daylight could be seen through it.

The chemist shook his head, "I never saw that before. But I never looked for it, either, sir."

Dr. Smith said nothing. He stepped back slowly and passed the thermostat, a parallelopiped of a box made out of thin sheet iron. The water in it moved swirlingly as the stirrer turned in motor-driven monomania, while the electric bulbs beneath the water, serving as heaters, flicked on and off distractingly, in time with the clicking of the mercury relay.

"Well, then, was this here?" And Dr. Smith scraped gently with his fingernail at a spot near the top of the wide side of the thermostat. It was a neat, tiny circle drilled through the metal. The water did not quite reach it.

The chemist's eyes widened. "No, sir, that *wasn't* there ever before. I'll guarantee that."

"Hmm. Is there one on the other side?"

"Well, I'll be damned. I mean, yes, sir!"

"All right, come round here and sight through the holes.... Shut the thermostat off, please. Now stay there." He placed his finger on the hole in the wall. "What do you see?" he called out.

"I see your finger, sir. Is that where the hole is?"

Dr. Smith did not answer. He said, with a calmness he was far from feeling, "Sight through in the other direction.... Now what do you see?"

"Nothing now."

"But that's the place where the crucible with the uranium was standing. You're looking at the exact place, aren't you?"

Reluctantly, "I think so, sir."

Dr. Smith said frostily, with a quick glance at the name plate on the still-open door, "Mr. Jennings, this is absolutely top-secret. I don't want you ever to speak about this to anyone. Do you understand?"

"Absolutely, sir!"

"Then let's get out of here. We'll send in the radiation men to check the place, and you and I will spend a siege in the infirmary."

"Radiation burns, you mean?" The chemist paled.

"We'll find out."

But there were no serious signs of radiation burns in either. Blood counts were normal and a study of the hair roots revealed nothing. The nausea that developed was eventually tabbed as psychosomatic and no other symptoms appeared.

Nor, in all the Institute, was anyone found, either then or in the future, to explain why a crucible of crude uranium, well below critical size, and under no direct neutronic bombardment, should suddenly melt and radiate that deadly and significant corona.

The only conclusion was that nuclear physics had queer and dangerous crannies left in it.

Yet Dr. Smith never brought himself to tell all the truth in the report he eventually prepared. He made no mention of the holes in the laboratory, no mention of the fact that the one nearest the spot where the crucible had been was barely visible, the one on the other side of the thermostat was a trace larger, while the one in the wall, three times as far away from that fearful spot, could have had a nail thrust through it.

A beam expanding in a straight line could travel several miles before the Earth's curvature made the surface fall away from it sufficiently to prevent further damage, and then it would be ten feet across. After that, flashing emptily into space, expanding and weakening, a queer strain in the fabric of the cosmos.

He never told anyone of that fancy.

He never told anyone that he called for the morning papers next day, while still in the infirmary, and searched the columns with a definite purpose in mind.

But so many people in a giant metropolis disappear every day. And nobody had gone screaming to the police with vague tales of how, before his eyes, a man (or would it be half a man?) had disappeared. At least no such case was reported.

Dr. Smith forced forgetfulness, eventually.

To Joseph Schwartz it had happened between one step and the next. He had lifted his right foot to clear the Raggedy Ann doll and for a moment he had felt dizzy—as though for the merest trifle of time a whirlwind had lifted him and turned him inside out. When he placed his right foot down again, all the breath went out of him in a gasp and he felt himself slowly crumple and slide down to the grass.

He waited a long time with his eyes closed—and then he opened them.

It was true! He was sitting on grass, where previously he had been walking on concrete.

The houses were gone! The white houses, each with its lawn, squatting there, row, on row, all gone!

And it was not a lawn he was sitting on, for the grass was growing rank, untended, and there were trees about, many of them, with more on the horizon.

That was when the worst shock of all came, because the leaves on those trees were ruddy, some of them, and in the curve of his hand he felt the dry brittleness of a dead leaf. He was a city man, but he knew autumn when he saw it.

Autumn! Yet when he had lifted his right foot it had been a June day, with everything a fresh and glistening green.

He looked toward his feet automatically as he thought that and, with a sharp cry, reached toward them. . . . The little cloth doll that he had stepped over, a little breath of reality, a——

Well, no! He turned it over in his trembling hands, and it was not whole. Yet it was not mangled; it was sliced. Now wasn't that queer! Sliced lengthwise very neatly, so that the waste-yarn stuffing wasn't stirred a hair. It lay there in interrupted threads, ending flatly.

The glitter on his left shoe caught Schwartz's eye. Still clutching the doll, he forced his foot over his raised knee. The extreme tip of the sole, the part that extended forward past the uppers, was smoothly sliced off. Sliced off as no earthly knife in the hand of an earthly cobbler could have duplicated. The fresh surface gleamed almost liquidly in its unbelievable smoothness.

Schwartz's confusion had reached up from his spinal cord and touched the cerebrum, where it finally froze him with horror.

At last, because even the sound of his own voice was a soothing element in a world otherwise completely mad, he spoke aloud. The voice he heard was low and tense and panting.

He said, "In the first place, I'm not crazy. I feel inside just the way I've always felt. . . . Of course, if maybe I were crazy, I wouldn't know it, or would I? No——" Inside, he felt the hysteria rise and forced it down. "There must be something else possible."

He considered, "A dream, maybe? How can I tell if it's a dream or not?" He pinched himself and felt the nip, but shook his head. "I can always dream I feel a pinch. That's no proof."

He looked about him despairingly. Could dreams be so clear, so detailed, so lasting? He had read once that most dreams last not more than five seconds, that they are induced by trifling disturbances to the sleeper, that the apparent length of the dreams is an illusion.

Cold comfort! He shifted the cuff of his shirt upward and stared at his wrist watch. The second hand turned and turned and turned. If it were a dream, the five seconds was going to stretch madly.

He looked away and wiped futilely at the cold dampness of his forehead. "What about amnesia?"

He did not answer himself, but slowly buried his head in both hands.

If he had lifted his foot and, as he did so, his mind had slipped the well-worn and well-oiled tracks it had followed so faithfully for so long...If three months later, in the autumn, or a year and three months later, or ten years and three months later, he had put his foot down in this strange place, just as his mind returned...Why, it would seem a single step, and all this...Then where had he been and what had he done in the interval?

"No!" The word came out in a loud cry. That couldn't be! Schwartz looked at his shirt. It was the one he had put on that morning, or what should have been that morning, and it was a fresh shirt. He bethought himself, plunged a fist into his jacket pocket, and brought out an apple.

He bit into it wildly. It was fresh and still had a lingering coolness from the refrigerator which had held it two hours earlier—or what should have been two hours.

And the little rag doll, what about that?

He felt himself beginning to go wild. It had to be a dream, or he really was insane.

It struck him that the time of day had changed. It was late afternoon, or at least the shadows were lengthening. The quiet desolation of the place flooded down upon him suddenly and freezingly.

He lurched to his feet. Obviously he would have to find people, any people. And, as obviously, he would have to find a house, and the best way to do that would be to find a road.

Automatically he turned in the direction in which the trees seemed thinnest, and walked.

The slight chill of evening was creeping inside his jacket and the tops of the trees were becoming dim and forbidding when he came upon that straight and impersonal streak of macadam. He lunged toward it with sobbing gratitude and loved the feel of the hardness beneath his feet.

But along either direction was absolute emptiness, and

for a moment he felt the cold clutch again. He had hoped for cars. It would have been the easiest thing to wave them down and say—he said it aloud in his eagerness—"Going toward Chicago, maybe?"

What if he was nowhere near Chicago? Well, any large city; anyplace he could reach a telephone line. He had only four dollars and twenty-seven cents in his pocket, but there was always the police . . .

He was walking along the highway, walking along the middle, watching in both directions. The setting of the sun made no impression upon him, or the fact that the first stars were coming out.

No cars. Nothing! And it was getting to be really dark.

He thought that first dizziness might be coming back, because the horizon at his left glimmered. Through the gaps in the trees there was a cold blue shine. It was not the leaping red he imagined a forest fire would be like, but a faint and creeping glow. And the macadam beneath his feet seemed to sparkle ever so faintly. He bent down to touch it, and it felt normal. But there was that tiny glimmer that caught the edges of his eyes.

He found himself running wildly along the highway, his shoes thudding in blunt and uneven rhythm. He was conscious of the damaged doll in his hand and he tossed it wildly over his head.

Leering, mocking remnant of life . . .

And then he stopped in a panic. Whatever it was, it was a proof of his sanity. And he needed it! So he felt about in the darkness, crawling on his knees till he found it, a dark patch on the ultra-faint glow. The stuffing was plumping out and, absently, he forced it back.

He was walking again—too miserable to run, he told himself.

He was getting hungry and really, really frightened when he saw that spark to the right.

It was a house, of course!

He shouted wildly and no one answered, but it was a house, a spark of reality blinking at him through the horrible, nameless wilderness of the last hours. He turned off the road and went plunging cross-country, across ditches, around trees, through the underbrush, and over a creek.

Queer thing! Even the creek glowed phosphorescently! But it was only the tiniest fragment of his mind that noted it.

Then he was there, with his hands reaching out to touch the hard white structure. It was neither brick nor stone nor wood, but he never paid that the least mind. It looked like a dull, strong porcelain, but he didn't give a hoot. He was just looking for a door, and when he came to it and saw no bell, he kicked at it and yelled like a demon.

He heard the stirring inside and the blessed, lovely sound of a human voice other than his own. He yelled again.

"Hey, in there!"

There was a faint, oiled whir, and the door opened. A woman emerged, a spark of alarm in her eyes. She was tall and wiry, and behind her was the gaunt figure of a hard-faced man in work clothes. . . . No, not work clothes. Actually they were like nothing Schwartz had ever seen, but, in some indefinable way, they looked like the kind of clothes men worked in.

But Schwartz was not analytical. To him they, and their clothes, were beautiful; beautiful only as the sight of friends to a man alone can be beautiful.

The woman spoke and her voice was liquid, but peremptory, and Schwartz reached for the door to keep himself upright. His lips moved, uselessly, and, in a rush, all the clammiest fears he had known returned to choke his windpipe and stifle his heart.

For the woman spoke in no language Schwartz had ever heard.

2. THE DISPOSAL OF A STRANGER

Loa Maren and her stolid husband, Arbin, played cards in the cool of the same evening, while the older man in the motor-driven wheel chair in the corner rustled his newspaper angrily and called, "Arbin!"

Arbin Maren did not answer at once. He fingered the thin, smooth rectangles carefully as he considered the next play. Then, as he slowly made a decision, he responded with an absent, "What do you want, Grew?"

The grizzled Grew regarded his son-in-law fiercely over the top of the paper and rustled it again. He found noise of that sort a great relief to his feelings. When a man teems with energy and finds himself spiked to a wheel chair with two dead sticks for legs, there must be something, by Space, he can do to express himself. Grew used his newspaper. He rustled it; he gestured with it; when necessary, he swatted at things with it.

Elsewhere than on Earth, Grew knew, they had telenews machines that issued rolls of microfilm as servings of current

11

news. Standard book viewers were used for them. But Grew
sneered silently at that. An effete and degenerate custom!

Grew said, "Did you read about the archaeological expedition they're sending to Earth?"

"No, I haven't," said Arbin calmly.

Grew knew that, since nobody but himself had seen the
paper yet, and the family had given up their video last year.
But then his remark had simply been in the nature of an
opening gambit, anyway.

He said, "Well, there's one coming. And on an Imperial
grant, too, and how do you like that?" He began reciting
in the queer unevenness of tone that most people somehow
assume automatically when reading aloud, "'Bel Arvardan,
Senior Research Associate at the Imperial Archaeological
Institute, in an interview granted the Galactic Press, spoke
hopefully of the expected valuable results of archaeological
studies which are being projected upon the planet Earth,
located on the outskirts of the Sirius Sector (see map).
"Earth," he said, "with its archaic civilization and its unique
environment, offers a freak culture which has been too long
neglected by our social scientists, except as a difficult ex-
ercise in local government. I have every expectation that
the next year or two will bring about revolutionary changes
in some of our supposed fundamental concepts of social
evolution and human history."' And so on and so on," he
finished with a flourish.

Arbin Maren had been listening with only half an ear.
He mumbled, "What does he mean, 'freak culture'?"

Loa Maren hadn't been listening at all. She simply said,
"It's your play, Arbin."

Grew went on, "Well, aren't you going to ask me why
the *Tribune* printed it? You know they wouldn't print a
Galactic Press release for a million Imperial Credits without
a good reason."

He waited uselessly for an answer, then said, "Because
they have an editorial on it. A full-page editorial that blasts
the living daylights out of this guy Arvardan. Here's a fellow
wants to come here for scientific purposes and they're choking themselves purple to keep him out. Look at this piece

of rabble-rousing. Look at it!" He shook the paper at them. "Read it, why don't you?"

Loa Maren put down her cards and clamped her thin lips firmly together. "Father," she said, "we've had a hard day, so let's not have politics just now. Later, maybe, eh? Please, Father."

Grew scowled and mimicked, "'Please, Father! Please, Father.' It appears to me you must be getting pretty tired of your old father when you begrudge him a few quiet words on current events. I'm in your way, I suppose, sitting here in the corner and letting you two work for three.... Whose fault is it? I'm strong. I'm willing to work. And you know I could get my legs treated and be as well as ever." He slapped them as he spoke: hard, savage, ringing slaps, which he heard but did not feel. "The only reason I can't is because I'm getting too old to make a cure worth their while. Don't you call that a 'freak culture'? What else could you call a world where a man can work but they won't let him? By the Stars, I think it's about time we stopped this nonsense about our so-called 'peculiar institutions.' They're not just peculiar; they're *cracked*! I think——"

He was waving his arms and angry blood was reddening his face.

But Arbin had risen from his chair, and his grip was strong on the older man's shoulder. He said, "Now where's the call to be upset, Grew? When you're through with the paper, I'll read the editorial."

"Sure, but you'll agree with them, so what's the use? You young ones are a bunch of milksops; just sponge rubber in the hands of the Ancients."

And Loa said sharply, "Quiet, Father. Don't start *that*." She sat there listening for a moment. She could not have said exactly what for, but...

Arbin felt that cold little prickle that always came when the Society of Ancients was mentioned. It just wasn't safe to talk as Grew did, to mock Earth's ancient culture, to—to——

Why, it was rank Assimilationism. He swallowed earnestly; the word was an ugly one, even when confined to thought.

Of course in Grew's youth there had been much of this foolish talk of abandoning the old ways, but these were different times. Grew should know that—and he probably did, except that it wasn't easy to be reasonable and sensible when you were in a wheel-chair prison, just waiting away your days for the next Census.

Grew was perhaps the least affected, but he said no more. And as the moments passed he grew quieter and the print became progressively more difficult to place in focus. He had not yet had time to give the sports pages a detailed and critical perusal when his nodding head lolled slowly down upon his chest. He snored softly, and the paper fell from his fingers with a final, unintentional rustle.

Then Loa spoke, in a worried whisper. "Maybe we're not being kind to him, Arbin. It's a hard life for a man like Father. It's like being dead compared to the life he used to lead."

"Nothing's like being dead, Loa. He has his papers and his books. Let him be! A bit of excitement like this peps him up. He'll be happy and quiet for days now."

Arbin was beginning to consider his cards again, and as he reached for one the pounding at the door sounded, with hoarse yells that didn't quite coalesce into words.

Arbin's hand lurched and stopped. Loa's eyes grew fearful; she stared at her husband with a trembling lower lip.

Arbin said, "Get Grew out of here. Quickly!"

Loa was at the wheel chair as he spoke. She made soothing sounds with her tongue.

But the sleeping figure gasped, startled awake at the first motion of the chair. He straightened and groped automatically for his paper.

"What's the matter?" he demanded irritably, and by no means in a whisper.

"Shh. It's *all* right," muttered Loa vaguely, and wheeled the chair into the next room. She closed the door and placed her back against it, thin chest heaving as her eyes sought those of her husband. There was that pounding again.

They stood close to each other as the door opened, almost defensively so, and hostility peeped from them as they faced the short, plump man who smiled faintly at them.

Loa said, "Is there anything we can do for you?" with a ceremonial courtesy, then jumped back as the man gasped and put out a hand to stop himself from falling.

"Is he sick?" asked Arbin bewilderedly. "Here, help me take him inside."

The hours after that passed, and in the quiet of their bedroom Loa and Arbin prepared slowly for bed.

"Arbin," said Loa.

"What is it?"

"Is it safe?"

"Safe?" He seemed to avoid her meaning deliberately.

"I mean, taking this man into the house. Who is he?"

"How should I know?" was the irritated response. "But, after all, we can't refuse shelter to a sick man. Tomorrow, if he lacks identification, we'll inform the Regional Security Board, and that will be the end of it." He turned away in an obvious attempt at breaking off the conversation.

But his wife broke the returning silence, her thin voice more urgent. "You don't think he might be an agent of the Society of Ancients, do you? There's Grew, you know."

"You mean because of what he said tonight? That's past the limit of reason. I won't argue about it."

"I don't mean that, and you know it. I mean that we've been keeping Grew illegally now for two years, and you know we're breaking just about the most serious Custom."

Arbin muttered, "We're harming no one. We're filling our quota, aren't we, even though it's set for three people— three *workers*? And if we are, why should they suspect anything? We don't even let him out of the house."

"They might trace the wheel chair. You had to buy the motor and fittings outside."

"Now don't start that again, Loa. I've explained many times that I've bought nothing but standard kitchen equipment for that chair. Besides, it does not make any sense at all to consider him an agent of the Brotherhood. Do you suppose that they would go through such an elaborate trick-

ery for the sake of a poor old man in a wheel chair? Couldn't
they enter by daylight and with legal search warrants? Please,
reason this thing out."

"Well, then, Arbin"—her eyes were suddenly bright and
eager—"if you really think so—and I've been so hoping
you would—he must be an Outsider. He *can't* be an Earthman."

"What do you mean, he can't be? That's more ridiculous
still. Why should a man of the Empire come here to Earth,
of all places?"

"I don't know why! Yes, I do; maybe he's committed a
crime out there." She was caught up instantly in her own
fancy. "Why not? It makes sense. Earth would be the natural
place to come to. Who would ever think of looking for him
here?"

"*If* he's an Outsider. What evidence do you have for
that?"

"He doesn't speak the language, does he? You'll have
to grant me that. Could you understand a single word? So
he *must* come from some far-off corner of the Galaxy where
the dialect is strange. They say the men of Fomalhaut have
to learn practically a new language to be understood at the
Emperor's court on Trantor. . . . But don't you see what all
this can mean? If he's a stranger on Earth, he will have no
registration with the Census Board, and he will be only too
glad to avoid reporting to them. We can use him on the
farm, in the place of Father, and it will be three people
again, not two, who will have to meet the quota for three
this next season. . . . He could even help with the harvest
now."

She looked anxiously at the uncertain face of her husband, who considered long, then said, "Well, go to bed,
Loa. We'll speak further in the common sense of daylight."

The whispering ended, the light was put out, and eventually sleep filled the room and the house.

The next morning it was Grew's turn to consider the
matter. Arbin put the question to him hopefully. He felt a
confidence in his father-in-law that he could not muster in
himself.

Grew said, "Your troubles, Arbin, obviously arise from the fact that I am registered as a worker, so that the produce quota is set at three. I'm tired of creating trouble. This is the second year I have lived past my time. It is enough."

Arbin was embarrassed. "Now that wasn't the point at all. I'm not hinting that you're a trouble to us."

"Well, after all, what's the difference? In two years there will be the Census, and I will go anyway."

"At least you will have two more years of your books and your rest. Why should you be deprived of that?"

"Because others are. And what of you and Loa? When they come to take me, they will take you two as well. What kind of a man would I be to live a few stinking years at the expense——"

"Stop it, Grew. I don't want histrionics. We've told you many times what we're going to do. We'll report you a week before the Census."

"And fool the doctor, I suppose?"

"We'll bribe the doctor."

"Hmp. And this new man—he'll double the offense. You'll be concealing him too."

"We'll turn him loose. For Earth's sake, why bother about this now? We have two years. What shall we do with him?"

"A stranger," mused Grew. "He comes knocking at the door. He's from nowhere. He speaks unintelligibly.... I don't know what to advise."

The farmer said, "He is mild-mannered; seems frightened to death. He can't do us any harm."

"Frightened, eh? What if he's feeble-minded? What if his babbling isn't a foreign dialect at all, but just insane mouthing?"

"That doesn't sound likely." But Arbin stirred uneasily.

"You tell yourself that because you want to use him.... All right, I'll tell you what to do. Take him into town."

"To Chica?" Arbin was horrified. "That would be ruin."

"Not at all," said Grew calmly. "The trouble with you is that you don't read the newspapers. Fortunately for this family, I do. It so happens that the Institute for Nuclear

Research has developed an instrument that is supposed to make it easier for people to learn. There was a full-page spread in the Week-end Supplement. And they want volunteers. Take this man. Let him be a volunteer."

Arbin shook his head firmly. "You're mad. I couldn't do anything like that, Grew. They'll ask for his registration number first thing. It's only inviting investigation to have things in improper order, and then they'll find out about you."

"No, they won't. It so happens you're all wrong, Arbin. The reason the Institute wants volunteers is that the machine is still experimental. It's probably killed a few people, so I'm sure they won't ask questions. And if the stranger dies, he'll probably be no worse off than he is now.... Here, Arbin, hand me the book projector and set the mark at reel six. And bring me the paper as soon as it comes, will you?"

When Schwartz opened his eyes, it was past noon. He felt that dull, heart-choking pain that feeds on itself, the pain of a wife no longer by his side at waking, of a familiar world lost . . .

Once before he had felt such a pain, and that momentary flash of memory came, lighting up a forgotten scene into sharp brilliance. There was himself, a youngster, in the snow of the wintry village . . . with the sleigh waiting . . . at the end of whose journey would be the train . . . and, after that, the great ship . . .

The longing, frustrating fear for the world of the familiar united him for the moment with that twenty-year-old who had emigrated to America.

The frustration was too real. This could not be a dream.

He jumped up as the light above the door blinked on and off and the meaningless baritone of his host sounded. Then the door opened and there was breakfast—a mealy porridge that he did not recognize but which tasted faintly like corn mush (with a savory difference) and milk.

He said, "Thanks," and nodded his head vigorously.

The farmer said something in return and picked up Schwartz's shirt from where it hung on the back of the chair. He inspected it carefully from all directions, paying particular attention to the buttons. Then, replacing it, he flung open the sliding door of a closet, and for the first time Schwartz became visually aware of the warm milkiness of the walls.

"Plastic," he muttered to himself, using that all-inclusive word with the finality laymen always do. He noted further that there were no corners or angles in the room, all planes fading into each other at a gentle curve.

But the other was holding objects out toward him and was making gestures that could not be mistaken. Schwartz obviously was to wash and dress.

With help and directions, he obeyed. Except that he found nothing with which to shave, nor could gestures to his chin elicit anything but an incomprehensible sound accompanied by a look of distinct revulsion on the part of the other. Schwartz scratched at his gray stubble and sighed windily.

And then he was led to a small, elongated, biwheeled car, into which he was ordered by gestures. The ground sped beneath them and the empty road moved backward on either side, until low, sparkling white buildings rose before him, and there, far ahead, was the blue water.

He pointed eagerly. "Chicago?"

It was the last gasp of hope within him, for certainly nothing he ever saw looked less like that city.

The farmer made no answer at all.

And the last hope died.

3. ONE WORLD—OR MANY?

Bel Arvardan, fresh from his interview with the press, on the occasion of his forthcoming expedition to Earth, felt at supreme peace with all the hundred million star systems that composed the all-embracing Galactic Empire. It was no longer a question of being known in this sector or that. Let his theories concerning Earth be proven and his reputation would be assured on every inhabited planet of the Milky Way, on every planet that Man had set foot through the hundreds of thousands of years of expansion through space.

These potential heights of renown, these pure and rarefied intellectual peaks of science were coming to him early, yet not easily. He was scarcely thirty-five, but already his career had been packed with controversy. It had begun with an explosion that had rocked the halls of the University of Arcturus when he first graduated as Senior Archaeologist from that institution at the unprecedented age of twenty-three. The explosion—no less effective for being immaterial—consisted of the rejection for publication, on the part of the *Journal of the Galactic Archaeological Society*, of his Senior Dissertation. It was the first time in the history of the university that a Senior Dissertation had been rejected. It was equally the first time in the history of that staid professional journal that a rejection had been couched in such blunt terms.

To a non-archaeologist, the reason for such anger against an obscure and dry little pamphlet, entitled *On the Antiquity of Artifacts in the Sirius Sector with Considerations of the Application Thereof to the Radiaton Hypothesis of Human Origin*, might seem mysterious. What was involved, however, was that from the first Arvardan adopted as his own the hypothesis advanced earlier by certain groups of mystics who were more concerned with metaphysics than with archaeology; *i.e.*, that Humanity had originated upon some single planet and had radiated by degrees throughout the Galaxy. This was a favorite theory of the fantasy writers of the day, and the bête noire of every respectable archaeologist of the Empire.

But Arvardan became a force to be reckoned with by even the most respectable, for within the decade he had become the recognized authority on the relics of the pre-Empire cultures still left in the eddies and quiet backwaters of the Galaxy.

For instance, he had written a monograph on the mechanistic civilization of the Rigel Sector, where the development of robots created a separate culture that persisted for centuries, till the very perfection of the metal slaves reduced the human initiative to the point where the vigorous fleets of the War Lord, Moray, took easy control. Orthodox archaeology insisted on the evolution of Human types independently on various planets and used such atypical cultures, as that on Rigel, as examples of race differences that had not yet been ironed out through intermarriage. Arvardan destroyed such concepts effectively by showing that Rigellian robot culture was but a natural outgrowth of the economic and social forces of the times and of the region.

Then there were the barbarous worlds of Ophiuchus, which the orthodox had long upheld as samples of primitive

Humanity not yet advanced to the stage of interstellar travel. Every textbook used those worlds as the best evidence of the Merger Theory; *i.e.*, that Humanity was the natural climax of evolution on any world based upon a water-oxygen chemistry with proper intensities of temperature and gravitation; that each independent strain of Humanity could intermarry; that with the discovery of interstellar travel, such intermarriage took place.

Arvardan, however, uncovered traces of the early civilization that had preceded the then thousand-year-old barbarism of Ophiuchus and proved that the earliest records of the planet showed traces of interstellar trade. The final touch came when he demonstrated beyond any doubt that Man had emigrated to the region in an already civilized state.

It was after that that the *J. Gal. Arch. Soc.* (to give the *Journal* its professional abbreviation) decided to print Arvardan's Senior Dissertation more than ten years after it had been presented.

And now the pursuit of his pet theory led Arvardan to probably the least significant planet of the Empire—the planet called Earth.

Arvardan landed at that one spot of Empire on all Earth, that patch among the desolate heights of the plateaus north of the Himalayas. There where radioactivity was not, and never had been, there gleamed a palace that was not of Terrestrial architecture. In essence it was a copy of the viceregal palaces that existed on more fortunate worlds. The soft lushness of the grounds was built for comfort. The forbidding rocks had been covered with topsoil, watered, immersed in an artificial atmosphere and climate—and converted into five square miles of lawns and flower gardens.

The cost in energy involved in this performance was terrific by Earthly calculations, but it had behind it the completely incredible resources of tens of millions of planets, continually growing in number. (It has been estimated that in the Year of the Galactic Era 827 an average of fifty new planets each day were achieving the dignity of provincial status, this condition requiring the attainment of a population of five hundred millions.)

In this spot of non-Earth lived the Procurator of Earth, and sometimes, in this artificial luxury, he could forget that he was a Procurator of a rathole world and remember that he was an aristocrat of great honor and ancient family.

His wife was perhaps less often deluded, particularly at such times as, topping a grassy knoll, she could see in the distance the sharp, decisive line separating the grounds from the fierce wilderness of Earth. It was then that not all the colored fountains (luminescent at night, with an effect of cold liquid fire), flowered walks, or idyllic groves could compensate for the knowledge of their exile.

So perhaps Arvardan was welcomed even more than protocol might call for. To the Procurator, after all, Arvardan was a breath of Empire, of spaciousness, of boundlessness.

And Arvardan for his part found much to admire.

He said, "This is done well—and with taste. It is amazing how a touch of the central culture permeates the most outlying districts of our Empire, Lord Ennius."

Ennius smiled. "I'm afraid the Procurator's court here on Earth is more pleasant to visit than to live in. It is but a shell that rings hollowly when touched. When you have considered myself and family, the staff, the Imperial garrison, both here and in the important planetary centers, together with an occasional visitor such as yourself, you have exhausted all the touch of the central culture that exists. It seems scarcely enough."

They sat in the colonnade in the dying afternoon, with the sun glinting downward toward the mist-purpled jags of the horizon and the air so heavy with the scent of growing things that its motions were merely sighs of exertion.

It was, of course, not quite suitable for even a Procurator to show too great a curiosity about the doings of a guest, but that does not take into account the inhumanity of day-to-day isolation from all the Empire.

Ennius said, "Do you plan to stay for some time, Dr. Arvardan?"

"As to that, Lord Ennius, I cannot surely say. I have

come ahead of the rest of my expedition in order to acquaint myself with Earth's culture and to fulfill the necessary legal requirements. For instance, I must obtain the usual official permission from you to establish camps at the necessary sites, and so on."

"Oh granted, granted! But when do you start digging? And whatever can you possibly expect to find on this miserable heap of rubble?"

"I hope, if all goes well, to be able to set up camp in a few months. And as to this world—why, it's anything but a miserable heap. It is absolutely unique in the Galaxy."

"Unique?" said the Procurator stiffly. "Not at all! It is a very ordinary world. It is more or less a pigpen of a world, or a horrible hole of a world, or a cesspool of a world, or almost any other particularly derogative adjective you care to use. And yet, with all its refinement of nausea, it cannot even achieve uniqueness in villainy, but remains an ordinary, brutish peasant world."

"But," said Arvardan, somewhat taken aback by the energy of the inconsistent statements thus thrown at him, "the world is radioactive."

"Well, what of that? Some thousands of planets in the Galaxy are radioactive, and some are considerably more so than Earth."

It was at this moment that the soft-gliding motion of the mobile cabinet attracted their attention. It came to a halt within easy hand reach.

Ennius gestured toward it and said to the other, "What would you prefer?"

"I'm not particular. A lime twist, perhaps."

"That can be handled. The cabinet will have the ingredients. . . . With or without Chensey?"

"Just about a tang of it," said Arvardan, and held up his forefinger and thumb, nearly touching.

"You'll have it in a minute."

Somewhere in the bowels of the cabinet (perhaps the most universally popular mechanical offspring of human ingenuity) a bartender went into action—a non-human bartender whose electronic soul mixed things not by jiggers but by atom counts, whose ratios were perfect every time, and who could not be matched by all the inspired artistry of anyone merely human.

The tall glasses appeared from nowhere, it seemed, as they waited in the appropriate recesses.

Arvardan took the green one and, for a moment, felt the chill of it against his cheek. Then he placed the rim to his lips and tasted.

"Just right," he said. He placed the glass in the well-fitted holder in the arm of his chair and said, "Thousands of radioactive planets, Procurator, just as you say, but only one of them is inhabited. *This* one, Procurator."

"Well"—Ennius smacked his lips over his own drink and seemed to lose some of his sharpness after contact with its velvet—"perhaps it *is* unique in that way. It's an unenviable distinction."

"But it is not just a question of statistical uniqueness." Arvardan spoke deliberately between occasional sips. "It goes further; it has tremendous potentialities. Biologists have shown, or claim to have shown, that on planets in which the intensity of radioactivity in the atmosphere and in the seas is above a certain point life will not develop. . . . Earth's radioactivity is above that point by a considerable margin."

"Interesting. I didn't know that. I imagine that this would constitute definite proof that Earth life is fundamentally different from that of the rest of the Galaxy. . . . That should suit you, since you're from Sirius." He seemed sardonically amused at this point and said in a confidential aside, "Do you know that the biggest single difficulty involved in ruling this planet lies in coping with the intense anti-Terrestrialism that exists throughout the entire Sirius Sector? And the feeling is returned with interest on the part of these Earthmen. I'm not saying, of course, that anti-Terrestrialism doesn't exist in more or less diluted form in many places in the Galaxy, but not like on Sirius."

Arvardan's response was impatient and vehement. "Lord Ennius, I reject the implication. I have as little intolerance in me as any man living. I believe in the oneness of humanity to my very scientific core, and that includes even Earth.

And all life *is* fundamentally one, in that it is all based upon nucleic acid molecules in chains and protein complexes in colloidal dispersion. The effect of radioactivity that I just talked of does not apply simply to some forms of human life, or to some forms of any life. It applies to *all* life, since it is based upon the quantum mechanics of these macromolecules. It applies to you, to me, to Earthmen, to spiders, and to germs.

"You see, proteins and nucleic acids, as I probably needn't tell you, are immensely complicated groupings of amino acids nucleotides, and certain other specialized compounds, arranged in intricate three-dimensional patterns that are as unstable as sunbeams on a cloudy day. It is this instability that is life, since it is forever changing its position in an effort to maintain its identity—in the manner of a long rod balanced on an acrobat's nose.

"But these marvelous chemicals must be first built up out of inorganic matter before life can exist. So, at the very beginning, by the influence of the sun's radiant energy upon those huge solutions we call oceans, organic molecules gradually increase in complexity from methane to formaldehyde and finally to sugars and starches in one direction, urea to nucleotides to nucleic acids in another direction and from urea to amino acids and proteins in still another direction. It's a matter of chance, of course, these combinations and disintegrations of atoms, and the process on one world may take millions of years while on another it may take only hundreds. Of course it is much more probable that it will take millions of years. In fact, it is most probable that it will end up never happening.

"Now physical organic chemists have worked out with great exactness all the reaction chain involved, particularly the energetics thereof; that is, the energy relationships involved in each atom shift. It is now known beyond the shadow of a doubt that several of the crucial steps in the building of life require the absence of radiant energy. If this strikes you as queer, Procurator, I can only say that photochemistry (the chemistry of reactions induced by radiant energy) is a well-developed branch of the science, and there are innumerable cases of very simple reactions which will go in one of two different directions depending upon whether it takes place in the presence or absence of quanta of light energy.

"In ordinary worlds the sun is the only source of radiant energy, or, at least, by far the major source. In the shelter of clouds, or at night, the carbon and nitrogen compounds combine and recombine, in the fashions made possible by the absence of those little bits of energy hurled into the midst of them by the sun—like bowling balls into the midst of an infinite number of infinitesimal tenpins.

"But on radioactive worlds, sun or no sun, every drop of water—even in the deepest night, even five miles under—sparkles and bursts with darting gamma rays, kicking up the carbon atoms—activating them, the chemists say—and forcing certain key reactions to proceed only in certain ways, ways that never result in life."

Arvardan's drink was gone. He placed the empty glass on the waiting cabinet. It was withdrawn instantly into the special compartment where it was cleaned, sterilized, and made ready for the next drink.

"Another one?" asked Ennius.

"Ask me after dinner," said Arvardan. "I've had quite enough for now."

Ennius tapped a tapering fingernail upon the arm of his chair and said, "You make the process sound quite fascinating, but if all is as you say, then what about the life on Earth? How did it develop?"

"Ah, you see, even you are beginning to wonder. But the answer, *I* think, is simple. Radioactivity, in excess of the minimum required to prevent life, is still not necessarily sufficient to destroy life already formed. It might modify it, but, except in comparatively huge excess, it will not destroy it. . . . You see, the chemistry involved is different. In the first case, simple molecules must be prevented from building up, while in the second, already-formed complex molecules must be broken down. Not at all the same thing."

"I don't get the application of that at all," said Ennius.

"Isn't it obvious? Life on Earth originated *before* the

planet became radioactive. My dear Procurator, it is the only possible explanation that does not involve denying either the fact of life on Earth or enough chemical theory to upset half the science."

Ennius gazed at the other in amazed disbelief. "But you can't mean that."

"Why not?"

"Because how can a world *become* radioactive? The life of the radioactive elements in the planet's crust are in the millions and billions of years. I've learned that, at least, during my university career, even in a pre-law course. They must have existed indefinitely in the past."

"But there is such a thing as artificial radioactivity, Lord Ennius—even on a huge scale. There are thousands of nuclear reactions of sufficient energy to create all sorts of radioactive isotopes. Why, if we were to suppose that human beings might use some applied nuclear reaction in industry, without proper controls, or even in war, if you can imagine anything like a war proceeding on a single planet, most of the topsoil could, conceivably, be converted into artificially radioactive materials. What do you say to that?"

The sun had expired in blood on the mountains, and Ennius's thin face was ruddy in the reflection of that process. The gentle evening wind stirred, and the drowsy murmur of the carefully selected varieties of insect life upon the palace grounds was more soothing than ever.

Ennius said, "It sounds very artificial to me. For one thing, I can't conceive using nuclear reactions in war or letting them get out of control to this extent in any manner——"

"Naturally, sir, you tend to underestimate nuclear reactions because you're living in the present, when they're so easily controlled. But what if someone—or some army— used such weapons before the defense had been worked out? For instance, it's like using fire bombs before anyone knew that water or sand would put out fire."

"Hmm," said Ennius, "you sound like Shekt."

"Who's Shekt?" Arvardan looked up quickly.

"An Earthman. One of the few decent ones—I mean,

one that a gentleman can speak to. He's a physicist. He told me once that Earth might not always have been radioactive."

"Ah. . . . Well, that's not unusual, since the theory is certainly not original with me. It's part of the *Book of the Ancients*, which contains the traditional, or mythical, history of prehistoric Earth. I'm saying what it says, in a way, except that I'm putting its rather elliptical phraseology into equivalent scientific statements."

"The Book of the Ancients?" Ennius seemed surprised, and a little upset. "Where did you get that?"

"Here and there. It wasn't easy, and I only obtained parts. Of course all this traditional information about non-radioactivity, even where completely unscientific, is important to my project. . . . Why do you ask?"

"Because the book is the revered text of a radical sect of Earthmen. It is forbidden for Outsiders to read it. I wouldn't broadcast the fact that you did, either, while you're here. Non-Earthmen, or Outsiders, as they call them, have been lynched for less."

"You make it sound as if the Imperial police power here is defective."

"It is in cases of sacrilege. A word to the wise, Dr. Arvardan!"

A melodious chime sounded a vibrant note that seemed to harmonize with the rustling whisper of the trees. It faded out slowly, lingering as though in love with its surroundings.

Ennius rose. "I believe it is time for dinner. Will you join me, sir, and enjoy such hospitality as this husk of Empire on Earth can afford?"

An occasion for an elaborate dinner came infrequently enough. An excuse, even a slim one, was not to be missed. So the courses were many, the surroundings lavish, the men polished, and the women bewitching. And, it must be added, Dr. B. Arvardan of Baronn, Sirius, was lionized to quite an intoxicating extent.

Arvardan took advantage of his dinner audience during the latter portion of the banquet to repeat much of what he had said to Ennius, but here his exposition met with markedly less success.

A florid gentleman in colonel's uniform leaned toward him with that marked condescension of the military man for the scholar and said, "If I interpret your expressions rightly, Dr. Arvardan, you are trying to tell us that these hounds of Earth represent an ancient race that may once have been the ancestors of all humanity?"

"I hesitate, Colonel, to make the flat assertion, but I think there is an interesting chance that it might be so. A year from now I confidently hope to be able to make a definite judgment."

"If you find that they are, Doctor, which I strongly doubt," rejoined the colonel, "you will astonish me beyond measure. I have been stationed on Earth now for four years, and my experience is not of the smallest. I find these Earthmen to be rogues and knaves, every one of them. They are definitely our inferiors intellectually. They lack that spark that has spread humanity throughout the Galaxy. They are lazy, superstitious, avaricious, and with no trace of nobility of soul. I defy you, or anyone, to show me an Earthman who can in any way be an equal of any true man—yourself or myself, for instance—and only then will I grant you that he may represent a race who once were our ancestors. But, until then, please excuse me from making any such assumption."

A portly man at the foot of the table said suddenly, "They say the only good Earthman is a dead Earthman, and that even then they generally stink," and laughed immoderately.

Arvardan frowned at the dish before him and said, without looking up, "I have no desire to argue racial differences, especially since it is irrelevant in this case. It is the Earthman of prehistory that I speak of. His descendants of today have been long isolated, and have been subjected to a most unusual environment—yet I still would not dismiss them too casually."

He turned to Ennius and said, "My Lord, I believe you mentioned an Earthman before dinner."

"I did? I don't recall."

"A physicist. Shekt."

"Oh yes. Yes."

"Affret Shekt, perhaps?"

"Why, yes. Have you heard of him?"

"I think I have. It's been bothering me all through dinner, ever since you mentioned him, but I think I've placed him. He wouldn't be at the Institute of Nuclear Research at—— Oh, what's the name of that damned place?" He struck at his forehead with the heel of his palm once or twice. "At Chica?"

"You have the right person. What about him?"

"Only this. There was an article by him in the August issue of *Physical Reviews*. I noticed it because I was looking for anything that had to do with Earth, and articles by Earthmen in journals of Galactic circulation are very rare.... In any case, the point I am trying to make is that the man claims to have developed something he calls a Synapsifier, which is supposed to improve the learning capacity of the mammalian nervous system."

"Really?" said Ennius a bit too sharply. "I haven't heard about it."

"I can find you the reference. It's quite an interesting article; though, of course, I can't pretend to understand the mathematics involved. What he has done, however, has been to treat some indigenous animal form on Earth—rats, I believe they call them—with the Synapsifier and then put them to solving a maze. You know what I mean: learning the proper pathway through a tiny labyrinth to some food supply. He used non-treated rats as controls and found that in every case the Synapsified rats solved the maze in less than one third the time.... Do you see the significance, Colonel?"

The military man who had initiated the discussion said indifferently, "No, Doctor, I do not."

"I'll explain, then, that I firmly believe that any scientist capable of doing such work, even an Earthman, is certainly my intellectual equal, at least, and, if you'll pardon my presumption, yours as well."

Ennius interrupted. "Pardon me, Dr. Arvardan. I would

like to return to the Synapsifier. Has Shekt experimented with human beings?"

Arvardan laughed. "I doubt it, Lord Ennius. Nine tenths of his Synapsified rats died during treatment. He would scarcely dare use human subjects until much more progress has been made."

So Ennius sank back into his chair with a slight frown on his forehead and, thereafter, neither spoke nor ate for the remainder of the dinner.

Before midnight the Procurator had quietly left the gathering and, with a bare word to his wife only, departed in his private cruiser on the two-hour trip to the city of Chica, with the slight frown still on his forehead and a raging anxiety in his heart.

Thus it was that on the same afternoon that Arbin Maren brought Joseph Schwartz into Chica for treatment with Shekt's Synapsifier, Shekt himself had been closeted with none less than the Procurator of Earth for over an hour.

4. THE ROYAL ROAD

Arbin was uneasy in Chica. He felt surrounded. Somewhere in Chica, one of the largest cities on Earth—they said it had fifty thousand human beings in it—somewhere there were officials of the great outer Empire.

To be sure, he had never seen a man of the Galaxy; yet here, in Chica, his neck was continually twisting in fear that he might. If pinned down, he could not have explained how he would identify an Outsider from an Earthman, even if he were to see one, but it was in his very marrow to feel that there was, somehow, a difference.

He looked back over his shoulder as he entered the Institute. His biwheel was parked in an open area, with a six-hour coupon holding a spot open for it. Was the extravagance itself suspicious?...Everything frightened him now. The air was full of eyes and ears.

If only the strange man would remember to remain hidden in the bottom of the rear compartment. He had nodded violently—but had he understood? He was suddenly impatient with himself. Why had he let Grew talk him into this madness?

And then somehow the door was open in front of him and a voice had broken in on his thoughts.

It said, "What do you want?"

It sounded impatient; perhaps it had already asked him that same thing several times.

He answered hoarsely, words choking out of his throat like dry powder, "Is this where a man can apply for the Synapsifier?"

The receptionist looked up sharply and said, "Sign here."

Arbin put his hands behind his back and repeated huskily, "Where do I see about the Synapsifier?" Grew had told him the name, but the word came out queerly, like so much gibberish.

But the receptionist said, with iron in her voice, "I can't do anything for you unless you sign the register as a visitor. It's in the rules."

Without a word, Arbin turned to go. The young woman behind the desk pressed her lips together and kicked the signal bar at the side of her chair violently.

Arbin was fighting desperately for a lack of notoriety and failing miserably in his own mind. This girl was looking hard at him. She'd remember him a thousand years later. He had a wild desire to run, run back to the car, back to the farm . . .

Someone in a white lab coat was coming rapidly out of another room, and the receptionist was pointing to him. "Volunteer for the Synapsifier, Miss Shekt," she was saying. "He won't give his name."

Arbin looked up. It was still another girl, young. He looked disturbed. "Are *you* in charge of the machine, miss?"

"No, not at all." She smiled in a very friendly fashion, and Arbin felt anxiety ebb slightly.

"I can take you to him, though," she went on. Then, eagerly, "Do you really want to volunteer for the Synapsifier?"

"I just want to see the man in charge," Arbin said woodenly.

"All right." She seemed not at all disturbed by the rebuff. She slipped back through the door from which she had come. There was a short wait. Then, finally, there was the beckon of a finger...

He followed her, heart pounding, into a small anteroom. She said gently, "If you will wait about half an hour or less, Dr. Shekt will be with you. He is very busy just now.... If you would like some book films and a viewer to pass the time, I'll bring them to you."

But Arbin shook his head. The four walls of the small room closed about him, and held him rigid, it seemed. Was he trapped? Were the Ancients coming for him?

It was the longest wait in Arbin's life.

Lord Ennius, Procurator of Earth, had experienced no comparable difficulties in seeing Dr. Shekt, though he had experienced an almost comparable excitement. In his fourth year as Procurator, a visit to Chica was still an event. As the direct representative of the remote Emperor, his social standing was, legalistically, upon a par with viceroys of huge Galactic sectors that sprawled their gleaming volumes across hundreds of cubic parsecs of space, but, actually, his post was little short of exile.

Trapped as he was in the sterile emptiness of the Himalayas, among the equally sterile quarrels of a population that hated him and the Empire he represented, even a trip to Chica was escape.

To be sure, his escapes were short ones. They had to be short, since here at Chica it was necessary to wear lead-impregnated clothes at all times, even while sleeping, and, what was worse, to dose oneself continually with metaboline.

He spoke bitterly of that to Shekt.

"Metaboline," he said, holding up the vermilion pill for inspection, "is perhaps a true symbol of all that your planet means to me, my friend. Its function is to heighten all metabolic processes while I sit here immersed in the radioactive cloud that surrounds me and which you are not even aware of."

He swallowed it. "There! Now my heart will beat more quickly; my breath will pump a race of its own accord; and my liver will boil away in those chemical syntheses that, medical men tell me, make it the most important factory in the body. And for that I pay with a siege of headaches and lassitude afterward."

Dr. Shekt listened with some amusement. He gave a strong impression of being nearsighted, did Shekt, not because he wore glasses or was in any way afflicted, but merely because long habit had given him the unconscious trick of peering closely at things, of weighing all facts anxiously before saying anything. He was tall and in his late middle age, his thin figure slightly stooped.

But he was well read in much of Galactic culture, and he was relatively free of the trick of universal hostility and suspicion that made the average Earthman so repulsive even to so cosmopolitan a man of the Empire as Ennius.

Shekt said, "I'm sure you don't need the pill. Metaboline is just one of your superstitions, and you know it. If I were to substitute sugar pills without your knowledge, you'd be none the worse. What's more, you would even psychosomaticize yourself into similar headaches afterward."

"You say that in the comfort of your own environment. Do you deny that your basal metabolism is higher than mine?"

"Of course I don't, but what of it? I know that it is a superstition of the Empire, Ennius, that we men of Earth are different from other human beings, but that's not really so in the essentials. Or are you coming here as a missionary of the anti-Terrestrians?"

Ennius groaned. "By the life of the Emperor, your comrades of Earth are themselves the best such missionaries. Living here, as they do, cooped up on their deadly planet, festering in their own anger, they're nothing but a standing ulcer in the Galaxy.

"I'm serious, Shekt. What planet has so much ritual in its daily life and adheres to it with such masochistic fury? Not a day passes but I receive delegations from one or another of your ruling bodies for the death penalty for some poor devil whose only crime has been to invade a forbidden area, to evade the Sixty, or perhaps merely to eat more than his share of food."

"Ah, but you always grant the death penalty. Your idealistic distaste seems to stop short at resisting."

"The Stars are my witness that I struggle to deny the death. But what can one do? The Emperor *will* have it that all the subdivisions of the Empire are to remain undisturbed in their local customs—and that is right and wise, since it removes popular support from the fools who would otherwise kick up rebellion on alternate Tuesdays and Thursdays. Besides, were I to remain obdurate when your Councils and Senates and Chambers insist on the death, such a shrieking would arise and such a wild howling and such denunciation of the Empire and all its works that I would sooner sleep in the midst of a legion of devils for twenty years than face such an Earth for ten minutes."

Shekt sighed and rubbed the thin hair back upon his skull. "To the rest of the Galaxy, if they are aware of us at all, Earth is but a pebble in the sky. To us it is home, and all the home we know. Yet we are no different from you of the outer worlds, merely more unfortunate. We are crowded here on a world all but dead, immersed within a wall of radiation that imprisons us, surrounded by a huge Galaxy that rejects us. What can we do against the feeling of frustration that burns us? Would you, Procurator, be willing that we send our surplus population abroad?"

Ennius shrugged. "Would I care? It is the outside populations themselves that would. They don't care to fall victim to Terrestrial diseases."

"Terrestrial diseases!" Shekt scowled. "It is a nonsensical notion that should be eradicated. We are not carriers of death. Are you dead for having been among us?"

"To be sure," smiled Ennius, "I do everything to prevent undue contact."

"It is because you yourself fear the propaganda created, after all, only by the stupidity of your own bigots."

"Why, Shekt, no scientific basis at all to the theory that Earthmen are themselves radioactive?"

"Yes, certainly they are. How could they avoid it? So are you. So is everyone on every one of the hundred million planets of the Empire. We are more so, I grant you, but scarcely enough to harm anyone."

"But the average man of the Galaxy believes the opposite, I am afraid, and is not desirous of finding out by experiment. Besides——"

"Besides, you're going to say, we're different. We're not human beings, because we mutate more rapidly, due to atomic radiation, and have therefore changed in many ways.... Also not proven."

"But believed."

"And as long as it is so believed, Procurator, and as long as we of Earth are treated as pariahs, you are going to find in us the characteristics to which you object. If you push us intolerably, is it to be wondered at that we push back? Hating us as you do, can you complain that we hate in our turn? No, no, we are far more the offended than the offending."

Ennius was chagrined at the anger he had raised. Even the best of these Earthmen, he thought, have the same blind spot, the same feeling of Earth versus all the universe.

He said tactfully, "Shekt, forgive my boorishness, will you? Take my youth and boredom as excuse. You see before you a poor man, a young fellow of forty—and forty is the age of a babe in the professional civil service—who is grinding out his apprenticeship here on Earth. It may be years before the fools in the Bureau of the Outer Provinces remember me long enough to promote me to something less deadly. So we are both prisoners of Earth and both citizens of the great world of the mind in which there is distinction of neither planet nor physical characteristics. Give me your hand, then, and let us be friends."

The lines on Shekt's face smoothed out, or, more exactly, were replaced by others more indicative of good humor. He laughed outright. "The words are the words of a suppliant, but the tone is still that of the Imperial career diplomat. You are a poor actor, Procurator."

"Then counter me by being a good teacher, and tell me of this Synapsifier of yours."

Shekt started visibly and frowned. "What, you have heard of the instrument? You are then a physicist as well as an administrator?"

"All knowledge is my province. But seriously, Shekt, I would really like to know."

The physicist peered closely at the other and seemed doubtful. He rose and his gnarled hand lifted to his lip, which it pinched thoughtfully. "I scarcely know where to begin."

"Well, Stars above, if you are considering at which point in the mathematical theory you are to begin, I'll simplify your problem. Abandon them all. I know nothing of your functions and tensors and what not."

Shekt's eyes twinkled. "Well, then, to stick to descriptive matter only, it is simply a device intended to increase the learning capacity of a human being."

"Of a human being? Really! And does it work?"

"I wish we knew. Much more work is necessary. I'll give you the essentials, Procurator, and you can judge for yourself. The nervous system in man—and in animals— is composed of neuroprotein material. Such material consists of huge molecules in very precarious electrical balance. The slightest stimulus will upset one, which will right itself by upsetting the next, which will repeat the process, until the brain is reached. The brain itself is an immense grouping of similar molecules which are connected among themselves in all possible ways. Since there are something like ten to the twentieth power—that is, a one with twenty zeros after it—such neuroproteins in the brain, the number of possible combinations are of the order of factorial ten to the twentieth power. This is a number so large that if all the electrons and protons in the universe were made universes themselves, and all the electrons and protons in all of these new universes again made universes, then all the electrons and protons in all the universes so created would still be nothing in comparison. . . . Do you follow me?"

"Not a word, thank the Stars. If I even attempted to, I should bark like a dog for sheer pain of the intellect."

"Hmp. Well, in any case, what we call nerve impulses are merely the progressive electronic unbalance that proceeds along the nerves to the brain and then from the brain back along the nerves. Do you get that?"

"Yes."

"Well, blessings on you for a genius, then. As long as this impulse continues along a nerve cell, it proceeds at a rapid rate, since the neuroproteins are practically in contact. However, nerve cells are limited in extent, and between each nerve cell and the next is a very thin partition of non-nervous tissue. In other words, two adjoining nerve cells do not actually connect with each other."

"Ah," said Ennius, "and the nervous impulse must jump the barrier."

"Exactly! The partition drops the strength of the impulse and slows the speed of its transmission according to the square of the thickness thereof. This holds for the brain as well. But imagine, now, if some means could be found to lower the dielectric constant of this partition between the cells."

"That what constant?"

"The insulating strength of the partition. That's all I mean. If that were decreased, the impulse would jump the gap more easily. You would think faster and learn faster."

"Well, then, I come back to my original question. Does it work?"

"I have tried the instrument on animals."

"And with what result?"

"Why, that most die very quickly of denaturation of brain protein—coagulation, in other words, like hard-boiling an egg."

Ennius winced. "There is something ineffably cruel about the cold-bloodedness of science. What about those that didn't die?"

"Not conclusive, since they're not human beings. The burden of the evidence seems to be favorable, for them. . . . But I need humans. You see, it is a matter of the natural electronic properties of the individual brain. Each brain gives rise to microcurrents of a certain type. None are exactly duplicates. They're like fingerprints, or the blood-vessel patterns of the retina. If anything, they're even more individual. The treatment, I believe, must take that into account, and, if I am right, there will be no more denaturation. . . . But I have no human beings on whom to experiment. I ask for volunteers, but——" He spread his hands.

"I certainly don't blame them, old man," said Ennius. "But seriously, should the instrument be perfected, what do you intend doing with it?"

The physicist shrugged. "That's not for me to say. It would be up to the Grand Council, of course."

"You would not consider making the invention available to the Empire?"

"I? I have no objections at all. But only the Grand Council has jurisdiction over——"

"Oh," said Ennius with impatience, "the devil with your Grand Council. I have had dealings with them before. Would you be willing to talk to them at the proper time?"

"Why, what influence could I possibly have?"

"You might tell them that if Earth could produce a Synapsifier that would be applicable to human beings in complete safety, and if the device were made available to the Galaxy, then some of the restrictions on emigration to other planets might be broken down."

"What," said Shekt sarcastically, "and risk epidemics and our differentness and our non-humanity?"

"You might," said Ennius quietly, "even be removed *en masse* to another planet. Consider it."

The door opened at this point and a young lady brushed her way in past the book-film cabinet. She destroyed the musty atmosphere of the cloistered study with an automatic breath of spring. At the sight of a stranger she reddened slightly and turned.

"Come in, Pola," called Shekt hastily. "My Lord," he said to Ennius, "I believe you have never met my daughter. Pola, this is Lord Ennius, Procurator of Earth."

The Procurator was on his feet with an easy gallantry that negated her first wild attempt at a curtsy.

"My dear Miss Shekt," he said, "you are an ornament I did not believe Earth capable of producing. You would, indeed, be an ornament on any world I can think of."

He took Pola's hand, which was quickly and somewhat bashfully extended to meet his gesture. For a moment Ennius made as if to kiss it, in the courtly fashion of the past generation, but the intention, if such it was, never came to fruition. Half lifted, the hand was released—a trace too quickly, perhaps.

Pola, with the slightest of frowns, said, "I'm over-whelmed at your kindness, my Lord, to a simple girl of Earth. You are brave and gallant to dare infection as you do."

Shekt cleared his throat and interrupted. "My daughter, Procurator, is completing her studies at the University of Chica and is obtaining some needed field credits by spending two days a week in my laboratory as a technician. A competent girl, and though I say it with the pride of a father, she may someday sit in my place."

"Father," said Pola gently, "I have some important information for you." She hesitated.

"Shall I leave?" said Ennius quietly.

"No, no," said Shekt. "What is it, Pola?"

The girl said, "We have a volunteer, Father."

Shekt stared, almost stupidly. "For the Synapsifier?"

"So he says."

"Well," said Ennius, "I bring you good fortune, I see."

"So it would seem." Shekt turned to his daughter. "Tell him to wait. Take him to Room C, and I'll be with him soon."

He turned to Ennius after Pola left. "Will you excuse me, Procurator?"

"Certainly. How long does the operation take?"

"It's a matter of hours, I'm afraid. Do you wish to watch?"

"I can imagine nothing more gruesome, my dear Shekt. I'll be in the State House till tomorrow. Will you tell me the result?"

Shekt seemed relieved. "Yes, certainly."

"Good.... And think over what I said about your Synapsifier. Your new royal road to knowledge."

Ennius left, less at ease than when he had arrived; his knowledge no greater, his fears much increased.

5. THE INVOLUNTARY VOLUNTEER

Once alone, Dr. Shekt, quietly and cautiously, touched the summoner, and a young technician entered hurriedly, white robe sparkling, long brown hair carefully bound back.

Dr. Shekt said, "Has Pola told you——"

"Yes, Dr. Shekt. I've observed him through the visiplate, and he must undoubtedly be a legitimate volunteer. He's certainly not a subject sent in the usual manner."

"Ought I refer to the Council, do you suppose?"

"I don't know what to advise. The Council wouldn't approve of any ordinary communication. Any beam can be tapped, you know." Then, eagerly, "Suppose I get rid of him. I can tell him we need men under thirty. The subject is easily thirty-five."

"No, no. I'd better see him." Shekt's mind was a cold whirl. So far things had been most judiciously handled. Just enough information to lend a spurious frankness, but no more. And now an actual volunteer—and immediately after Ennius's visit. Was there a connection? Shekt himself had but the vaguest knowledge of the giant misty forces that

44

were now beginning to wrestle back and forth across the blasted face of Earth. But, in a way, he knew enough. Enough to feel himself at the mercy of them, and certainly more than any of the Ancients suspected he knew.

Yet what could he do, since his life was doubly in danger?

Ten minutes later Dr. Shekt was peering helplessly at the gnarled farmer standing before him, cap in hand, head half averted, as though attempting to avoid a too-close scrutiny. His age, thought Shekt, was certainly under forty, but the hard life of the soil was no flatterer of men. The man's cheeks were reddened beneath the leathery brown, and there were distinct traces of perspiration at the hairline and the temples, though the room was cool. The man's hands were fumbling at each other.

"Now, my dear sir," said Shekt kindly, "I understand you refuse to give your name."

Arbin's was a blind stubbornness. "I was told no questions would be asked if you had a volunteer."

"Hmm. Well, is there anything at all you *would* like to say? Or do you just want to be treated immediately?"

"Me? Here, now?" in sudden panic. "It's not myself that's the volunteer. I didn't say anything to give that impression."

"No? You mean someone else is the volunteer?"

"Certainly. What would *I* want——"

"I understand. Is the subject, this other man, with you?"

"In a way," said Arbin cautiously.

"All right. Now, look, just tell us whatever you wish. Everything you say will be held in strict confidence, and we'll help you in whatever way we can. Agreed?"

The farmer ducked his head, as a sort of rudimentary gesture of respect. "Thank you. It's like this, sir. We have a man about the farm, a distant—uh—relative. He helps, you understand——"

Arbin swallowed with difficulty, and Shekt nodded gravely.

Arbin continued. "He's a very willing worker and a very *good* worker—we had a son, you see, but he died—and my good woman and myself, you see, need the help—she's

not well—we could not get along without him, scarcely."
He felt that somehow the story was a complete mess.

But the gaunt scientist nodded at him. "And this relative
of yours is the one you wish treated?"

"Why, yes, I thought I had said that—but you'll pardon
me if this takes me some time. You see, the poor fellow is
not—exactly—right in his head." He hurried on, furiously.
"He is not sick, you understand. He is not wrong so that
he has to be put away. He's just *slow*. He doesn't talk, you
see."

"He can't talk?" Shekt seemed startled.

"Oh—he can. It's just that he doesn't like to. He doesn't
talk *well*."

The physicist looked dubious. "And you want the Synapsifier to improve his mentality, eh?"

Slowly, Arbin nodded. "If he knew a bit more, sir, why,
he could do some of the work my wife can't, you see."

"He might die. Do you understand that?"

Arbin looked at him helplessly, and his fingers writhed
furiously.

Shekt said, "I'd need his consent."

The farmer shook his head slowly, stubbornly. "He won't
understand." Then, urgently, almost beneath his breath,
"Why, look, sir, I'm sure you'll understand me. You don't
look like a man who doesn't know what a hard life is. This
man is getting old. It's not a question of the Sixty, you see,
but what if, in the next Census, they think he's a half-wit
and—and take him away? We don't like to lose him, and
that's why we bring him here.

"The reason I'm trying to be secret-like is that maybe—
maybe"—and Arbin's eyes swiveled involuntarily at the
walls, as if to penetrate them by sheer will and detect the
listeners that might be behind—"well, maybe the Ancients
won't like what I'm doing. Maybe trying to save an afflicted
man can be judged as against the Customs, but life is hard,
sir. . . . And it would be useful to you. You *have* asked for
volunteers."

"I know. Where is your relative?"

Arbin took the chance. "Out in my biwheel, if no one's

found him. He wouldn't be able to take care of himself if anyone has——"

"Well, we'll hope he's safe. You and I will go out right now and bring the car around to our basement garage. I'll see to it that no one knows of his presence but ourselves and my helpers. And I assure you that you won't be in trouble with the Brotherhood."

His arm dropped in friendly fashion to Arbin's shoulder, who grinned spasmodically. To the farmer it was like a rope loosening from about his neck.

Shekt looked down at the plump, balding figure upon the couch. The patient was unconscious, breathing deeply and regularly. He had spoken unintelligibly, had understood nothing. Yet there had been none of the physical stigmata of feeblemindedness. Reflexes had been in order, for an old man.

Old! Hmm.

He looked across at Arbin, who watched everything with a glance like a vise.

"Would you like us to take a bone analysis?"

"No," cried Arbin. Then, more softly, "I don't want anything that might be identification."

"It might help us—be safer, you know—if we knew his age," said Shekt.

"He's fifty," said Arbin shortly.

The physicist shrugged. It didn't matter. Again he looked at the sleeper. When brought in, the subject had been, or certainly seemed, dejected, withdrawn, uncaring. Even the Hypno-pills had apparently aroused no suspicion. They had been offered him; there had been a quick, spasmodic smile in response, and he had swallowed them.

The technician was already rolling in the last of the rather clumsy units which together made up the Synapsifier. At the touch of a push button the polarized glass in the windows of the operating room underwent molecular rearrangement and became opaque. The only light was the white one that blazed its cold brilliance upon the patient suspended, as he was, in the multihundred-kilowatt diamagnetic field some two inches above the operating table to which he was transferred.

Arbin still sat in the dark there, understanding nothing, but determined in deadly fashion to prevent, somehow, by his presence, the harmful tricks he knew he had not the knowledge to prevent.

The physicists paid no attention to him. The electrodes were adjusted to the patient's skull. It was a long job. First there was the careful study of the skull formation by the Ullster technique that revealed the winding, tight-knit fissures. Grimly, Shekt smiled to himself. Skull fissures weren't an unalterable quantitative measure of age, but they were good enough in this case. The man was older than the claimed fifty.

And then, after a while, he did not smile. He frowned. There was something wrong with the fissures. They seemed odd—not quite . . .

For a moment he was ready to swear that the skull formation was a primitive one, a throwback, but then . . . Well, the man was subnormal in mentality. Why not?

And suddenly he exclaimed in shock, "Why, I hadn't noticed! This man has hair on his face!" He turned to Arbin. "Has he always been bearded?"

"Bearded?"

"Hair on his face! Come here! Don't you see it?"

"Yes, sir." Arbin thought rapidly. He *had* noticed it that morning and then had forgotten. "He was born like that," he said, and then weakened it by adding, "I think."

"Well, let's remove it. You don't want him going around like a brute beast, do you?"

"No, sir."

The hair came off smoothly at the application of a depilatory salve by the carefully gloved technician.

The technician said, "He has hair on his chest too, Dr. Shekt."

"Great Galaxy," said Shekt, "let me see! Why, the man is a rug! Well, let it be. It won't show with a shirt, and I want to get on with the electrodes. Let's have wires here and here, and here." Tiny pricks and the insertion of the platinum hair-lets. "Here and here."

A dozen connections, probing through skin to the fissures, through the tightness of which could be felt the delicate shadow echoes of the microcurrents that surged from cell to cell in the brain.

Carefully they watched the delicate ammeters stir and leap, as the connections were made and broken. The tiny needlepoint recorders traced their delicate spider webs across the graphed paper in irregular peaks and troughs.

Then the graphs were removed and placed on the illuminated opal glass. They bent low over it, whispering.

Arbin caught disjointed flashes: ". . . remarkably regular . . . look at the height of the quinternary peak . . . think it ought to be analyzed . . . clear enough to the eye . . ."

And then, for what seemed a long time, there was a tedious adjustment of the Synapsifier. Knobs were turned, eyes on vernier adjustments, then clamped and their readings recorded. Over and over again the various electrometers were checked and new adjustments were made necessary.

Then Shekt smiled at Arbin and said, "It will all be over very soon."

The large machinery was advanced upon the sleeper like a slow-moving and hungry monster. Four long wires were dangled to the extremities of his limbs, and a dull black pad of something that looked like hard rubber was carefully adjusted at the back of his neck and held firmly in place by clamps that fitted over the shoulders. Finally, like two giant mandibles, the opposing electrodes were parted and brought downward over the pale, pudgy head, so that each pointed at a temple.

Shekt kept his eyes firmly on the chronometer; in his other hand was the switch. His thumb moved; nothing visible happened—not even to the fear-sharpened sense of the watching Arbin. After what might have been hours, but was actually less than three minutes, Shekt's thumb moved again.

His assistant bent over the still-sleeping Schwartz hurriedly, then looked up triumphantly. "He's alive."

There remained yet several hours, during which a library

of recordings were taken, to an undertone of almost wild excitement. It was well past midnight when the hypodermic was pressed home and the sleeper's eyes fluttered.

Shekt stepped back, bloodless but happy. He dabbed at his forehead with the back of a hand. "It's *all* right."

He turned to Arbin firmly. "He must stay with us a few days, sir."

The look of alarm grew madly in Arbin's eyes. "But—but——"

"No, no, you must rely on me," urgently. "He will be safe; I will stake my life on it. I *am* staking my life on it. Leave him to us; no one will see him but ourselves. If you take him with you now, he may not survive. What good will that do you?... And if he does die, you may have to explain the corpse to the Ancients."

It was the last that did the trick. Arbin swallowed and said, "But look, how am I to know when to come and take him? I won't give you my name!"

But it was submission. Shekt said, "I'm not asking you for your name. Come a week from today at ten in the evening. I'll be waiting for you at the door of the garage, the one we took in your biwheel at. You must believe me, man; you have nothing to fear."

It was evening when Arbin arrowed out of Chica. Twenty-four hours had passed since the stranger had pounded at his door, and in that time he had doubled his crimes against the Customs. Would he ever be safe again?

He could not help but glance over his shoulder as his biwheel sped along the empty road. Would there be someone to follow? Someone to trace him home? Or was his face already recorded? Were matchings being leisurely made somewhere in the distant files of the Brotherhood at Wash-enn, where all living Earthmen, together with their vital statistics, were listed, for purposes of the Sixty.

The Sixty, which must come to all Earthmen eventually. He had yet a quarter of a century before it came to him, yet he lived daily with it on Grew's account, and now on the stranger's account.

What if he never returned to Chica?

No! He and Loa could not long continue producing for three, and once they failed, their first crime, that of concealing Grew, would be discovered. And so crimes against the Customs, once begun, *must* be compounded.

Arbin knew that he would be back, despite any risk.

It was past midnight before Shekt thought of retiring, and then only because the troubled Pola insisted. Even then he did not sleep. His pillow was a subtle smothering device, his sheets a pair of maddening snarls. He arose and took his seat by the window. The city was dark now, but there on the horizon, on the side opposite the lake, was the faint trace of that blue glow of death that held sway over all but a few patches of Earth.

The activities of the hectic day just past danced madly before his mind. His first action after having persuaded the frightened farmer to leave had been to televise the State House. Ennius must have been waiting for him, for he himself had answered. He was still encased in the heaviness of the lead-impregnated clothing.

"Ah, Shekt, good evening. Your experiment is over?"

"And nearly my volunteer as well, poor man."

Ennius looked ill. "I thought well when I thought it better not to stay. You scientists are scarcely removed from murderers, it seems to me."

"He is not yet dead, Procurator, and it may be that we will save him, but——" And he shrugged his shoulders.

"I'd stick to rats exclusively henceforward, Shekt. . . . But you don't look at all your usual self, friend. Surely you, at least, must be hardened to this, even if I am not."

"I am getting old, my Lord," said Shekt simply.

"A dangerous pastime on Earth," was the dry reply. "Get you to bed, Shekt."

And so Shekt sat there, looking out at the dark city of a dying world.

For two years now the Synapsifier had been under test, and for two years he had been the slave and sport of the

Society of Ancients, or the Brotherhood, as they called themselves.

He had seven or eight papers that might have been published in the *Sirian Journal of Neurophysiology*, that might have given that Galaxy-wide fame to him that he so wanted. These papers moldered in his desk. Instead there was that obscure and deliberately misleading paper in *Physical Reviews*. That was the way of the Brotherhood. Better a half-truth than a lie.

And still Ennius was inquiring. Why?

Did it fit in with other things he had learned? Was the Empire suspecting what he himself suspected?

Three times in two hundred years Earth had risen. Three times, under the banner of a claimed ancient greatness, Earth had rebelled against the Imperial garrisons. Three times they had failed—of course—and had not the Empire been, essentially, enlightened, and the Galactic Councils, by and large, statesmanlike, Earth would have been bloodily erased from the roll of inhabited planets.

But now things might be different. . . . Or *could* they be different? How far could he trust the words of a dying madman, three quarters incoherent?

What was the use? In any case, he dared do nothing. He could only wait. He was getting old, and, as Ennius had said, that was a dangerous pastime on Earth. The Sixty was almost upon him, and there were few exceptions to its inevitable grasp.

And even on this miserable, burning mud ball of Earth, he wanted to live.

He went to bed once more at that point, and just before falling asleep he wondered feebly if his call to Ennius might have been tapped by the Ancients. He did not know at the time that the Ancients had other sources of information.

It was morning before Shekt's young technician had completely made up his mind.

He admired Shekt, but he knew well that the secret treatment of a non-authorized volunteer was against the direct order of the Brotherhood. And that order had been given the status of a Custom, which made disobedience a capital offense.

He reasoned it out. After all, who was this man who had been treated? The campaign for volunteers had been carefully worked out. It was designed to give enough information about the Synapsifier to remove suspicion on the part of possible Imperial spies without giving any real encouragement to volunteers. The Society of Ancients sent their own men for treatment, and that was enough.

Who had sent this man, then? The Society of Ancients in secret? In order to test Shekt's reliability?

Or was Shekt a traitor? He had been closeted with someone earlier in the day—someone in bulky clothes, such as Outsiders wore in fear of radioactive poisoning.

In either case Shekt might go down in doom, and why should he himself be dragged down as well? He was a young man with nearly four decades of life before him. Why should he anticipate the Sixty?

Besides, it would mean promotion for him. . . . And Shekt was so old, the next Census would probably get him anyway, so it would involve very little harm for him. Practically none at all.

The technician had decided. His hand reached for the communicator, and he punched the combination that would lead directly to the private room of the High Minister of all Earth, who, under the Emperor and Procurator, held the power of life and death over every man on Earth.

It was evening again before the misty impressions within Schwartz's skull sharpened through the pink pain. He remembered the trip to the low, huddling structures by the lakeside, the long crouching wait in the rear of the car.

And then—what? What? His mind yanked away at the sluggish thoughts. . . . Yes, they had come for him. There was a room, with instruments and dials, and two pills. . . . That was it. They had given him pills, and he had taken them cheerfully. What had he to lose? Poisoning would have been a favor.

And then—nothing.

Wait! There had been flashes of consciousness . . . People bending over him . . . Suddenly he remembered the cold motion of a stethoscope over his chest. . . . A girl had been feeding him.

It flashed upon him that he had been operated upon and, in panic, he flung the bed sheets from him and sat up.

A girl was upon him, hands on his shoulders, forcing him back onto the pillows. She spoke soothingly, but he did not understand her. He tensed himself against the slim arms, but uselessly. He had no strength.

He held his hands before his face. They seemed normal. He moved his legs and heard them brush against the sheets. They couldn't have been amputated.

He turned to the girl and said, without much hope, "Can you understand me? Do you know where I am?" He scarcely recognized his own voice.

The girl smiled and suddenly poured out a rapid patter of liquid sound. Schwartz groaned. Then an older man entered, the one who had given him the pills. The man and the girl spoke together, the girl turning to him after a while, pointing to his lips, and making little gestures of invitation to him.

"What?" he said.

She nodded eagerly, her pretty face glowing with pleasure, until, despite himself, Schwartz felt glad to look at it.

"You want me to talk?" he asked.

The man sat down upon his bed and motioned him to open his mouth. He said, "Ah-h-h," and Schwartz repeated "Ah-h-h" while the man's fingers massaged Schwartz's Adam's apple.

"What's the matter?" said Schwartz peevishly, when the pressure was removed. "Are you surprised I can talk? What do you think I am?"

The days passed, and Schwartz learned a few things. The man was Dr. Shekt—the first human being he knew by name since he had stepped over the rag doll. The girl was his daughter, Pola. Schwartz found that he no longer needed to shave. The hair on his face never grew. It frightened him. Did it ever grow?

His strength came back quickly. They were letting him put on clothes and walk about now, and were feeding him something more than mush.

Was his trouble amnesia, then? Were they treating him for that? Was all this world normal and natural, while the world he thought he remembered was only the fantasy of an amnesic brain?

And they never let him step out of the room, not even into the corridor. Was he a prisoner, then? Had he committed a crime?

There never can be a man so lost as one who is lost in the vast and intricate corridors of his own lonely mind, where none may reach and none may save. There never was a man so helpless as one who cannot remember.

Pola amused herself by teaching him words. He was not at all amazed at the ease with which he picked them up and remembered. He remembered that he had had a trick memory in the past; that memory, at least, seemed accurate. In two days he could understand simple sentences. In three he could make himself understood.

On the third day, however, he did become amazed. Shekt taught him numbers and set him problems. Schwartz would give answers, and Shekt would look at a timing device and record with rapid strokes of his stylus. But then Shekt explained the term "logarithm" to him and asked for the logarithm of two.

Schwartz picked his words carefully. His vocabulary was still minute and he reinforced it with gestures. "I—not— say. Answer—not—number."

Shekt nodded his head excitedly and said, "Not number. Not this, not that; part this, part that."

Schwartz understood quite well that Shekt had confirmed his statement that the answer was not an even number but a fraction and therefore said, "Point three zero one zero three—and—more—numbers."

"Enough!"

Then came the amazement. How had he known the answer to that? Schwartz was certain that he had never heard of logarithms before, yet in his mind the answer had come as soon as the question was put. He had no idea of the process by which it had been calculated. It was as if his mind were an independent entity, using him only as its mouthpiece.

Or had he once been a mathematician, in the days before his amnesia?

He found it exceedingly difficult to wait the days out. Increasingly he felt he must venture out into the world and force an answer from it somehow. He could never learn in the prison of this room, where (the thought suddenly came to him) he was but a medical specimen.

The chance came on the sixth day. They were beginning to trust him too much, and one time when Shekt left he did not lock the door. Where usually the door so neatly closed itself that the very crack of its joining the wall became invisible, this time a quarter inch of space showed.

He waited to make sure Shekt was not returning on the instant, and then slowly put his hand over the little gleaming light as he had seen them often do. Smoothly and silently the door slid open. . . . The corridor was empty.

And so Schwartz "escaped."

How was he to know that for the six days of his residence there the Society of Ancients had its agents watching the hospital, his room, himself?

6. APPREHENSION IN THE NIGHT

The Procurator's palace was scarcely less a fairyland at night. The evening flowers (none native to Earth) opened their fat white blossoms in festoons that extended their delicate fragrance to the very walls of the palace. Under the polarized light of the moon, the artificial silicate strands woven cleverly into the stainless aluminum alloy of the palace structure sparked a faint violet against the metallic sheen of their surroundings.

Ennius looked at the stars. They were the real beauty to him, since they were the Empire.

Earth's sky was of an intermediate type. It had not the unbearable glory of the skies of the Central Worlds, where star elbowed star in such blinding competition that the black of night was nearly lost in a coruscant explosion of light. Nor did it possess the lonely grandeur of the skies of the Periphery, where the unrelieved blackness was broken at great intervals by the dimness of an orphaned star—with the milky lens shape of the Galaxy spreading across the sky, the individual stars thereof lost in diamond dust.

On Earth two thousand stars were visible at one time. Ennius could see Sirius, round which circled one of the ten most populous planets of the Empire. There was Arcturus, capital of the sector of his birth. The sun of Trantor, the Empire's capital world, was lost somewhere in the Milky Way. Even under a telescope it was just part of a general blaze.

He felt a soft hand on his shoulder, and his own went up to meet it.

"Flora?" he whispered.

"It had better be," came his wife's half-amused voice. "Do you know that you haven't slept since you returned from Chica? Do you know further that it is almost dawn?... Shall I have breakfast sent out here?"

"Why not?" He smiled fondly up at her and felt in the darkness for the brown ringlet that hovered next to her cheek. He tugged at it. "And must you wait up with me and shadow the most beautiful eyes in the Galaxy?"

She freed her hair and replied gently, "You are trying to shadow them yourself with your sugar syrup, but I've seen you this way before and am not in the tiniest hoodwinked. What worries you tonight, dear?"

"Why, that which always worries me. That I have buried you here uselessly, when there's not a viceregal society in the Galaxy you could not grace."

"Besides that! Come, Ennius, I will not be played with."

Ennius shook his head in the shadows and said, "I don't know. I think an accumulation of little puzzling things has finally sickened me. There's the matter of Shekt and his Synapsifier. And there's this archaeologist, Arvardan, and his theories. And other things, other things. Oh, what's the use, Flora—I'm doing no good here at all."

"Surely this time of the morning isn't quite the moment for putting your morale to the test."

But Ennius was speaking through clenched teeth. "These Earthmen! Why should so few be such a burden to the Empire? Do you remember, Flora, when I was first appointed to the Procuracy, the warnings I received from old Faroul, the last Procurator, as to the difficulties of the position?...He was right. If anything, he did not go far enough in his warnings. Yet I laughed at him at the time and privately thought him the victim of his own senile incapacity. I was young, active, daring. I would do better..." He paused, lost in himself, then continued, apparently at a disconnected point. "Yet so many independent pieces of evidence seem to show that these Earthmen are once again being misled into dreams of rebellion."

He looked up at his wife. "Do you know that it is the doctrine of the Society of Ancients that Earth was at one time the sole home of Humanity, that it is the appointed center of the race, the true representation of Man?"

"Why, so Arvardan told us two evenings ago, didn't he?" It was always best at these times to let him talk himself out.

"Yes, so he did," said Ennius gloomily, "but even so, he spoke only of the past. The Society of Ancients speaks of the future as well. Earth, once more, they say, will be the center of the race. They even claim that this mythical Second Kingdom of Earth is at hand; they warn that the Empire will be destroyed in a general catastrophe which will leave Earth triumphant in all its pristine glory"—and his voice shook—"as a backward, barbarous, soil-sick world. Three times before this same nonsense has raised rebellion, and the destruction brought down upon Earth has never served in the least to shake their stupid faith."

"They are but poor creatures," said Flora, "these men of Earth. What should they have, if not their Faith? They are certainly robbed of everything else—of a decent world, of a decent life. They are even robbed of the dignity of acceptance on a basis of equality by the rest of the Galaxy. So they retire to their dreams. Can you blame them?"

"Yes, I can blame them," cried Ennius with energy. "Let them turn from their dreams and fight for assimilation. They don't deny they are different. They simply wish to replace 'worse' by 'better,' and you can't expect the rest of the Galaxy to let them do that. Let them abandon their cliquishness, their outdated and offensive 'Customs.' Let them be *people*, and they will be considered people. Let them be Earthers and they will be considered only as such.

"But never mind that. For instance, what's going on with the Synapsifier? Now there's a little thing that is keeping me from sleep." Ennius frowned thoughtfully at the dullness which was overcoming the polished darkness of the eastern sky.

"The Synapsifier? . . . Why, isn't that the instrument Dr. Arvardan spoke of at dinner? Did you go to Chica to see about that?"

Ennius nodded.

"And what did you find out there?"

"Why nothing at all," said Ennius. "I know Shekt. I know him well. I can tell when he's at ease; I can tell when he isn't. I tell you, Flora, that man was dying of apprehension all the time he was speaking to me. And when I left he broke into a sweat of thankfulness. It is an unhappy mystery, Flora."

"But will the machine work?"

"Am I a neurophysicist? Shekt says it will not. He called me up to tell me that a volunteer was nearly killed by it. But I don't believe that. He was excited! He was more than that. He was triumphant! His volunteer had lived and the experiment had been successful, or I've never seen a happy man in my life. . . . Now why do you suppose he lied to me, then? Do you suppose that the Synapsifier is in operation? Do you suppose that it can be creating a race of geniuses?"

"But then why keep it secret?"

"Ah! Why? It isn't obvious to you. Why has Earth failed in its rebellions? There are fairly tremendous odds against it, aren't there? Increase the average intelligence of the Earthman. Double it. Triple it. And where may your odds be then?"

"Oh, Ennius."

"We may be in the position of apes attacking human beings. What price numerical odds?"

"You're really jumping at shadows. They couldn't hide a thing like that. You can always have the Bureau of Outer Provinces send in a few psychologists and keep testing random samples of Earthmen. Surely any abnormal rise in I.Q. could be detected instantly."

"Yes. I suppose so. . . . But that may not be it. I'm not sure of anything, Flora, except that a rebellion is in the cards. Something like the last one, except that it will probably be worse."

"Are we prepared for it? I mean, if you're so certain——"

"Prepared?" Ennius's laughter was a bark. "*I* am. The garrison is in readiness and fully supplied. Whatever can possibly be done with the material at hand, I have done. But, Flora, I don't want to have a rebellion. I don't want my Procuracy to go down in history as the Procuracy of the Rebellion. I don't want my name linked with death and slaughter. I'll be decorated for it, but a century from now the history books will call me a bloody tyrant. What about the Viceroy of Santanni in the sixth century? Could he have done other than he did, though millions died? He was honored then, but who has a good word for him now? *I* would rather be known as the man who prevented a rebellion and saved the worthless lives of twenty million fools." He sounded quite hopeless about it.

"Are you so sure you can't, Ennius—even yet?" She sat down beside him and brushed her finger tips along the line of his jaw.

He caught them and held them tightly. "How can I? Everything works against me. The Bureau itself rushes into the struggle on the side of the fanatics of Earth by sending this Arvardan here."

"But, dear, I don't see that this archaeologist will do anything so awful. I'll admit he sounds like a faddist, but what harm can he do?"

"Why, isn't it plain? He wants to be allowed to prove that Earth *is* the original home of Humanity. He wants to bring scientific authority to the aid of subversion."

"Then stop him."

"I can't. There you have it, frankly. There's a theory about that viceroys can do anything, but that just isn't so. That man, Arvardan, has a writ of permission from the

Bureau of Outer Provinces. It is approved by the Emperor. That supersedes me completely. I could do nothing without appealing to the Central Council, and that would take months. . . . And what reasons could I give? If I tried to stop him by force, on the other hand, it would be an act of rebellion; and you know how ready the Central Council is to remove any executive they think is overstepping the line, ever since the Civil War of the eighties. And then what? I'd be replaced by someone who wouldn't be aware of the situation at all, and Arvardan would go ahead anyway.

"And that *still* isn't the worst, Flora. Do you know how he intends to prove the antiquity of Earth? Suppose you guess."

Flora laughed gently. "You're making fun of me, Ennius. How should I guess? I'm no archaeologist. I suppose he'll try to dig up old statues or bones and date them by their radioactivity or something like that."

"I wish it were like that. What Arvardan intends to do, he told me yesterday, is to enter the radioactive areas on Earth. He intends to find human artifacts there, show that they exist from a time previous to that at which Earth's soil became radioactive—since he insists the radioactivity is man-made—and date it in that fashion."

"But that's almost what I said."

"Do you know what it means to enter the radioactive areas? They're Forbidden. It's one of the strongest Customs these Earthmen have. No one can enter the Forbidden Areas, and all radioactive areas are Forbidden."

"But then that's good. Arvardan will be stopped by the men of Earth themselves."

"Oh, fine. He'll be stopped by the High Minister! And then how will we ever convince him that all this was not a Government-sponsored project, that the Empire is not conniving at deliberate sacrilege?"

"The High Minister can't be that touchy."

"Can't he?" Ennius reared back and stared at his wife. The night had lightened to a slatiness in which she was just visible. "You have the most touching naïveté. He certainly *can* be that touchy. Do you know what happened—oh, about fifty years ago? I'll tell you, and then you can judge for yourself.

"Earth, it so happens, will allow no outward sign of Imperial domination on their world because of their insistence that Earth is the rightful ruler of the Galaxy. But it so happened that young Stannell II—the boy emperor who was somewhat insane and who was removed by assassination after a reign of two years; you remember!—ordered that the Emperor's insignia be raised in their Council Chamber at Washenn. In itself the order was reasonable, since the insignia is present in every planetary Council Chamber in the Galaxy as a symbol of the Imperial unity. But what happened in this case? The day the insignia was raised, the town became a mass of riots.

"The lunatics of Washenn tore down the insignia and took up arms against the garrison. Stannell II was sufficiently mad to demand that his order be complied with if it meant the slaughter of every Earthman alive, but he was assassinated before that could be put into effect, and Edard, his successor, canceled the original order. All was peace again."

"You mean," said Flora incredulously, "that the Imperial insignia was not replaced?"

"I mean that exactly. By the Stars, Earth is the only one of the millions and millions of planets in the Empire that has no insignia in its Council Chamber. This miserable planet we are on now. And if even today we were to try again, they would fight to the last man to prevent us. And you ask me if they're touchy. I tell you they're mad."

There was silence in the slowly graying light of dawn, until Flora's voice sounded again, little and unsure of itself.

"Ennius?"

"Yes."

"You're not just concerned about the rebellion that you're expecting because of its effect on your reputation. I wouldn't be your wife if I couldn't half read your thoughts, and it seems to me that you expect something actually dangerous to the Empire. . . . You shouldn't hide anything from me, Ennius. You're afraid these Earthmen will *win*."

"Flora, I can't talk about it." There was something tortured in his eyes. "It isn't even a hunch.... Maybe four years on this world is too long for any sane man. But why are these Earthmen so confident?"

"How do you know they are?"

"Oh, they are. I have *my* sources of information too. After all, they've been crushed three times. They *can't* have illusions left. Yet they face two hundred million worlds, each one singly stronger than they, and they are confident. Can they really be so firm in their faith in some Destiny or some supernatural Force—something that has meaning only to them? Maybe—maybe—maybe——"

"Maybe what, Ennius?"

"Maybe they have their weapons."

"Weapons that will allow one world to defeat two hundred millions? You *are* panicky. No weapon could do that."

"I have already mentioned the Synapsifier."

"And I have told you how to take care of that. Do you know of any other type of weapon they could use?"

Reluctantly, "No."

"Exactly. There isn't any such weapon possible. Now I'll tell you what to do, dear. Why don't you get in touch with the High Minister and, in earnest of your good faith, warn him of Arvardan's plans? Urge, unofficially, that he not be granted permission. This will remove any suspicion—or should—that the Imperial Government has any hand in this silly violation of their customs. At the same time you will have stopped Arvardan without having appeared in the mess yourself. Then have the Bureau send out two good psychologists—or, better, ask for four, so they'll be sure to send at least two—and have them check on the Synapsifier possibility.... And anything else can be taken care of by our soldiers, while we allow posterity to take care of itself.

"Now why don't you sleep right here? We can put the chair back down, you can use my fur piece as a blanket, and I'll have a breakfast tray wheeled out when you awake. Things will seem different in the sun."

And so it was that Ennius, after waking the night through, fell asleep five minutes before sunrise.

Thus it was eight hours later that the High Minister first learned of Bel Arvardan and his mission from the Procurator himself.

7. CONVERSATION WITH MADMEN?

As for Arvardan, he was concerned only with making holiday. His ship, the *Ophiuchus*, was not to be expected for at least a month, therefore he had a month to spend as lavishly as he might wish.

So it was that on the sixth day after his arrival at Everest, Bel Arvardan left his host and took passage on the Terrestrial Air Transport Company's largest jet Stratospheric, traveling between Everest and the Terrestrial capital, Washenn.

If he took a commercial liner, rather than the speedy cruiser placed at his service by Ennius, it was done deliberately, out of the reasonable curiosity of a stranger and an archaeologist toward the ordinary life of men inhabiting such a planet as Earth.

And for another reason too.

Arvardan was from the Sirian Sector, notoriously the sector above all others in the Galaxy where anti-Terrestrian prejudice was strong. Yet he had always liked to think he had not succumbed to that prejudice himself. As a scientist, as an archaeologist, he couldn't afford to. Of course he had grown into the habit of thinking of Earthmen in certain set caricature types, and even now the word "Earthman" seemed an ugly one to him. But he wasn't really prejudiced.

At least he didn't think so. For instance, if an Earthman had ever wished to join an expedition of his or work for him in any capacity—and had the training and the ability— he would be accepted. If there were an opening for him, that was. And if the other members of the expedition didn't mind too much. That *was* the rub. Usually the fellow workers objected, and then what could you do?

He pondered the matter. Now certainly he would have no objection to be eating with an Earthman, or even bunking with one in case of need—assuming the Earthman were reasonably clean, and healthy. In fact, he would in all ways treat him as he would treat anyone else, he thought. Yet there was no denying that he would always be conscious of the fact that an Earthman was an Earthman. He couldn't help that. That was the result of a childhood immersed in an atmosphere of bigotry so complete that it was almost invisible, so entire that you accepted its axioms as second nature. Then you left it and saw it for what it was when you looked back.

But here was his chance to test himself. He was in a plane with only Earthmen about him, and he felt perfectly natural, almost. Well, just a little self-conscious.

Arvardan looked about at the undistinguished and normal faces of his fellow passengers. They were supposed to be different, these Earthmen, but could he have told these from ordinary men if he had met them casually in a crowd? He didn't think so. The women weren't bad-looking...His brows knit. Of course even tolerance must draw the line somewhere. Intermarriage, for instance, was quite unthinkable.

The plane itself was, in his eyes, a small affair of imperfect construction. It was, of course, nuclear-powered, but the application of the principle was far from efficient. For one thing, the power unit was not well shielded. Then it occurred to Arvardan that the presence of stray gamma rays and a high neutron density in the atmosphere might well strike Earthmen as less important than it might strike others.

Then the view caught his eyes. From the dark wine-purple of the extreme stratosphere, Earth presented a fabulous appearance. Beneath him the vast and misted land areas in sight (obscured here and there by the patches of sun-bright clouds) showed a desert orange. Behind them, slowly receding from the fleeing stratoliner, was the soft and fuzzy night line, within whose dark shadow there was the sparking of the radioactive areas.

His attention was drawn from the window by the laughter among the others. It seemed to center about an elderly couple, comfortably stout and all smiles.

Arvardan nudged his neighbor. "What's going on?"

His neighbor paused to say, "They've been married forty years, and they're making the Grand Tour."

"The Grand Tour?"

"You know. All around the Earth."

The elderly man, flushed with pleasure, was recounting in voluble fashion his experiences and impressions. His wife joined in periodically, with meticulous corrections involving completely unimportant points; these being given and taken in the best of humor. To all this the audience listened with the greatest attention, so that to Arvardan it seemed that Earthmen were as warm and human as any people in the Galaxy.

And then someone asked, "And when is it that you're scheduled for the Sixty?"

"In about a month," came the ready, cheerful answer. "Sixteenth November."

"Well," said the questioner, "I hope you have a nice day for it. My father reached his Sixty in a damned pouring rain. I've never seen one like it since. I was going with him—you know, a fellow likes company on a day like that—and he complained about the rain every step of the way. We had an open biwheel, you see, and we got soaked. 'Listen,' I said, 'what are *you* complaining about, Dad? *I've* got to come back.'"

There was a general howl of laughter which the anniversary couple were not backward in joining. Arvardan, however, felt plunged in horror as a distinct and uncomfortable suspicion entered his mind.

He said to the man sharing his seat, "This Sixty, this subject of conversation here—I take it they're referring to euthanasia. I mean, you're put out of the way when you reach your sixtieth birthday, aren't you?"

Arvardan's voice faded somewhat as his neighbor choked off the last of his chuckles to turn in his seat and favor the questioner with a long and suspicious stare. Finally he said, "Well, what do you think he meant?"

Arvardan made an indefinite gesture with his hand and smiled rather foolishly. He had known of the custom, but only academically. Something in a book. Something discussed in a scientific paper. But it was now borne in upon him that it actually applied to living beings, that the men and women surrounding him could, by custom, live only to sixty.

The man next to him was still staring. "Hey, fella, where you from? Don't they know about the Sixty in your home town?"

"We call it the 'Time,'" said Arvardan feebly. "I'm from back there." He jerked his thumb hard over his shoulder, and after an additional quarter minute the other withdrew that hard, questioning stare.

Arvardan's lips quirked. These people were suspicious. That facet of the caricature, at least, was authentic.

The elderly man was talking again. "She's coming with me," he said, nodding toward his genial wife. "She's not due for about three months after that, but there's no point in her waiting, she thinks, and we might as well go together. Isn't that it, Chubby?"

"Oh yes," she said, and giggled rosily. "Our children are all married and have homes of their own. I'd just be a bother to them. Besides, I couldn't enjoy the time anyway without the old fellow—so we'll just leave off together."

Whereupon the entire list of passengers seemed to engage themselves in a simultaneous arithmetical calculation of the time remaining to each—a process involving conversion factors from months to days that occasioned several disputes among the married couples involved.

One small fellow with tight clothes and a determined expression said fiercely, "I've got exactly twelve years, three months, and four days left. Twelve years, three months, and four days. Not a day more, not a day less."

Which someone qualified by saying, reasonably, "Unless you die first, of course."

"Nonsense," was the immediate reply. "I have no intention of dying first. Do I look like the sort of man who would die first? I'm living twelve years, three months, and four days, and there's not a man here with the hardihood to deny it." And he looked very fierce indeed.

A slim young man took a long, dandyish cigarette from between his lips to say darkly, "It's well for them that can calculate it out to a day. There's many a man living past his time."

"Ah, surely," said another, and there was a general nod and a rather inchoate air of indignation arose.

"Not," continued the young man, interspersing his cigarette puffs with a complicated flourish intended to remove the ash, "that I see any objection to a man—or woman—wishing to continue on past their birthday to the next Council day, particularly if they have some business to clean up. It's these sneaks and parasites that try to go past to the next Census, eating the food of the next generation——" He seemed to have a personal grievance there.

Arvardan interposed gently, "But aren't the ages of everyone registered? They can't very well pass their birthday too far, can they?"

A general silence followed, admixtured not a little with contempt at the foolish idealism expressed. Someone said at last, in diplomatic fashion, as though attempting to conclude the subject, "Well, there isn't much point living past the Sixty, I suppose."

"Not if you're a farmer," shot back another vigorously. "After you've been working in the fields for half a century, you'd be crazy not to be glad to call it off. How about the administrators, though, and the businessmen?"

Finally the elderly man, whose fortieth wedding anniversary had begun the conversation, ventured his own opinion, emboldened perhaps by the fact that, as a current victim of the Sixty, he had nothing to lose.

"As to that," he said, "it depends on who you know." And he winked with a sly innuendo. "I knew a man once who was sixty the year after the 810 Census and lived till the 820 Census caught him. He was sixty-nine before he left off. Sixty-nine! Think of that!"

"How did he manage that?"

"He had a little money, and his brother was one of the Society of Ancients. There's nothing you can't do if you've got that combination."

There was general approval of that sentiment.

"Listen," said the young man with the cigarette emphatically, "I had an uncle who lived a year past—just a year. He was just one of these selfish guys who don't feel like going, you know. A lot he cared for the rest of us. . . . And I didn't know about it, you see, or I would have reported him, believe me, because a guy should go when it's his time. It's only fair to the next generation. Anyway, he got caught all right, and the first thing *I* knew, the Brotherhood calls on me and my brother and wants to know how come we didn't report him. I said, hell, I didn't know anything about it; nobody in my family knew anything about it. I said we hadn't seen him in ten years. My old man backed us up. But we got fined five hundred credits just the same. That's when you don't have any pull."

The look of discomposure on Arvardan's face was growing. Were these people madmen to accept death so—to resent their friends and relatives who tried to escape death? Could he, by accident, be on a ship carrying a cargo of lunatics to asylum—or euthanasia? Or were these simply Earthmen?

His neighbor was scowling at him again, and his voice broke in on Arvardan's thoughts. "Hey fella, where's 'back there'?"

"Pardon me?"

"I said—where are you from? You said 'back there.' What's 'back there'? Hey?"

Arvardan found the eyes of all upon him now, each with its own sudden spark of suspicion in it. Did they think him a member of this Society of Ancients of theirs? Had his questioning seemed the cajolery of an *agent provocateur*?

So he met that by saying, in a burst of frankness, "I'm not from anywhere on Earth. I'm Bel Arvardan from Baronn, Sirius Sector. What's your name?" And he held out his hand.

He might as well have dropped a nuclear micro-bomb into the middle of the plane.

The first silent horror on every face turned rapidly into angry, bitter hostility that flamed at him. The man who had shared his seat rose stiffly and crowded into another, where the pair of occupants squeezed closely together to make room for him.

Faces turned away. Shoulders surrounded him, hemmed him in. For a moment Arvardan burned with indignation. Earthmen to treat *him* so! *Earthmen!* He had held out the hand of friendship to them. He, a Sirian, had condescended to treat with them and they had rebuffed him.

And then, with an effort, he relaxed. It was obvious that bigotry was never a one-way operation, that hatred bred hatred!

He was conscious of a presence beside him, and he turned toward it resentfully. "Yes?"

It was the young man with the cigarette. He was lighting a new one as he spoke. "Hello," he said. "My name's Creen. . . . Don't let those jerks get you."

"No one's getting me," said Arvardan shortly. He was not too pleased with the company, nor was he in the mood for patronizing advice from an Earthman.

But Creen was not trained to the detection of the more delicate nuances. He puffed his cigarette to life in man-sized drags and tapped its ashes over the arm of the seat into the middle aisle.

"Provincials!" he whispered with contempt. "Just a bunch of farmers. . . . They lack the Galactic view. Don't bother with them.... Now you take me. I got a different philosophy. Live and let live, I say. I got nothing against Outsiders. If they want to be friendly with me, I'll be friendly with them. What the hell——They can't help being an Outsider just like I can't help being an Earthman. Don't you think I'm right?" And he tapped Arvardan familiarly on the wrist.

Arvardan nodded and felt a crawling sensation at the other's touch. Social contact with a man who felt resentful over losing a chance to bring about his uncle's death was not pleasant, quite regardless of planetary origin.

Creen leaned back. "Heading for Chica? What did you say your name was? Albadan?"

"Arvardan. Yes, I'm going to Chica."

"That's my home town. Best damned city on Earth. Going to stay there long?"

"Maybe. I haven't made any plans."

"Umm.... Say, I hope you don't object to my saying that I've been noticing your shirt. Mind if I take a close look? Made in Sirius, huh?"

"Yes, it is."

"It's very good material. Can't get anything like that on Earth.... Say, bud, you wouldn't have a spare shirt like that in your luggage, would you? I'd pay for it if you wanted to sell it. It's a snappy number."

Arvardan shook his head emphatically. "Sorry, but I don't have much of a wardrobe. I am planning to buy clothes here on Earth as I go along."

"I'll pay you fifty credits," said Creen.... Silence. He added, with a touch of resentment, "That's a good price."

"A very good price," said Arvardan, "but, as I told you, I have no shirts to sell."

"Well..." Creen shrugged. "Expect to stay on Earth quite a while, I suppose?"

"Maybe."

"What's your line of business?"

The archaeologist allowed irritation to rise to the surface. "Look, Mr. Creen, if you don't mind, I'm a little tired and would like to take a nap. Is that all right with you?"

Creen frowned. "What's the matter with *you*? Don't your kind believe in being civil to people? I'm just asking you a polite question; no need to bite my ear off."

The conversation, hitherto conducted in a low voice, had suddenly amplified itself into a near shout. Hostile expressions turned Arvardan's way, and the archaeologist's lips compressed themselves into a thin line.

He had asked for it, he decided bitterly. He would not have gotten into this mess if he had held aloof from the beginning, if he hadn't felt the necessity of vaunting his damned tolerance and forcing it on people who didn't want it.

He said levelly, "Mr. Creen, I didn't ask you to join me, and I haven't been uncivil. I repeat, I am tired and would like to rest. I think there's nothing unusual in that."

"Listen"—the young man rose from his seat, threw his cigarette away with a violent gesture, and pointed a finger— "you don't have to treat me like I'm a dog or something. You stinking Outsiders come here with your fine talk and standoffishness and think it gives you the right to stamp all over us. We don't have to stand for it, see. If you don't like it here, you can go back where you came from, and it won't take much more of your lip to make me light into you, either. You think I'm afraid of you?"

Arvardan turned his head away and stared stonily out the window.

Creen said no more, but took his original seat once again. There was an excited buzz of conversation round and about the plane which Arvardan ignored. He felt, rather than saw, the sharpened and envenomed glances being cast at him. Until, gradually, it passed, as all things did.

He completed the journey, silent and alone.

The landing at the Chica airport was welcome. Arvardan smiled to himself at the first sight from the air of the "best damned city on Earth," but found it, nevertheless, an immense improvement over the thick, unfriendly atmosphere of the plane.

He supervised the unloading of his luggage and had it

transferred into a biwheel cab. At least he would be the only passenger here, so that if he took care not to speak unnecessarily to the driver, he could scarcely get into trouble.

"State House," he told the cabby, and they were off.

Arvardan thus entered Chica for the first time, and he did so on the day that Joseph Schwartz escaped from his room at the Institute for Nuclear Reasearch.

Creen watched Arvardan leave with a bitter half-smile. He took out his little book and studied it closely between puffs at his cigarette. He hadn't gotten much out of the passengers, despite his story about his uncle (which he had used often before to good effect). To be sure, the old guy had complained about a man living past his time and had blamed it on "pull" with the Ancients. That would come under the heading of slander against the Brotherhood. But then the geezer was heading for the Sixty in a month, anyway. No use putting his name down.

But this Outsider, that was different. He surveyed the item with a feeling of pleasure: "Bel Arvardan, Baronn, Sirius Sector—curious about the Sixty—secretive about own affairs—entered Chica by commercial plane 11 A.M. Chica time, 12 October—anti-Terrestrian attitude very marked."

This time maybe he had a real haul. Picking up these little squealers who made incautious remarks was dull work, but things like this made it pay off.

The Brotherhood would have his report before half an hour was up. He made his way leisurely off the field.

8. CONVERGENCE AT CHICA

For the twentieth time Dr. Shekt leafed through his latest volume of research notes, then looked up as Pola entered his office. She frowned as she slipped on her lab coat.

"Now, Father, haven't you eaten yet?"

"Eh? Certainly I have ... Oh, what's this?"

"This is lunch. Or it was, once. What you ate must have been breakfast. Now there's no sense in my buying meals and bringing them here if you're not going to eat them. I'm just going to make you go home for them."

"Don't get excited. I'll eat it. I can't interrupt a vital experiment every time you think I ought to eat, you know."

He grew cheerful again over the dessert. "You have no idea," he said, "the kind of man this Schwartz is. Did I ever tell you about his skull sutures?"

"They're primitive. You told me."

"But that's not all. He's got thirty-two teeth: three molars up and down, left and right, counting one false one that must be homemade. At least I've never seen a bridge that has metal prongs hooking it onto adjacent teeth instead of being grafted to the jawbone. . . . But have you ever seen anyone with thirty-two teeth?"

"I don't go about counting people's teeth, Father. What's the right number—twenty-eight?"

"It sure is. . . . I'm still not finished, though. We took an internal analysis yesterday. What do you suppose we found? . . . Guess!"

"Intestines?"

"Pola, you're being deliberately annoying, but I don't care. You needn't guess; I'll tell you. Schwartz has a vermiform appendix, three and a half inches long, and it's open. Great Galaxy, it's completely unprecedented! I have checked with the Medical School—cautiously, of course— and appendixes are practically never longer than half an inch, and they're never open."

"And just what does that mean?"

"Why, he's a complete throwback, a living fossil." He had risen from his chair and paced the distance to the wall and back with hasty steps. "I tell you what, Pola, I don't think we ought to give Schwartz up. He's too valuable a specimen."

"No, no, Father," said Pola quickly, "you can't do that. You promised that farmer to return Schwartz, and you must for Schwartz's own sake. He's unhappy."

"Unhappy! Why, we're treating him like a rich Outsider."

"What difference does that make? The poor fellow is used to his farm and his people. He's lived there all his life. And now he's had a frightening experience—a painful one, for all I know—and his mind works differently now. He can't be expected to understand. We've got to consider his human rights and return him to his family."

"But, Pola, the cause of science——"

"Oh, slush! What is the cause of science worth to me? What do you suppose the Brotherhood will say when they hear of your unauthorized experiments? Do you think *they* care about the cause of science? I mean, consider yourself if you don't wish to consider Schwartz. The longer you keep him, the greater the chance of being caught. You send him home tomorrow night, the way you originally planned to, do you hear?...I'll go down and see if Schwartz wants anything before dinner."

But she was back in less than five minutes, face damp and chalky. "Father, he's gone!"

"Who's gone?" he asked, startled.

"Schwartz!" she cried, half in tears. "You must have forgotten to lock the door when you left him."

Shekt was on his feet, throwing a hand out to steady himself. "How long?"

"I don't know. But it can't be very long. When were you last there?"

"Not fifteen minutes. I had just been here a minute or two when you came in."

"Well, then," with sudden decision, "I'll run out. He may simply be wandering about the neighborhood. *You* stay here. If someone else picks him up, they mustn't connect him with you. Understand?"

Shekt could only nod.

Joseph Schwartz felt no lifting of the heart when he exchanged the confines of his prison hospital for the expanses of the city outside. He did not delude himself to the effect that he had a plan of action. He knew, and knew well, that he was simply improvising.

If any rational impulse guided him (as distinct from mere blind desire to exchange inaction for action of any sort), it was the hope that by chance encounter some facet of life would bring back his wandering memory. That he was an amnesiac he was now fully convinced.

The first glimpse of the city, however, was disheartening. It was late afternoon and, in the sunlight, Chica was a milky white. The buildings might have been constructed of porcelain, like that farmhouse he had first stumbled upon.

Stirrings deep within told him that cities should be brown and red. And they should be much dirtier. He was sure of that.

He walked slowly. He felt, somehow, that there would be no organized search for him. He knew that, without knowing how he knew. To be sure, in the last few days he had found himself growing increasingly sensitive to "atmosphere," to the "feel" of things about him. It was part of the strangeness in his mind, since—since . . .

His thought trailed away.

In any case, the "atmosphere" at the hospital prison was one of secrecy; a frightened secrecy, it seemed. So they could not pursue him with loud outcry. He *knew* that. Now why should he know that? Was this queer activity of his mind part of what went on in cases of amnesia?

He crossed another intersection. Wheeled vehicles were relatively few. Pedestrians were—well, pedestrians. Their clothes were rather laughable: seamless, buttonless, colorful. But then so were his own. He wondered where his old clothes were, then wondered if he had ever really owned such clothes as he remembered. It is very difficult to be sure of anything, once you begin doubting your memory on principle.

But he remembered his wife so clearly; his children. They *couldn't* be fictions. He stopped in the middle of the walk to regain a composure suddenly lost. Perhaps they were distorted versions of real people, in this so unreal-seeming real life, whom he *must* find.

People were brushing past him and several muttered unamiably. He moved on. The thought occurred to him, suddenly and forcibly, that he was hungry, or would be soon, and that he had no money.

He looked about. Nothing like a restaurant in sight. Well, how did he know? He couldn't read the signs.

He gazed into each store front he passed. . . . And then he found an interior which consisted in part of small alcoved tables, at one of which two men sat and another at which a single man sat. And the men were eating.

At least that hadn't changed. Men who ate still chewed and swallowed.

He stepped in and, for a moment, stopped in considerable bewilderment. There was no counter, no cooking going on, no signs of any kitchen. It had been his idea to offer to wash the dishes for a meal, but—to whom could he make the offer?

Diffidently, he stepped up to the two diners. He pointed, and said painstakingly, "Food! Where? Please."

They looked up at him, rather startled. One spoke fluently, and quite incomprehensibly, patting a small structure at the wall end of the table. The other joined in, impatiently.

Schwartz's eyes fell. He turned to leave, and there was a hand upon his sleeve——

Granz had seen Schwartz while the latter was still only a plump and wistful face at the window.

He said, "What's *he* want?"

Messter, sitting across the little table, with his back to the street, turned, looked, shrugged his shoulders, and said nothing.

Granz said, "He's coming in," and Messter replied, "So what?"

"Nothing. Just mentioning it."

But a few moments later the newcomer, after looking about helplessly, approached and pointed to their beef stew, saying in a queer accent, "Food! Where? Please."

Granz looked up. "Food right here, bud. Just pull up a chair at any table you want and use the Foodo-mat....Foodomat! Don't you know what a Foodomat is?...Look at the poor jerk, Messter. He's looking at me as if he doesn't understand a word I say. Hey, fella—this thing, see. Just put a coin in and let me eat, will you?"

"Leave him alone," grunted Messter. "He's just a bum, looking for a handout."

"Hey, hold on." Granz seized Schwartz's sleeve as the latter turned to go. He added in an aside to Messter, "Space, let the guy eat. He's probably getting the Sixty soon. It's the least I can do to give him a break.... Hey, bud, you got any money?... Well, I'll be damned, he still doesn't understand me. Money, pal, money! This——" And he drew a shining half-credit piece out of his pocket, flipping it so that it sparkled in the air.

"Got any?" he asked.

Slowly Schwartz shook his head.

"Well, then, have this on me!" He replaced the half-credit piece in his pocket and tossed over a considerably smaller coin.

Schwartz held it uncertainly.

"All right. Don't just stand there. Stick it in the Foodomat. This thing here."

Schwartz suddenly found himself understanding. The Foodomat had a series of slits for coins of different sizes and a series of knobs opposite little milky rectangles, the writing upon which he could not read. Schwartz pointed to the food on the table and ran a forefinger up and down the knobs, raising his eyebrows in question.

Messter said in annoyance, "A sandwich isn't good enough for him. We're getting classy bums in this burg nowadays. It doesn't pay to humor them, Granz."

"All right, so I lose point eight five credits. Tomorrow's payday, anyway. . . . Here," he said to Schwartz. He placed coins of his own into the Foodomat and withdrew the wide metal container from the recess in the wall. "Now take it to another table. . . . Nah, keep that tenth piece. Buy yourself a cup of coffee with it."

Schwartz carried the container gingerly to the next table. It had a spoon attached to the side by means of a transparent, filmy material, which broke with a slight pop under the pressure of a fingernail. As it did so, the top of the container parted at a seam and curled back upon itself.

The food, unlike that which he saw the others eating, was cold; but that was a detail. It was only after a minute or so that he realized the food was getting warmer and that the container had grown hot to the touch. He stopped, in alarm, and waited.

The gravy first steamed, then bubbled gently for a moment. It cooled again and Schwartz completed the meal.

Granz and Messter were still there when he left. So was the third man, to whom, throughout, Schwartz had paid no attention.

Nor had Schwartz noticed, at any time since he had left

the Institute, the thin, little man who, without seeming to, had managed to remain always within eyeshot.

Bel Arvardan, having showered and changed his clothes, promptly followed his original intention of observing the human animal, subspecies Earth, in its native habitat. The weather was mild, the light breeze refreshing, the village itself—pardon, the city—bright, quiet, and clean.

Not so bad.

Chica first stop, he thought. Largest collection of Earthmen on the planet. Washenn next; local capital. Senloo! Senfran! Bonair! . . . He had plotted an itinerary all over the western continents (where most of the meager scattering of Earth's population lived) and, allowing two or three days at each, he would be back in Chica just about the time his expeditionary ship was due.

It would be educational.

As afternoon began to decline he stepped into a Foodomat and, as he ate, observed the small drama that played itself out between the two Earthmen who had entered shortly after himself and the plump, elderly man who came in last of all. But his observation was detached and casual, simply noting it as an item to set against his unpleasant experience on the jet transport. The two men at the table were obviously air-cab drivers and not wealthy, yet they could be charitable.

The begger left, and two minutes later Arvardan left as well.

The streets were noticeably fuller, as the workday was approaching its end.

He stepped hastily aside to avoid colliding with a young girl.

"Pardon me," he said.

She was dressed in white, in clothing which bore the stereotyped lines of a uniform. She seemed quite oblivious of the near collision. The anxious look on her face, the sharp turning of her head from side to side, her utter preoccupation, made the situation quite obvious.

He laid a light finger on her shoulder. "May I help you, miss? Are you in trouble?"

She stopped and turned startled eyes upon him. Arvardan found himself judging her age at nineteen to twenty-one, observing carefully her brown hair and dark eyes, her high cheekbones and little chin, her slim waist and graceful carriage. He discovered, suddenly, that the thought of this little female creature being an Earthwoman lent a sort of perverse piquancy to her attractiveness.

But she was still staring, and almost at the moment of speaking she seemed to break down. "Oh, it's no use. Please don't bother about me. It's silly to expect to find someone when you don't have the slightest idea where he could have gone." She was drooping in discouragement, her eyes wet. Then she straightened and breathed deeply. "Have you seen a plump man about five-four, dressed in green and white, no hat, rather bald?"

Arvardan looked at her in astonishment. "What? Green and white? . . . Oh, I don't believe this. . . . Look, this man you're referring to—does he speak with difficulty?"

"Yes, yes. Oh yes. You have seen him, then?"

"Not five minutes ago he was in there eating with two men. . . . Here they are. . . . Say, you two." He beckoned them over.

Granz reached them first. "Cab, sir?"

"No, but if you tell the young lady what happened to the man you were eating with, you'll stand to make the fare, anyway."

Granz paused and looked chagrined. "Well, I'd like to help you, but I never saw him before in my life."

Arvardan turned to the girl. "Now look, miss, he can't have gone in the direction you came from or you'd have seen him. And he can't be far away. Suppose we move north a bit. I'll recognize him if I see him."

His offer of help was an impulse, yet Arvardan was not, ordinarily, an impulsive man. He found himself smiling at her.

Granz interrupted suddenly. "What's he done, lady? He hasn't broken any of the Customs, has he?"

"No, no," she replied hastily. "He's only a little sick, that's all."

Messter looked after them as they left. "A little sick?" He shoved his visored cap back upon his head, then pinched balefully at his chin. "How d'ya like that, Granz? A little sick."

His eyes looked askance at the other for a moment.

"What's got into *you*?" asked Granz uneasily.

"Something that's making *me* a little sick. That guy must've been straight out of the hospital. That was a nurse looking for him, and a plenty worried nurse, too. Why should she be worried if he was just a *little* sick? He couldn't hardly talk, and he didn't hardly understand. You noticed that, didn't you?"

There was a sudden panicky light in Granz's eyes. "You don't think it's Fever?"

"I sure *do* think it's Radiation Fever—and he's far gone. He was within a foot of us, too. It's never any good——"

There was a little thin man next to them. A little thin man with bright, sharp eyes and a twittering voice, who had stepped out of nowhere. "What's that, gents? Who's got Radiation Fever?"

He was regarded with disfavor. "Who are you?"

"Ho," said the sharp little man, "you want to know, do you? It so happens that I'm a messenger of the Brotherhood, to be sure." He flashed a little glowing badge on the inner lapel of his jacket. "Now, in the name of the Society of Ancients, what's all this about Radiation Fever?"

Messter spoke in cowed and sullen tones. "*I* don't know nothing. There's a nurse looking for somebody who's sick, and I was wondering if it was Radiation Fever. That's not against the Customs, is it?"

"Ho! You're telling *me* about the Customs, are you? You better go about your business and let *me* worry about the Customs."

The little man rubbed his hands together, gazed quickly about him, and hurried northward.

"There he is!" and Pola clutched feverishly at her companion's elbow. It had happened quickly, easily, and accidentally. Through the despairing blankness he had suddenly materialized just within the main entrance of the self-service department store, not three blocks from the Foodomat.

"I see him," whispered Arvardan. "Now stay back and let me follow him. If he sees you and dashes into the mob, we'll never locate him."

Casually they followed in a sort of nightmare chase. The human contents of the store was a quicksand which could absorb its prey slowly—or quickly—keep it hidden impenetrably, spew it forth unexpectedly, set up barriers that somehow would not yield. The mob might almost have had a malevolent conscious mind of its own.

And then Arvardan circled a counter watchfully, playing Schwartz as though he were at the end of a fishing line. His huge hand reached out and closed on the other's shoulder.

Schwartz burst into incomprehensible prose and jerked away in panic. Arvardan's grip, however, was unbreakable to men far stronger than Schwartz, and he contented himself with smiling and saying, in normal tones, for the benefit of the curious spectator, "Hello, old chap, haven't seen you in months. How are you?"

A palpable fraud, he supposed, in the face of the other's gibberish, but Pola had joined them.

"Schwartz," she whispered, "come back with us."

For a moment Schwartz stiffened in rebellion, then he drooped.

He said wearily, "I—go—along—you," but the statement was drowned in the sudden blare of the store's loudspeaker system.

"*Attention! Attention! Attention!* The management requests that all patrons of the store leave by the Fifth Street exit in orderly fashion. You will present your registration cards to the guards at the door. It is essential that this be done rapidly. *Attention! Attention! Attention!*"

The message was repeated three times, the last time over the sound of scuffling feet as crowds were beginning to line up at the exits. A many-tongued cry was making itself heard, asking in various fashions the forever-unanswerable question of "What's happened? What's going on?"

Arvardan shrugged and said, "Let's get on line, miss. We're leaving anyway."

But Pola shook her head. "We can't. We can't——"

"Why not?" The archaeologist frowned.

The girl merely shrank away from him. How could she tell him that Schwartz had no registration card? Who was he? Why had he been helping her? She was in a whirl of suspicion and despair.

She said huskily, "You'd better go, or you'll get into trouble."

They were pouring out the elevators as the upper floors emptied. Arvardan, Pola, and Schwartz were a little island of solidity in the human river.

Looking back on it later, Arvardan realized that at this point he could have left the girl. Left her! Never seen her again! Have nothing to reproach himself with!... And all would have been different. The great Galactic Empire would have dissolved in chaos and destruction.

He did not leave the girl. She was scarcely pretty in her fear and despair. No one could be. But Arvardan felt disturbed at the sight of her helplessness.

He had taken a step away, and now he turned. "Are you going to stay here?"

She nodded.

"But why?" he demanded.

"Because"—and the tears now overflowed—"I don't know what else to do."

She was just a little, frightened girl, even if she was an Earthie. Arvardan said, in a softer voice, "If you'll tell me what's wrong, I'll try to help."

There was no answer.

The three formed a tableau. Schwartz had sunk to the floor in a squatting posture, too sick at heart to try to follow the conversation, to be curious at the sudden emptiness of the store, to do anything but bury his head in his hands in the last unspoken and unuttered whimper of despair. Pola, weeping, knew only that she was more frightened than she had ever thought it possible for anyone to be. Arvardan, puzzled and waiting, tried clumsily and ineffectually to pat Pola's shoulder in encouraging fashion, and he was conscious only of the fact that for the first time he had touched an Earthgirl.

The little man came upon them thus.

9. CONFLICT AT CHICA

Lieutenant Marc Claudy of the Chica garrison yawned slowly and gazed into the middle distance with an ineffable boredom. He was completing his second year of duty on Earth and waited yearningly for replacement.

Nowhere in the Galaxy was the problem of maintaining a garrison quite so complicated as it was on this horrible world. On other planets there existed a certain camaraderie between soldier and civilian, particularly female civilian. There was a sense of freedom and openness.

But here the garrison was a prison. There were the radiation-proof barracks and the filtered atmosphere, free of radioactive dust. There was the lead-impregnated clothing, cold and heavy, which could not be removed without grave risk. As a corollary to that, fraternization with the population (assuming that the desperation of loneliness could drive a soldier to the society of an "Earthie" girl) was out of the question.

What was left, then, but short snorts, long naps, and slow madness?

Lieutenant Claudy shook his head in a futile attempt to clear it, yawned again, sat up and began dragging on his shoes. He looked at his watch and decided it was not yet quite time for evening chow.

And then he jumped to his feet, only one shoe on, acutely conscious of his uncombed hair, and saluted.

The colonel looked about him disparagingly but said nothing directly on the subject. Instead he directed crisply, "Lieutenant, there are reports of rioting in the business district. You will take a decontamination squad to the Dunham department store and take charge. You will see to it that all your men are thoroughly protected against infection by Radiation Fever."

"Radiation Fever!" cried the lieutenant. "Pardon me, sir, but——"

"You will be ready to leave in fifteen minutes," said the colonel coldly.

Arvardan saw the little man first, and stiffened as the other made a little gesture of greeting. "Hi, guv'ner. Hi, big fella. Tell the little lady there ain't no call for the waterworks."

Pola's head had snapped up, her breath sucked in. Automatically she leaned toward the protecting bulk of Arvardan, who, as automatically, put a protective arm about her. It did not occur to him that that was the second time he had touched an Earthgirl.

He said sharply, "What do you want?"

The little man with the sharp eyes stepped diffidently out from behind a counter piled high with packages. He spoke in a manner which managed to be both ingratiating and impudent simultaneously.

"Here's a weird go outside," he said, "but it don't need to bother you, miss. I'll get your man back to the Institute for you."

"What institute?" demanded Pola fearfully.

"Aw, come off it," said the little man. "I'm Natter, fella with the fruit stand right across the street from the Institute for Nuclear Research. I seen you here lots of times."

"See here," said Arvardan abruptly, "what's all this about?"

Natter's little frame shook with merriment. "They think this fella here has Radiation Fever——"

"Radiation Fever?" It came from both Arvardan and Pola at once.

Natter nodded. "That's right. Two cabbies ate with him and that's what they said. News like that kind spreads, you know."

"The guards outside," demanded Pola, "are just looking for someone with fever?"

"That's right."

"And just why aren't you afraid of the fever?" demanded Arvardan abruptly. "I take it that it was fear of contagion that caused the authorities to empty the store."

"Sure. The authorities are waiting outside, afraid to come in, too. They're waiting for the Outsiders' decontamination squad to get here."

"And you're not afraid of the fever, is that it?"

"Why should I be? This guy don't have no fever. Look at him. Where's the sores on his mouth? He isn't flushed. His eyes are all right. I know what fever looks like. Come on, miss, we'll march out of here, then."

But Pola was frightened again. "No, no. We can't. He's— he's——" She couldn't go on.

Natter said insinuatingly, "*I* could take him out. No questions asked. No registration card necessary——"

Pola failed to suppress a little cry, and Arvardan said, with considerable distaste, "What makes *you* so important?"

Natter laughed hoarsely. He flipped his lapel. "Messenger for the Society of Ancients. Nobody'll ask me questions."

"And what's in it for you?"

"Money! You're anxious and I can help you. There ain't no fairer than that. It's worth, say, a hundred credits to you, and it's worth a hundred credits to me. Fifty credits now, fifty on delivery."

But Pola whispered in horror, "You'll take him to the Ancients."

"What for? He's no good to them, and he's worth a hundred credits to me. If you wait for the Outsiders, they're liable to kill the fella before they find out he's fever-free. You know Outsiders—they don't care if they kill an Earthman or not. They'd rather, in fact."

Arvardan said, "Take the young lady with you."

But Natter's little eyes were very sharp and very sly. "Oh no. Not that guv'ner. I take what you call calculated risks. I can get by with one, maybe not with two. And if I only take one, I take the one what's worth more. Ain't that reasonable to you?"

"What," said Arvardan, "if I pick you up and pull your legs off? What'll happen then?"

Natter flinched, but found his voice, nevertheless, and managed a laugh. "Why, then, you're a dope. They'll get you anyway, and there'll be murder, too, on the list. . . . All right, guv'ner. Keep your hands off."

"Please"—Pola was dragging at Arvardan's arm—"we *must* take a chance. Let him do as he says. . . . You'll be honest with us, w-won't you, Mr. Natter?"

Natter's lips were curling. "Your big friend wrenched my arm. He had no call to do that, and I don't like nobody to push me around. I'll just take an extra hundred credits for that. Two hundred in all."

"My father'll pay you——"

"One hundred in advance," he replied obdurately.

"But I don't have a hundred credits," Pola wailed.

"That's all right, miss," said Arvardan stonily. "I can swing it."

He opened his wallet and plucked out several bills. He threw them at Natter. "Get going!"

"Go with him, Schwartz," whispered Pola.

Schwartz did, without comment, without caring. He would have gone to hell at that moment with as little emotion.

And they were alone, staring at each other blankly. It was perhaps the first time that Pola had actually looked at Arvardan, and she was amazed to find him tall and craggily handsome, calm and self-confident. She had accepted him till now as an inchoate, unmotivated helper, but now——

She grew suddenly shy, and all the events of the last hour or two were enmeshed and lost in a scurry of heartbeating.

They didn't even know each other's name.

She smiled and said, "I'm Pola Shekt."

Arvardan had not seen her smile before, and found himself interested in the phenomenon. It was a glow that entered her face, a radiance. It made him feel—— But he put that thought away roughly. An Earthgirl!

So he said, with perhaps less cordiality than he intended, "My name is Bel Arvardan." He held out a bronzed hand, into which her little one was swallowed up for a moment.

She said, "I must thank you for all your help."

Arvardan shrugged it away. "Shall we leave? I mean, now that your friend is gone; safely, I trust."

"I think we would have heard quite a noise if they had caught him, don't you think so?" Her eyes were pleading for confirmation of her hope, and he refused the temptation toward softness.

"Shall we go?"

She was somehow frozen. "Yes, why not?" sharply.

But there was a whining in the air, a shrill moan on the horizon, and the girl's eyes were wide and her outstretched hand suddenly withdrawn again.

"What's the matter now?" asked Arvardan.

"It's the Imperials."

"And are you frightened of them too?" It was the self-consciously non-Earthman Arvardan who spoke—the Sirian archaeologist. Prejudice or not, however the logic might be chopped and minced, the approach of Imperial soldiers meant a trace of sanity and humanity. There was room for condescension here, and he grew kind.

"Don't worry about the Outsiders," he said, even stooping to use their term for non-Earthmen. "I'll handle them, Miss Shekt."

She was suddenly concerned. "Oh no, don't try anything like that. Just don't talk to them at all. Do as they say, and don't even look at them."

Arvardan's smile broadened.

* * *

The guards saw them while they were still a distance from the main entrance and fell back. They emerged into a little space of emptiness and a strange hush. The whine of the army cars was almost upon them.

And then there were armored cars in the square and groups of glass-globe-headed soldiers springing out therefrom. The crowds scattered before them in panic, aided in their scramblings by clipped shouts and thrusts with the butt ends of the neuronic whips.

Lieutenant Claudy, in the lead, approached an Earthman guard at the main entrance. "All right, you, who's got the fever?"

His face was slightly distorted within the enclosing glass, with its content of pure air. His voice was slightly metallic as a result of radioamplification.

The guard bent his head in deep respect. "If it please your honor, we have isolated the patient within the store. The two who were with the patient are now standing in the doorway before you."

"They are, are they? Good! Let them stand there. Now— in the first place, I want this mob out of here. Sergeant! Clear the square!"

There was a grim efficiency in the proceedings thereafter. The deepening twilight gloomed over Chica as the crowd melted into the darkening air. The streets were beginning to gleam in soft, artificial lighting.

Lieutenant Claudy tapped his heavy boots with the butt of his neuronic whip. "You're sure the sick Earthie is inside?"

"He has not left, your honor. He must be."

"Well, we'll assume he is and waste no time about it. Sergeant! Decontaminate the building!"

A contingent of soldiers, hermetically sealed away from all contact with Terrestrial environment, charged into the building. A slow quarter hour passed, while Arvardan watched all in absorbed fashion. It was a field experiment in intercultural relationships that he was professionally reluctant to disturb.

The last of the soldiers were out again, and the store was shrouded in deepening night.

"Seal the doors!"

Another few minutes and then the cans of disinfectant which had been placed in several spots on each floor were discharged at long distance. In the recesses of the building those cans were flung open and the thick vapors rolled out and curled up the walls, clinging to every square inch of surface, reaching through the air and into the inmost crannies. No protoplasm, from germ to man, could remain alive in its presence, and chemical flushing of the most painstaking type would be required eventually for decontamination.

But now the lieutenant was approaching Arvardan and Pola.

"What was his name?" There was not even cruelty in his voice, merely utter indifference. An Earthman, he thought, had been killed. Well, he had killed a fly that day also. That made two.

He received no answer, Pola bending her head meekly and Arvardan watching curiously. The Imperial officer did not take his eyes off them. He beckoned curtly. "Check them for infection."

An officer bearing the insignia of the Imperial Medical Corps approached them, and was not gentle in his investigation. His gloved hands pushed hard under their armpits and yanked at the corners of their mouths so that he might investigate the inner surfaces of their cheeks.

"No infection, Lieutenant. If they had been exposed this afternoon, the stigmata would be clearly visible by now if infection had occurred."

"Umm." Lieutenant Claudy carefully removed his glove and enjoyed the touch of "live" air, even that of Earth. He tucked the ungainly glass object into the crook of his left elbow and said harshly, "Your name, Earthie-squaw?"

The term itself was richly insulting; the tone in which it was uttered added disgrace to it, but Pola showed no sign of resentment.

"Pola Shekt, sir," she responded in a whisper.

"Your papers!"

She reached into the small pocket of her white jacket and removed the pink folder.

He took it, flared it open in the light of his pocket flash, and studied it. Then he tossed it back. It fell, fluttering, to the floor, and Pola bent quickly for it.

"Stand up," the officer ordered impatiently, and kicked the booklet out of reach. Pola, white-faced, snatched her fingers away.

Arvardan frowned and decided it was time to interfere. He said, "Say, look here, now."

The lieutenant turned on him in a flash, his lips drawn back. "What did you say, Earthie?"

Pola was between them at once. "If you please, sir, this man has nothing to do with anything that has happened today. I never saw him before——"

The lieutenant yanked her aside. "I said, What did you say, Earthie?"

Arvardan returned his stare coolly. "I said, Look here, now. And I was going to say further that I don't like the way you treat women and that I'd advise you to improve your manners."

He was far too irritated to correct the lieutenant's impression of his planetary origin.

Lieutenant Claudy smiled without humor. "And where have *you* been brought up, Earthie? Don't you believe in saying 'sir' when you address a man? You don't know your place, do you? Well, it's been a while since I've had the pleasure of teaching the way of life to a nice big Earthie-buck. Here, how's this——"

And quickly, like the flick of a snake, his open palm was out and across Arvardan's face, back and forth, once, twice. Arvardan stepped back in surprise and then felt the roaring in his ears. His hand shot out to catch the extended arm that pecked at him. He saw the other's face twist in surprise——

The muscles in his shoulders writhed easily.

The lieutenant was on the pavement with a crashing thud that sent the glass globe rolling into shattered fragments.

He lay still, and Arvardan's half-smile was ferocious. He dusted his hands lightly. "Any other bastard here think he can play pattycake on my face?"

But the sergeant had raised his neuronic whip. The contact closed and there was the dim violet flash that reached out and licked at the tall archaeologist.

Every muscle in Arvardan's body stiffened in unbearable pain, and he sank slowly to his knees. Then, with total paralysis upon him, he blacked out.

When Arvardan swam out of the haze he was conscious first of all of a wash of welcome coolness on his forehead. He tried to open his eyes and found his lids reacting as if swinging on rusty hinges. He let them remain closed and, with infinitely slow jerks (each fragmentary muscular movement shooting pins through him), lifted his arm to his face.

A soft, damp towel, held by a little hand . . .

He forced an eye open and battled with the mist.

"Pola," he said.

There was a little cry of sudden joy. "Yes. How do you feel?"

"As if I were dead," he croaked, "without the advantage of losing pain. . . . What happened?"

"We were carted off to the military base. The colonel's been in here. They've searched you—and I don't know what they're going to do, but—— Oh, Mr. Arvardan, you shouldn't ever have struck the lieutenant. I think you broke his arm."

A faint smile wrenched at Arvardan's face. "Good! I wish I'd broken his back."

"But resisting an Imperial officer—it's a capital offense." Her voice was a horrified whisper.

"Indeed? We'll see about that."

"Ssh. They're coming back."

Arvardan closed his eyes and relaxed. Pola's cry was faint and far-off in his ears, and when he felt the hypodermic's thrust he could not gather his muscles into motion.

And then there was the wash of wonderful soothing non-pain along his veins and nerves. His arms unknotted and his back released itself slowly from its rigid arch, settling down. He fluttered his eyelids rapidly and, with a thrust of his elbow, sat up.

The colonel was regarding him thoughtfully; Pola, apprehensively, yet, somehow, joyfully.

The colonel said, "Well, Dr. Arvardan, we seem to have had an unpleasant contretemps in the city this evening."

Dr. Arvardan. Pola realized the little she knew about him, not even his occupation. . . . She had never felt quite like this.

Arvardan laughed shortly. "Unpleasant, you say. I consider that a rather inadequate adjective."

"You have broken the arm of an officer of the Empire about the performance of his duty."

"That officer struck me first. His duty in no way included the necessity for grossly insulting me, both verbally and physically. In doing so he forfeited any claim he might have to treatment as an officer and gentleman. As a free citizen of the Empire, I had every right to resent such cavalier, not to say illegal, treatment."

The colonel harumphed and seemed at a loss for words. Pola stared at both of them with wide, unbelieving eyes.

Finally the colonel said softly, "Well, I need not say that I consider the whole incident to have been unfortunate. Apparently the pain and indignity involved have been equally spread on both sides. It may be best to forget this matter."

"Forget? I think not. I have been a guest at the Procurator's palace, and he may be interested in hearing exactly in what manner his garrison maintains order on Earth."

"Now, Dr. Arvardan, if I assure you that you will receive a public apology——"

"To hell with that. What do you intend doing with Miss Shekt?"

"What would you suggest?"

"That you free her instantly, return her papers, and tender your apologies—right now."

The colonel reddened, then said with an effort, "Of course." He turned to Pola. "If the young lady will accept my deepest regrets . . ."

* * *

They had left the dark garrison walls behind them. It had been a short and silent ten-minute air-taxi ride to the city proper, and now they stood at the deserted blackness of the Institute. It was past midnight.

Pola said, "I don't think I quite understand. You must be very important. It seems silly of me not to know your name. I didn't ever imagine that Outsiders could treat an Earthman so."

Arvardan felt oddly reluctant and yet compelled to end the fiction. "I'm not an Earthman, Pola. I'm an archaeologist from the Sirian Sector."

She turned on him quickly, her face white in the moonlight. For the space of a slow count to ten she said nothing. "Then you outfaced the soldiers because you were safe, after all, and knew it. And I thought—— I should have known."

There was an outraged bitterness about her. "I humbly beg your pardon, sir, if at any time today, in my ignorance, I affected any disrespectful familiarity with you——"

"Pola," he cried angrily, "what's the matter? What if I'm not an Earthman? How does that make me different from what I seemed to you to be five minutes ago?"

"You might have told me, sir."

"I'm not asking you to call me 'sir.' Don't be like the rest of them, will you?"

"Like the rest of whom, sir? The rest of the disgusting animals that live on Earth? . . . I owe you a hundred credits."

"Forget it," said Arvardan disgustedly.

"I cannot follow that order. If you'll give me your address, I will send you a money order for the amount tomorrow."

Arvardan was suddenly brutal. "You owe me much more than a hundred credits."

Pola bit her lip and said in lowered tones, "It is the only part of my great debt, sir, that I can repay. Your address?"

"State House," he flung at her across his shoulder. He was lost in the night.

And Pola found herself weeping!

* * *

Shekt met Pola at the door of his office.

"He's back," he said. "A little thin man brought him."

"Good!" She was having difficulty speaking.

"He asked for two hundred credits. I gave it to him."

"He was to ask for one hundred, but never mind."

She brushed past her father. He said wistfully, "I was terribly worried. The commotions in the neighborhood ——I dared not ask; I might have endangered you."

"It's all right. Nothing's happened. . . . Let me sleep here tonight, Father."

But not all her weariness could make her sleep, for something *had* happened. She had met a man, and he was an Outsider.

But she had his address. She had his address.

10. INTERPRETATION OF EVENTS

They presented a complete contrast, these two Earth-men—one with the greatest semblance of power on Earth, and one with the greatest reality.

Thus the High Minister was the most important Earthman on Earth, the recognized ruler of the planet by direct and definite decree of the Emperor of all the Galaxy—subject, of course, to the orders of the Emperor's Procurator. His Secretary seemed no one at all, really—merely a member of the Society of Ancients, appointed, theoretically, by the High Minister to take care of certain unspecified details, and dismissable, theoretically, at will.

The High Minister was known to all the Earth and was looked up to as the supreme arbiter on matters of Custom. It was he who announced the exemptions to the Sixty and it was he who judged the breakers of ritual, the defiers of rationing and of production schedules, the invaders of re-stricted territory and so on. The Secretary, on the other hand, was known to nobody, not even by name, except to the Society of Ancients and, of course, to the High Minister himself.

The High Minister had a command of language and made frequent speeches to the people, speeches of high emotional content and copious flow of sentiment. He had fair hair, worn long, and a delicate and patrician countenance. The Secretary, snub-nosed and wry-faced, preferred a short word to a long one, a grunt to a word, and silence to a grunt—at least in public.

It was the High Minister, of course, who had the semblance of power; the Secretary who had the reality. And in the privacy of the High Minister's office that circumstance was quite plain.

For the High Minister was pettishly puzzled and the Secretary coolly indifferent.

"What I don't see," said the High Minister, "is the connection of all these reports you bring me. Reports, reports!" He lifted an arm above his head and struck viciously at an imaginary heap of paper. "I don't have the time for them."

"Exactly," said the Secretary coldy. "It is why you hire me. I read them, digest them, transmit them."

"Well, good Balkis, about your business, then. And quickly, since these are minor matters."

"Minor? Your Excellency may lose a great deal someday if your judgment is not sharpened. . . . Let us see what these reports mean, and I shall then ask you if you still consider them minor. First we have the original report, now seven days old, from Shekt's underling, and it is that which first put me on the trail."

"What trail?"

Balkis's smile was faintly bitter. "May I recall to Your Excellency certain important projects which have been nurtured here on Earth for several years."

"Ssh!" The High Minister, in sudden loss of dignity, could not forbear looking about hastily.

"Your Excellency, it is not nervousness but confidence that will win for us. . . . You know further that the success of this project has depended upon the judicious use of Shekt's little toy, the Synapsifier. Until now, at least as far as we

know, it has been utilized under our direction only, and for
definite purposes. And now, without warning, Shekt has
Synapsified an unknown man, in complete violation of our
orders."

"This," said the High Minister, "is a simple matter. Discipline Shekt, take the treated man into custody, and end
the matter."

"No, no. You are far too straightforward, Your Excellency. You miss the point. It is not *what* Shekt has done,
buy *why* he has done so. Note that there exists a coincidence
about the matter, one of a considerable series of subsequent
coincidences. The Procurator of Earth had visited Shekt that
same day, and Shekt himself reported to us, in loyal and
trustworthy fashion, all that had passed between them. Ennius had wanted the Synapsifier for Imperial use. He made
promise, it seems, of great help and gracious assistance
from the Emperor."

"Hmm," said the High Minister.

"You are intrigued? A compromise such as that seems
attractive as compared to the dangers attending our present
course?...Do you remember the promises of food to us
during the famine five years ago? Do you? Shipments were
refused because we lacked Imperial credits, and Earth-man-
ufactured products could not be accepted, as being radio-
actively contaminated. Was there a free gift of food as
promised? Was there even a loan? A hundred thousand died
of starvation. Don't put your trust in Outsider promises.

"But that does not matter. What does is that Shekt made
a great display of loyalty. Surely we could never doubt him
again. With compounded certainty, we could not suspect
him of treason that very day. Yet so it came to pass."

"You mean in this unauthorized experiment, Balkis?"

"I do, Your Excellency. Who was the man treated? We
have photographs of him and, with the help of Shekt's
technician, retinal patterns. A check with the Planetary Reg-
istry shows no record of him. The conclusion must therefore
be reached that he is no Earthman, but an Outsider. Fur-
thermore, Shekt must have been aware of it, since a registration card cannot be forged or transferred, if checked

with retinal patterns. So, in simple fashion, the unalterable facts lead us to the conclusion that Shekt has Synapsified, knowingly, an Outsider. And why?...

"The answer to that may be disturbingly simple. Shekt is not an ideal instrument for our purposes. In his youth he was an Assimilationist; he even once stood for election to the Washenn Council on a platform of conciliation with the Empire. He was defeated, by the way."

The High Minister interrupted. "I didn't know that."

"That he was defeated?"

"No, that he ran. Why wasn't I informed of this? Shekt is a very dangerous man in the position he now holds."

Balkis smiled softly and tolerantly. "Shekt invented the Synapsifier and still represents the one man truly experienced in its operation. He has always been watched, and will now be watched more closely than ever. Do not forget that a traitor within our ranks, *known to us*, can do more harm to the enemy than a loyal man can do good to us.

"Now, let us continue to deal with the facts. Shekt has Synapsified an Outsider. Why? There is only one reason why a Synapsifier can possibly be used—to improve a mind. And why that? Because only so can the minds of our scientists, already improved by Synapsification, be overtaken. Eh? This means that the Empire has at least a faint suspicion of what is going on upon Earth. Is that minor, Your Excellency?"

There was a scattered dew on the High Minister's forehead. "Do you really think so?"

"The facts are a jigsaw puzzle that can fit only one way. The Outsider so treated was a man of undistinguished, even contemptible, appearance. A good stroke, too, since a bald and fat old man can still be the Empire's most skilled espionage agent. Oh yes. Yes. Who else could be trusted on a mission such as this?... But we have followed this stranger, whose alias, by the way, is Schwartz, as far as we can. Let us take this second file of reports."

The High Minister cast an eye upon them. "The ones concerning Bel Arvardan?"

"Dr. Bel Arvardan," assented Balkis, "eminent archaeologist of the gallant Sirian Sector, those worlds of brave and chivalrous bigots." He spat the last out. Then, "Well, never mind. In any case, we have here a queer mirror image to Schwartz, an almost poetic contrast. He is not unknown, but, instead, a famous figure. He is not a secret intruder, but one who comes floating on a tidal wave of publicity. We are warned of him not by an obscure technician, but by the Procurator of Earth himself."

"Do you think there is a connection, Balkis?"

"Your Excellency may suppose it possible that one may be designed to distract our attention from the other. Or else, since the ruling classes of the Empire are skilled enough in intrigue, we have an example of two methods of camouflage. In the case of Schwartz, the lights are put out. In the case of Arvardan, the lights are flashed in our eyes. In neither case are we intended to see anything? . . . Come, of what did Ennius warn us concerning Arvardan?"

The High Minister rubbed his nose thoughtfully. "Arvardan, he said, was on an archaeological expedition under Imperial sponsorship and wished to enter the Forbidden Areas for scientific purposes. No sacrilege, he said, was intended, and if we could stop him in gentle fashion, he would back our action to the Imperial Council. Something like that."

"So then we will watch Arvardan closely, but for what purpose? Why, to see that he makes no unauthorized entry into the Forbidden Areas. Here's the head of an archaeological expedition without men, ships, or equipment. Here's an Outsider who does not remain at Everest, where he belongs, but wanders about Earth, for some reason—and goes to Chica first. And how is our attention distracted from all these most curious and suspicious circumstances? Why, by urging us to watch carefully something that is of no importance.

"But notice, Your Excellency, that Schwartz was kept hidden in the Institute for Nuclear Research for six days. And then he escaped. Isn't that strange? The door, suddenly, wasn't locked. The corridor, suddenly, wasn't guarded. What queer negligence. And on what day was it that he escaped?

Why, on the same day that Arvardan arrived at Chica. A second peculiar coincidence."

"You think, then..." said the High Minister tensely.

"I think that Schwartz is the Outsider agent on Earth, that Shekt is the contact man with the Assimilationist traitors among us, and that Arvardan is the contact man with the Empire. Observe the skill with which the meeting between Schwartz and Arvardan was arranged. Schwartz is allowed to escape, and after an appropriate interval his nurse—Shekt's daughter, by a not-too-surprising additional coincidence—is out after him. If anything were to go wrong with their split-second timetable, it is obvious that she would have found him suddenly; that he would have become a poor, sick patient for the benefit of anyone's curiosity; that he would have been brought back to safety for another attempt later. In fact, two overcurious cabbies were told that he was a sick man, and that, ironically enough, backfired upon them.

"Follow it closely, now. Schwartz and Arvardan meet first in a Foodomat. They are, apparently, unaware of each other's existence. It is a preliminary meeting, designed, simply, to indicate that all has gone well so far and that the next step may be taken.... At least they don't underestimate us, which is gratifying.

"Then Schwartz leaves; a few minutes later Arvardan leaves and the Shekt girl meets him. It is stop-watch timing. Together, after playing a little part for the benefit of the afore-mentioned cabbies, they head for the Dunham department store, and now all three are together. Where else but a department store? It is an ideal meeting place. It has a secrecy no cave in the mountains could duplicate. Too open to be suspected. Too crowded to be stalked. Wonderful—wonderful——I give credit to my opponent."

The High Minister writhed in his chair. "If our opponent deserves too much credit, he will win."

"Impossible. He is already defeated. And in that respect we must give credit to the excellent Natter."

"And who is Natter?"

"An insignificant agent who must be used to the limit

after this. His actions yesterday could not have been improved upon. His long-range assignment has been to watch
Shekt. For the purpose, he keeps a fruit stand across the
street from the Institute. For the last week he has been
specifically instructed to watch the development of the
Schwartz affair.

"He was on hand when the man, known to him through
photographs and through a glimpse at the time he was first
brought to the Institute, escaped. He observed every action,
himself unobserved, and it is his report that details yesterday's events. With incredible intuition, he decided that the
entire purpose of the 'escape' was to arrange a meeting with
Arvardan. He felt himself to be not in a position, singlehanded, to exploit that meeting, so he decided to prevent
it. The cabbies, to whom the Shekt girl had described
Schwartz as being sick, speculated on Radiation Fever. Natter seized on that with the swiftness of genius. As soon as
he observed the meeting in the department store, he reported
the case of fever and the local authorities at Chica were,
praised be Earth, intelligent enough to co-operate quickly.

"The store was emptied, and the camouflage which they
counted upon to hide their conversation was stripped from
them. They were alone and very conspicuous in the store.
Natter went further. He approached them and talked them
into allowing him to escort Schwartz back to the Institute.
They agreed. What could they do? . . . So that the day ended
without a single word passing between Arvardan and
Schwartz.

"Nor did he commit the folly of arresting Schwartz. The
two are still in ignorance of their detection and will yet lead
us to bigger game.

"And Natter went further still. He notified the Imperial
garrison, and that is beyond praise. It presented Arvardan
with a situation he could not possibly have counted upon.
He must either reveal himself to be an Outsider and destroy
his usefulness, which apparently depends upon conducting
himself upon Earth as though he were an Earthman, or he
must keep the fact secret and subject himself to whatever
unpleasantness might result. He took the more heroic al-

ternative, and even broke the arm of an officer of the Empire, in his passion for realism. That, at least, must be remembered in his favor.

"It is significant that his actions were as they were. Why should he, an Outsider, expose himself to the neuronic whip for an Earthgirl if the matter at stake was not supremely important?"

Both fists of the High Minister were on the desk before him. He glowered savagely, the long, smooth lines of his face crumpled in distress. "It is well for you, Balkis, from such meager details, to construct the spider web you do. It is skillfully done, and I feel that it is as you say. Logic leaves us no other alternative. . . . But it means that they are too close, Balkis. They are too close. . . . And they will have no mercy this time."

Balkis shrugged. "They cannot be too close, or, in a case of such potential destructiveness for all the Empire, they would have already struck. . . . And their time is running short. Arvardan must still meet with Schwartz if anything is to be accomplished, and so I can predict for you the future."

"Do so—do so."

"Schwartz must be sent away now and events allowed to quiet down from their current high pitch."

"But where will he be sent?"

"We know that too. Schwartz was brought to the Institute by a man, obviously a farmer. Descriptions reached us from both Shekt's technician and from Natter. We went through the registration data of every farmer within sixty miles of Chica, and Natter identified one Arbin Maren as the man. The technician supported that decision independently. We investigated the man quietly, and it seems that he is supporting a father-in-law, a helpless cripple, in evasion of the Sixty."

The High Minister pounded the table. "Such cases are entirely too frequent, Balkis. The laws must be tightened——"

"It is not now the point, Your Excellency. What is important is the fact that since the farmer is violating the Customs, he can be blackmailed."

"Oh..."

"Shekt, and his Outsider allies, need a tool for just such a case—that is, where Schwartz must remain in seclusion for a longer period than he can safely stay hidden in the Institute. This farmer, probably helpless and innocent, is perfect for the purpose. Well, he will be watched. Schwartz will never be out of sight. . . . Now, eventually another meeting between him and Arvardan will have to be arranged, and that time we will be prepared. Do you understand everything now?"

"I do."

"Well, praise Earth. Then I will leave you now." And, with a sardonic smile, he added, "With your permission, of course."

And the High Minister, completely oblivious to the sarcasm, waved a hand in dismissal.

The Secretary, on his way to his own small office, was alone, and, when alone, his thoughts sometimes escaped from beneath his firm control and disported themselves in the secrecy of his mind.

They concerned themselves very little with Dr. Shekt, Schwartz, Arvardan—least of all with the High Minister.

Instead there was the picture of a planet, Trantor—from whose huge, planet-wide metropolis all the Galaxy was ruled. And there was the picture of a palace whose spires and sweeping arches he had never seen in reality; that no other Earthman had ever seen. He thought of the invisible lines of power and glory that swept from sun to sun in gathering strings, ropes, and cables to that central palace and to that abstraction, the Emperor, who was, after all, merely a man.

His mind held that thought fixedly—the thought of that power which could alone bestow a divinity during life—concentrated in one who was merely human.

Merely human! Like himself!

He could be——

11. THE MIND THAT CHANGED

The coming of the change was dim in Joseph Schwartz's mind. Many times, in the absolute quiet of the night—how much more quiet the nights were now; were they ever noisy and bright and clanging with the life of energetic millions?—in the new quiet, he traced it back. He would have liked to say that here, here was the moment.

There was first that old, shattering day of fear when he was alone in a strange world—a day as misty in his mind now as the memory of Chicago itself. There was the trip to Chica, and its strange, complicated ending. He thought of that often.

Something about a machine—pills he had taken. Days of recuperation and then the escape, the wandering, the inexplicable events that last hour in the department store. He couldn't possibly remember that part correctly. Yet, in the two months since, how clear everything was, how unfaulted his memory.

Even then things had begun to seem strange. He had been sensitive to atmosphere. The old doctor and his daughter had been uneasy, even frightened. Had he known that then? Or had it just been a fugitive impression, strengthened by the hindsight of his thoughts since?

But then, in the department store, just before that big man had reached out and trapped him—just *before* that— he had become conscious of the coming snatch. The warning had not been soon enough to save him, but it was a definite indication of the change.

And, since then, the headaches. No, not quite headaches. Throbbings rather, as though some hidden dynamo in his brain had started working and, with its unaccustomed action, was vibrating every bone of his skull. There had been nothing like it in Chicago—supposing his fantasy of Chicago had meaning—or even during his first few days here in reality.

Had they done something to him that day in Chica? The machine? The pills—that had been anesthetic. An operation? And his thoughts, having reached that point for the hundredth time, stopped once more.

He had left Chica the day after his abortive escape, and now the days passed easily.

There had been Grew in his wheel chair, repeating words and pointing, or making motions, just as the girl, Pola, had done before him. Until one day Grew stopped speaking nonsense and began talking English. Or no, he himself— he, Joseph Schwartz—had stopped speaking English and had begun talking nonsense. Except that it wasn't nonsense, any more.

It was so easy. He learned to read in four days. He surprised himself. He had had a phenomenal memory once, in Chicago, or it seemed to him that he had. But he had not been capable of *such* feats. Yet Grew did not seem surprised.

Schwartz gave it up.

Then, when the autumn had become really golden, things were clear again, and he was out in the fields working. It was amazing, the way he picked it up. There it was again— he *never* made a mistake. There were complicated machines that he could run without trouble after a single explanation.

He waited for the cold weather and it never quite came. The winter was spent in clearing ground, in fertilizing, in preparing for the spring planting in a dozen ways.

He questioned Grew, tried to explain what snow was, but the latter only stared and said, "Frozen water falling like rain, eh? Oh! The word for that is snow! I understand it does that on other planets but not on Earth."

Schwartz watched the temperature thereafter and found that it scarcely varied from day to day—and yet the days shortened, as would be expected from a northerly location, say as northerly as Chicago. He wondered if he was on Earth.

He tried reading some of Grew's book films but gave up. People were people still, but the minutiae of daily life, the knowledge of which was taken for granted, the historical and sociological allusions that meant nothing to him, forced him back.

The puzzles continued. The uniformly warm rains, the wild instructions he received to remain away from certain regions. For instance, there had been the evening that he had finally become too intrigued by the shining horizon, the blue glow to the south...

He had slipped off after supper, and when not a mile had passed, the almost noiseless whir of the biwheel engine came up behind him and Arbin's angry shout rang out in the evening air. He had stopped and had been taken back.

Arbin had paced back and forth before him and had said, "You must stay away from anywhere that it shines at night."

Schwartz had asked mildly, "Why?"

And the answer came with biting incision. "Because it is forbidden." A long pause, then, "You really don't know what it's like out there, Schwartz?"

Schwartz spread his hands.

Arbin said, "Where do you come from? Are you an—an Outsider?"

"What's an Outsider?"

Arbin shrugged and left.

But that night had had a great importance for Schwartz, for it was during that short mile toward the shiningness that the strangeness in his mind had coalesced into the Mind Touch. It was what he called it, and the closest he had come, either then or thereafter, to describing it.

He had been alone in the darkling purple. His own footsteps against the springy pavement were muted. He hadn't seen anybody. He hadn't heard anybody. He hadn't touched anything.

Not exactly... It had been *something* like a touch, but not anywhere on his body. It was in his mind.... Not exactly a touch, but a presence—a somethingness there like a velvety tickle.

Then there had been two—*two* touches, distinct, apart. And the second—how could he tell them apart?—had grown louder (no, that wasn't the right word); it had grown distincter, more definite.

And then he knew it was Arbin. He knew it five minutes, at least, before he caught the sound of the biwheel, ten minutes before he laid eyes on Arbin.

Thereafter it occurred again and again with increasing frequency.

It began to dawn on him that he always knew when Arbin, Loa, or Grew was within a hundred feet of himself, even when he had no reason for knowing, even when he had every reason to suppose the opposite. It was a hard thing to take for granted, yet it began to seem so natural.

He experimented, and found that he knew exactly where any of them were, at any time. He could distinguish between them, for the Mind Touch differed from person to person. Not once had he the nerve to mention it to the others.

And sometimes he would wonder what that first Mind Touch on the road to the Shiningness had been. It had been neither Arbin, Loa, nor Grew. Well? Did it make a difference?

It did later. He had come across the Touch again, the same one, when he brought in the cattle one evening. He came to Arbin then and said:

"What about that patch of woods past the South Hills, Arbin?"

"Nothing about it," was the gruff answer. "It's Ministerial Ground."

"What's that?"

Arbin seemed annoyed. "It's of no importance to you, is it? They call it Ministerial Ground because it is the property of the High Minister."

"Why isn't it cultivated?"

"It's not intended for that." Arbin's voice was shocked. "It was a great Center. In ancient days. It is very sacred and must not be disturbed. Look, Schwartz, if you want to remain here safely, curb your curiosity and tend to your job."

"But if it's so sacred, then nobody can live there?"

"Exactly. You're right."

"Are you sure?"

"I'm sure. . . . And you're not to trespass. It will mean the end for you."

"I won't."

Schwartz walked away, wondering and oddly uneasy. It was from that wooded ground that the Mind Touch came, quite powerfully, and now something additional had been added to the sensation. It was an unfriendly Touch, a threatening Touch.

Why? Why?

And still he dared not speak. They would not have believed him, and something unpleasant would happen to him as a consequence. He knew that too. He knew too much, in fact.

He was younger these days, also. Not so much in the physical sense, to be sure. He was thinner in his stomach and broader in his shoulders. His muscles were harder and springier and his digestion was better. That was the result of work in the open. But it was something else he was chiefly conscious of. It was his way of thinking.

Old men tend to forget what thought was like in their youth; they forget the quickness of the mental jump, the daring of the youthful intuition, the agility of the fresh insight. They become accustomed to the more plodding varieties of reason, and because this is more than made up by the accumulation of experience, old men think themselves wiser than the young.

But to Schwartz experience remained, and it was with a sharp delight that he found he could understand things at a bound, that he gradually progressed from following Arbin's explanations to anticipating them, to leaping on ahead. As a result, he felt young in a far more subtle way than any amount of physical excellence could account for.

Two months passed, and it all came out—over a game of chess with Grew in the arbor.

Chess, somehow, hadn't changed, except for the names of the pieces. It was as he remembered it, and therefore it was always a comfort to him. At least, in this one respect, his poor memory did not play him false.

Grew told him of variations of chess. There was four-handed chess, in which each player had a board, touching each other at the corners, with a fifth board filling the hollow in the center as a common No Man's Land. There were three-dimensional chess games in which eight transparent boards were placed one over the other and in which each piece moved in three dimensions as they formerly moved in two, and in which the number of pieces and pawns were doubled, the win coming only when a simultaneous check of both enemy kings occurred. There were even the popular varieties, in which the original position of the chessmen were decided by throws of the dice, or where certain squares conferred advantages or disadvantages to the pieces upon them, or where new pieces with strange properties were introduced.

But chess itself, the original and unchangeable, was the same—and the tournament between Schwartz and Grew had completed its first fifty games.

Schwartz had a bare knowledge of the moves when he began, so that he lost constantly in the first games. But that had changed and losing games were becoming rarer. Gradually Grew had grown slow and cautious, had taken to smoking his pipe into glowing embers in the intervals between moves, and had finally subsided into rebellious and querulous losses.

Grew was White and his pawn was already on King 4.

"Let's go," he urged sourly. His teeth were clamped hard on his pipe and his eyes were already searching the board tensely.

Schwartz took his seat in the gathering twilight and sighed. The games were really becoming uninteresting as more and more he became aware of the nature of Grew's moves before they could be made. It was as if Grew had a misty window in his skull. And the fact that he himself knew, almost instinctively, the proper course of chess play to take was simply of a piece with the rest of his problem.

They used a "night-board," one that glowed in the darkness in a checkered blue-and-orange glimmer. The pieces, ordinary lumpish figures of a reddish clay in the sunlight, were metamorphosed at night. Half were bathed in a creamy whiteness that lent them the look of cold and shining porcelain, and the others sparked in tiny glitters of red.

The first moves were rapid. Schwartz's own King's Pawn met the enemy advance head on. Grew brought out his King's Knight to Bishop 3; Schwartz countered with Queen's Knight to Bishop 3. Then the White Bishop leaped to Queen's Knight 5, and Schwartz's Queen's Rook's Pawn slid ahead a square to drive it back to Rook 4. He then advanced his other Knight to Bishop 3.

The shining pieces slid across the board with an eery volition of their own as the grasping fingers lost themselves in the night.

Schwartz was frightened. He might be revealing insanity, but he *had to know*. He said abruptly, "Where am I?"

Grew looked up in the midst of a deliberate move of his Queen's Knight to Bishop 3 and said, "What?"

Schwartz didn't know the word for "country," or "nation." He said, "What world is this?" and moved his Bishop to King 2.

"Earth," was the short reply, and Grew castled with great emphasis, first the tall figurine that was the King, moving, and then the lumpish Rook topping it and resting on the other side.

That was a thoroughly unsatisfactory answer. The word

Grew had used Schwartz translated in his mind as "Earth." But what was "Earth"? Any planet is "Earth" to those that live on it. He advanced his Queen's Knight's Pawn two spaces, and again Grew's Bishop had to retreat, to Knight 3 this time. Then Schwartz and Grew, each in turn, advanced the Queen's Pawn one space, each freeing his Bishop for the battle in the center that was soon to begin.

Schwartz asked, as calmly and casually as he could, "What year is this?" He castled.

Grew paused. He might have been startled. "What *is* it you're harping on today? Don't you want to play? If it will make you happy, this is 827." He added sarcastically, "G.E." He stared frowningly at the board, then slammed his Queen's Knight to Queen 5, where it made its first assault.

Schwartz dodged quickly, moving his own Queen's Knight to Rook 4 in counterattack. The skirmish was on in earnest. Grew's Knight seized the Bishop, which leaped upward in a bath of red fire to be dropped with a sharp click into the box where it might lie, a buried warrior, until the next game. And then the conquering Knight fell instantly to Schwartz's Queen. In a moment of overcaution, Grew's attack faltered and he moved his remaining Knight back to the haven of King 1, where it was relatively useless. Schwartz's Queen's Knight now repeated the first exchange, taking the Bishop and falling prey in its turn to the Rook's Pawn.

Now another pause, and Schwartz asked mildly, "What's G.E.?"

"What?" demanded Grew bad-humoredly. "Oh—you mean you're still wondering what year this is? Of all the fool——Well, I keep forgetting you just learned to talk a month or so ago. But you're intelligent. Don't you really know? Well, it's 827 of the Galactic Era. Galactic Era: G.E.—see? It's 827 years since the foundation of the Galactic Empire; 827 years since the coronation of Frankenn the First. Now, *please*, it's your move."

But the Knight that Schwartz held was swallowed up in the grip of his hand for the moment. He was in a fury of frustration. He said, "Just one minute," and put the Knight down on Queen 2. "Do you recognize any of these names? America, Asia, the United States, Russia, Europe——" He groped for identification.

In the darkness Grew's pipe was a sullen red glow and the dim shadow of him hunched over the shining chessboard as if it had the less life of the two. He might have shaken his head curtly, but Schwartz could not see that. He didn't have to. He sensed the other's negation as clearly as though a speech had been delivered.

Schwartz tried again. "Do you know where I can get a map?"

"No maps," growled Grew, "unless you want to risk your neck in Chica. I'm no geographer. I never heard of the names you mention, either. What are they? People?"

Risk his neck? Why that? Schwartz felt the coldness gather. Had he committed a crime? Did Grew know about it?

He asked doubtfully, "The sun has nine planets, hasn't it?"

"Ten," was the uncompromising answer.

Schwartz hesitated. Well, they *might* have discovered another that he hadn't heard about. But then why should Grew have heard about it? He counted on his fingers, and then, "How about the sixth planet? Has it got rings?"

Grew was slowly moving the King's Bishop's Pawn forward two squares, and Schwartz instantly did the same.

Grew said, "Saturn, you mean? Of course it has rings." He was calculating now. He had the choice of taking either the Bishop's Pawn or the King's Pawn, and the consequences of the choice were not too clear.

"And is there an asteroid belt—little planets—between Mars and Jupiter? I mean between the fourth and fifth planets?"

"Yes," mumbled Grew. He was relighting his pipe and thinking feverishly. Schwartz caught that agonized uncertainty and was annoyed at it. To him, now that he was sure of Earth's identity, the chess game was less than a trifle. Questions quivered along the inner surface of his skull, and one slipped out.

"Your book films are real, then? There are other worlds? With people?"

And now Grew looked up from the board, eyes probing uselessly in the darkness. "Are you serious?"

"Are there?"

"By the Galaxy! *I believe you really don't know.*"

Schwartz felt humiliated in his ignorance. "Please——"

"Of course there are worlds. Millions of them! Every star you see has worlds, and most of those you don't see. It's all part of the Empire."

Delicately, inside, Schwartz felt the faint echo of each of Grew's intense words as they sparked directly from mind to mind. Schwartz felt the mental contacts growing stronger with the days. Maybe, soon, he could hear those tiny words in his mind even when the person thinking them *wasn't* talking.

And now, for the first time, he finally thought of an alternative to insanity. Had he passed through time, somehow? Slept through, perhaps?

He said huskily, "How long since it's all happened, Grew? How long since the time when there was only one planet?"

"What do you mean?" He was suddenly cautious. "Are you a member of the Ancients?"

"Of the what? I'm not a member of anything, but wasn't Earth once the only planet?... Well, wasn't it?"

"The Ancients say so," said Grew grimly, "but who knows? Who really knows? The worlds up there have been existing all history long as far as I know."

"But how long is that?"

"Thousands of years, I suppose. Fifty thousand, a hundred—I can't say."

Thousands of years! Schwartz felt a gurgle in his throat and pressed it down in panic. All that between two steps? A breath, a moment, a flicker of time—and he had jumped thousands of years? He felt himself shrinking back to amnesia. His identification of the Solar System must have been the result of imperfect memories penetrating the mist.

But now Grew was making his next move—he was taking the other's Bishop's Pawn, and it was almost mechanically that Schwartz noted mentally the fact that it was the wrong choice. Move fitted to move now with no conscious effort. His King's Rook swooped forward to take the foremost of the now-doubled White Pawns. White's Knight advanced again to Bishop 3. Schwartz's Bishop moved to Knight 2, freeing itself for action. Grew followed suit by moving his own Bishop to Queen 2.

Schwartz paused before launching the final attack. He said, "Earth is boss, isn't it?"

"Boss of what?"

"Of the Emp——"

But Grew looked up with a roar at which the chessmen quivered. "Listen, you, I'm tired of your questions. Are you a complete fool? Does Earth look as if it's boss of anything?" There was a smooth whir as Grew's wheel chair circled the table. Schwartz felt grasping fingers on his arm.

"Look! Look there!" Grew's voice was a whispered rasp. "You see the horizon? You see it shine?"

"Yes."

"*That* is Earth—all Earth. Except here and there, where a few patches like this one exist."

"I don't understand."

"Earth's crust is radioactive. The soil glows, always glowed, will glow forever. Nothing can grow. No one can live——You really didn't know that? Why do you suppose we have the Sixty?"

The paralytic subsided. He circled his chair about the table again. "It's your move."

The Sixty! Again a Mind Touch with an indefinable aura of menace. Schwartz's chess pieces played themselves, while he wondered about it with a tight-pressed heart. His King's Pawn took the opposing Bishop's Pawn. Grew moved his Knight to Queen 4 and Schwartz's Rook side-stepped the attack to Knight 4. Again Grew's Knight attacked, moving to Bishop 3, and Schwartz's Rook avoided the issue again to Knight 5. But now Grew's King's Rook's Pawn advanced one timorous square and Schwartz's Rook slashed forward. It took the Knight's Pawn, checking the enemy King. Grew's King promptly took the Rook, but Schwartz's Queen plugged the hole instantly, moving to Knight 4 and checking. Grew's King scurried to Rook 1, and Schwartz brought up his Knight, placing it on King 4. Grew moved his Queen to King 2 in a strong attempt to mobilize his defenses, and Schwartz countered by marching his Queen forward two squares to Knight 6, so that the fight was now in close quarters. Grew had no choice; he moved his Queen to Knight 2, and the two female majesties were now face to face. Schwartz's Knight pressed home, taking the opposing Knight on Bishop 6, and when the now-attacked White Bishop moved quickly to Bishop 3, the Knight followed to Queen 5. Grew hesitated for slow minutes, then advanced his outflanked Queen up the long diagonal to take Schwartz's Bishop.

Then he paused and drew a relieved breath. His sly opponent had a Rook in danger with a check in the offing and his own Queen ready to wreak havoc. And he was ahead a Rook to a Pawn.

"Your move," he said with satisfaction.

Schwartz said finally, "What—what is the Sixty?"

There was a sharp unfriendliness to Grew's voice. "Why do you ask that? What are you after?"

"Please," humbly. He had little spirit left in him. "I am a man with no harm in me. I don't know who I am or what happened to me. Maybe I'm an amnesia case."

"Very likely," was the contemptuous reply. "Are you escaping from the Sixty? Answer truthfully."

"But I tell you I don't know what the Sixty is!"

It carried conviction. There was a long silence. To Schwartz, Grew's Mind Touch was ominous, but he could not, quite, make out words.

Grew said slowly, "The Sixty is your sixtieth year. Earth supports twenty million people, no more. To live, you must produce. If you cannot produce, you cannot live. Past Sixty— you cannot produce."

"And so . . ." Schwartz's mouth remained open.

"You're put away. It doesn't hurt."

"You're killed?"

"It's not murder," stiffly. "It *must* be that way. Other worlds won't take us, and we must make room for the children some way. The older generation must make room for the younger."

"Suppose you don't tell them you're sixty?"

"Why shouldn't you? Life after sixty is no joke. . . . And there's a Census every ten years to catch anyone who is foolish enough to try to live. Besides, they have your age on record."

"Not mine." The words slipped out. Schwartz couldn't stop them. "Besides, I'm only fifty—next birthday."

"It doesn't matter. They can check by your bone structure. Don't you know that? There's no way of masking it. They'll get me next time. . . . Say, it's your move."

Schwartz disregarded the urging. "You mean they'll——"

"Sure, I'm only fifty-five, but look at my legs. I can't work, can I? There are three of us registered in our family, and our quota is adjusted on a basis of three workers. When I had the stroke I should have been reported, and then the quota would have been reduced. But I would have gotten a premature Sixty, and Arbin and Loa wouldn't do it. They're fools, because it has meant hard work for them—till you came along. And they'll get me next year, anyway. . . . Your move."

"Is next year the Census?"

"That's right. . . . Your move."

"Wait!" urgently. "Is *everyone* put away after sixty? No exceptions at all?"

"Not for you and me. The High Minister lives a full life, and members of the Society of Ancients; certain scientists or those performing some great service. Not many qualify. Maybe a dozen a year. . . . *It's your move!*"

"Who decides who qualifies?"

"The High Minister, of course. Are you moving?"

But Schwartz stood up. "Never mind. It's checkmate in five moves. My Queen is going to take your Pawn to check you; you've got to move to Knight 1; I bring up the Knight to check you at King 2; you must move to Bishop 2; my Queen checks you at King 6; you must move to Knight 2; my Queen goes to Knight 6, and when you're then forced to Rook 1, my Queen mates you at Rook 6.

"Good game," he added automatically.

Grew stared long at the board, then, with a cry, dashed it from the table. The gleaming pieces rolled dejectedly about on the lawn.

"You and your damned distracting chatter," yelled Grew.

But Schwartz was conscious of nothing. Nothing except the overwhelming necessity of escaping the Sixty. For though Browning said:

> *Grow old along with me!*
> *The best is yet to be ...*

that was in an Earth of teeming billions and of unlimited food. The best that was *now* to be was the Sixty—and death.

Schwartz was sixty-two.

Sixty-two ...

12. THE MIND THAT KILLED

It worked out so neatly in Schwartz's methodical mind. Since he did not want to die, he would have to leave the farm. If he stayed where he was, the Census would come, and with it, death.

Leave the farm, then. But where would he go?

There was the—what was it, a hospital?—in Chica. They had taken care of him before. And why? Because he had been a medical "case." But wasn't he still a case? And he could talk now; he could give them the symptoms, which he couldn't before. He could even tell them about the Mind Touch.

Or did everyone have the Mind Touch? Was there any way he could tell? . . . None of the others had it. Not Arbin or Loa or Grew. He knew that. They had no way of telling where he was unless they saw or heard him. Why, he couldn't beat Grew in Chess if Grew could——

Wait, now, chess was a popular game. And it couldn't be played if people had the Mind Touch. Not really.

So that made him a peculiarity—a psychological spec-

imen. It might not be a particularly gay life, being a specimen, but it would keep him alive.

And suppose one considered the new possibility that had
just arisen. Suppose he were not an amnesiac but a man
who had stumbled through time. Why, then, in addition
to the Mind Touch, he was a man from the past. He was a
historical specimen, an archaeological specimen; they
couldn't kill him.

If they believed him.

Hmm, *if* they believed him.

That doctor would believe. He had needed a shave that
morning Arbin took him to Chica. He remembered that very
well. After that his hair never grew, so they must have done
something to him. That meant that the doctor knew that
he—*he*, Schwartz—had had hair on his face. Wouldn't that
be significant? Grew and Arbin never shaved. Grew had
once told him that only animals had hair on their face.

So he had to get to the doctor.

What was his name? Shekt? . . . Shekt, that was right.

But he knew so little of this horrible world. To leave by
night or cross-country would have entangled him in mys-
teries, would have plunged him into radioactive danger
pockets of which he knew nothing. So, with the boldness
of one with no choice, he struck out upon the highway in
the early afternoon.

They wouldn't be expecting him back before suppertime,
and by that time he would be well away. *They* would have
no Mind Touch to miss.

For the first half hour he experienced a feeling of elation,
the first sensation he had had since all this had started. He
was finally doing something; he was making an attempt to
fight back at his environment. Something with a *purpose*,
and not mere unreasoning flight as that time in Chica.

Ah, for an old man he wasn't bad. He'd show them.

And then he stopped——He stopped in the middle of
the highway, because something obtruded itself upon his
notice, something he had forgotten.

There was the strange Mind Touch, the unknown Mind

Touch; the one he had detected first when he had tried to reach the shining horizon and had been stopped by Arbin; the one that had been watching from the Ministerial Ground.

It was with him now—behind him and watching.

He listened closely—or, at least, he did that which was the equivalent of listening with regard to the Mind Touch. It came no closer, but it was fastened upon himself. It had within it watchfulness and enmity, but not desperation.

Other things became clear. The follower must not lose sight of him, and the follower was armed.

Cautiously, almost automatically, Schwartz turned, picking apart the horizon with eager eyes.

And the Mind Touch changed instantly.

It became doubtful and cautious, dubious as to its own safety, and the success of its own project, whatever that was. The fact of the follower's weapons became more prominent, as though he were speculating upon using it if trapped.

Schwartz knew that he himself was unarmed and helpless. He knew that the follower would kill him rather than allow him to get out of sight; kill him at the first false move. . . . And he saw no one.

So Schwartz walked on, knowing that his follower remained close enough to kill him. His back was stiff in the anticipation of he knew not what. How does death feel? . . . How does death feel? . . . The thought jostled him in time to his steps, jounced in his mind, jiggled in the subconscious, until it went nearly past endurance.

He held onto the follower's Mind Touch as the one salvation. He would detect that instant's increase in tension that would mean that a weapon was being leveled, a trigger being pulled, a contact being closed. At that instant he would drop, he would run——

But why? If it were the Sixty, why not kill him out of hand?

The time-slip theory was fading out in his mind; amnesia again. He was a criminal, perhaps—a dangerous man, who must be watched. Maybe he had once been a high official, who could not be simply killed but must be tried. Perhaps his amnesia was the method used by his unconscious to escape the realization of some tremendous guilt.

And so now he was walking down an empty highway toward a doubtful destination, with death walking at his back.

It was growing dark, and the wind had a dying chill to it. As usual, it didn't seem right. Schwartz judged it to be December, and certainly sunset at four-thirty was right for it, but the wind's chill was not the iciness of a midwestern winter.

Schwartz had long decided that the reason for the prevalent mildness was that the planet (Earth?) did not depend on the sun entirely for its heat. The radioactive soil itself gave off heat, small by the square foot but huge by the million square miles.

And in the darkness the follower's Mind Touch grew nearer. Still attentive, and keyed up to a gamble. In the darkness, following was harder. He had followed him that first night—toward the shiningness. Was he afraid to take the risk again?

"Hey! Hey, fella——"

It was a nasal, high-pitched voice. Schwartz froze.

Slowly, in one piece, he turned around. The small figure coming up to him waved its hand, but in the sunless time of day he could not make it out clearly. It approached, unhurrying. He waited.

"Hey, there. Glad to see you. It ain't much fun beating it along the road without company. Mind if I go along with you?"

"Hello," said Schwartz dully. It was the correct Mind Touch. It was the follower. And the face was familiar. It belonged to that hazy time, in Chica.

And then the follower gave every sign of recognition. "Say, I know you. Sure!...Don't you remember me?"

It was impossible for Schwartz to say whether under ordinary conditions, in another time, he might or might not have believed the other to be sincere. But now how could he avoid seeing that thin, ragged layer of synthetic recognition that overlay the deep currents of a Touch that told him—shouted at him—that the little man with the very sharp eyes had known him from the start? Knew him and had a death weapon ready for him, if necessary.

Schwartz shook his head.

"Sure," insisted the little man. "It was in the department store. I got you away from that mob." He seemed to double up in artificial laughter. "They thought you had Radiation Fever. *You* remember."

Schwartz did, too, vaguely—dimly. A man like this, for a few minutes, and a crowd, which had first stopped them and then parted for them.

"Yes," he said. "Pleased to meet you." It wasn't very brilliant conversation, but Schwartz could do no better, and the little man did not seem to mind.

"My name's Natter," he said, shoving out a limp hand at the other. "I didn't get a chance to talk much with you that first time—overlooked it in the crisis of things, you might say—but I'm sure glad to get a second chance. . . . Let's have the mitt."

"I'm Schwartz." And he touched palms with the other, briefly.

"How come you're walking?" asked Natter. "Going somewheres?"

Schwartz shrugged. "Just walking."

"A hiker, huh? That's for me too. All year round I'm on the road—puts the old kibosh on the grummlies."

"What?"

"You know. Makes you full of life. You get to breathe that air and feel the blood pumping, hey? . . . Walked too far this time. Hate to get back after night by my lonesome. Always glad for the company. Where you going?"

It was the second time Natter had asked the question, and the Mind Touch made plain the importance attached to it. Schwartz wondered how long he could evade the issue. There was a questing anxiety in the follower's mind. And no lie would do. Schwartz didn't know enough about this new world to lie.

He said, "I'm going to the hospital."

"The hospital? What hospital?"

"I was there when I was in Chica."

"You mean the Institute. Ain't that it? That's where I took you before, that time in the department store, I mean." Anxiety and increasing tension.

"To Dr. Shekt," said Schwartz. "Do you know him?"

"I've heard of him. He's a big shot. Are you sick?"

"No, but I'm supposed to report once in a while." Did that sound reasonable?

"Walking?" said Natter. "Doesn't he send a car for you?" Apparently it did not seem reasonable.

Schwartz said nothing now—a clammy silence.

Natter, however, was buoyant. "Look here, chum, soon's I pass a public Communi-wave, I'll order a taxi from the city. It'll meet us on the road."

"A Communi-wave?"

"Sure. They have 'em all along the highway. See, there's one."

He took a step away from Schwartz, and the latter found himself in a sudden shriek. "Stop! Don't move."

Natter stopped. There was a queer coldness in his expression as he turned. "What's eating you, bud?"

Schwartz found the new language almost inadequate for the rapidity with which he hurled words at the other. "I'm tired of this acting. I know you, and I know what you're going to do. You're going to call somebody to tell them I'm going to Dr. Shekt. They'll be ready for me in the city and they'll send out a car to pick me up. And you'll kill me if I try to get away."

There was a frown on Natter's face. He muttered, "You're sure right on the gizzbo with that last——" It was not intended for Schwartz's ears, nor did it reach them, but the words rested lightly on the very surface of his Mind Touch.

Aloud he said, "Mister, you've got me confused. You're shoving a fast one right past my nose." But he was making room, and his hand was drifting toward his hip.

And Schwartz lost control of himself. He waved his arms in a wild fury. "Leave me alone, why don't you? What have I done to you? . . . Go away! *Go away!*"

He ended in a voice-cracked shriek, his forehead ridged with hate and fear of the creature who stalked him and whose mind was so alive with enmity. His own emotions heaved and thrust at the Mind Touch, attempting to evade the clingingness of it, rid itself of the breath of it——

And it was gone. Suddenly and completely gone. There had been the momentary consciousness of overwhelming pain—not in himself, but in the other—then nothing. No Mind Touch. It had dropped away like the grip of a fist growing lax and dead.

Natter was a crumpled smear on the darkening highway. Schwartz crept toward him. Natter was a little man, easy to turn over. The look of agony on his face might have been stamped on, deeply, deeply. The lines remained, did not relax. Schwartz felt for the heartbeat and did not find it.

He straightened in a deluge of self-horror.

He had murdered a man!

And then a deluge of amazement——

Without touching him! He had killed this man just by hating him, by striking somehow at the Mind Touch.

What other powers did he have?

He made a quick decision. He searched the other's pockets and found money. Good! He could use that. Then he dragged the corpse into the fields and let the high grass cover it.

He walked on for two hours. No other Mind Touch disturbed him.

He slept in an open field that night, and the next morning, after two hours more, reached the outskirts of Chica.

Chica was only a village to Schwartz, and by comparison with the Chicago he remembered, the motion of the populace was still thin and sporadic. Even so, the Mind Touches were for the first time numerous. They amazed and confused him.

So many! Some drifting and diffuse; some pointed and intense. There were men who passed with their minds popping in tiny explosions; others with nothing inside their skulls but, perhaps, a gentle rumination on the breakfast just completed.

At first Schwartz turned and jumped with every Touch that passed, taking each as a personal contact; but within the hour he learned to ignore them.

He was hearing words now, even when they were not actually mouthed. This was something new, and he found himself listening. They were thin, eery phrases, disconnected and wind-whipped; far off, far off . . . And with them, living, crawling emotion and other subtle things that cannot be described—so that all the world was a panorama of boiling life visible to himself only.

He found he could penetrate buildings as he walked, sending his mind in as though it were something he held on a leash, something that could suck its way into crannies invisible to the eye and bring out the bones of men's inner thoughts.

It was before a huge stone-fronted building that he halted, and considered. They (whoever they were) were after him. He had killed the follower, but there must be others—the others that the follower had wanted to call. It might be best for him to make no move for a few days, and how to do that best? . . . A job? . . .

He probed the building before which he had stopped. In there was a distant Mind Touch that to him might mean a job. They were looking for textile workers in there—and he had once been a tailor.

He stopped inside, where he was promptly ignored by everyone. He touched someone's shoulder.

"Where do I see about a job, please?"

"Through that door!" The Mind Touch that reached him was full of annoyance and suspicion.

Through the door, and then a thin, point-chin fellow fired questions at him and fingered the classifying machine onto which he punched the answers.

Schwartz stammered his lies and truths with equal uncertainty.

But the personnel man began, at least, with a definite unconcern. The questions were fired rapidly: "Age? . . . Fifty-two? Hmm. State of health? . . . Married? . . . Experience?

...Worked with textiles?...Well, what kind?...Thermoplastic? Elastomeric?...What do you mean, you think all kinds?...Whom did you work with last?...Spell his name....You're not from Chica, are you?...Where are your papers?...You'll have to bring them here if you want action taken....What's your registration number?..."

Schwartz was backing away. He hadn't forseen this end when he had begun. And the Mind Touch of the man before him was changing. It had become suspicious to the point of single-trackedness, and cautious too. There was a surface layer of sweetness and good-fellowship that was so shallow, and which overlay animosity so thinly, as to be the most dangerous feature of all.

"I think," said Schwartz nervously, "that I'm not suited for this job."

"No, no, come back." And the man beckoned at him. "We have something for you. Just let me look through the files a bit." He was smiling, but his Mind Touch was clearer now and even more unfriendly.

He had punched a buzzer on his desk——

Schwartz, in a sudden panic, rushed for the door.

"Hold him!" cried the other instantly, dashing from behind his desk.

Schwartz struck at the Mind Touch, lashing out violently with his own mind, and he heard a groan behind him. He looked quickly over his shoulder. The personnel man was seated on the floor, face contorted and temples buried in his palms. Another man bent over him; then, at an urgent gesture, headed for Schwartz. Schwartz waited no more.

He was out on the street, fully aware now that there must be an alarm out for him with a complete description made public, and that the personnel man, at least, had recognized him.

He ran and doubled along the streets blindly. He attracted attention; more of it now, for the streets were filling up—suspicion, suspicion everywhere—suspicion because he ran—suspicion because his clothes were wrinkled and ill-fitting——

In the multiplicity of Mind Touches and in the confusion

of his own fear and despair, he could not identify the true enemies, the ones in which there was not only suspicion but certainty, and so he hadn't the slightest warning of the neuronic whip.

There was only that awful pain, which descended like the whistle of a lash and remained like the crush of a rock. For seconds he coasted down the slope of that descent into agony before drifting into the black.

13. SPIDER WEB AT WASHENN

The grounds of the College of Ancients in Washenn are nothing if not sedate. Austerity is the key word, and there is something authentically grave about the clustered knots of novices taking their evening stroll among the trees of the Quadrangle—where none but Ancients might trespass. Occasionally the green-robed figure of a Senior Ancient might make its way across the lawn, receiving reverences graciously.

And, once in a long while, the High Minister himself might appear.

But not as now, at a half run, almost in a perspiration, disregarding the respectful raising of hands, oblivious to the cautious stares that followed him, the blank looks at one another, the slightly raised eyebrows.

He burst into the Legislative Hall by the private entrance and broke into an open run down the empty, step-ringing ramp. The door that he thundered at opened at the foot pressure of the one within, and the High Minister entered.

His Secretary scarcely looked up from behind his small,

plain desk, where he hunched over a midget Field-shielded Televisor, listening intently and allowing his eyes to rove over a quire or so of official-looking communcations that piled high before him.

The High Minister rapped sharply on the desk. "What is this? What is going on?"

The Secretary's eyes flicked coldly at him, and the Televisor was put to one side. "Greetings, Your Excellency."

"Greet me no greetings!" retorted the High Minister impatiently. "I want to know what is going on."

"In a sentence, our man has escaped."

"You mean the man who was treated by Shekt with the Synapsifier—the Outsider—the spy—the one on the farm outside Chica——"

It is uncertain how many qualifications the High Minister, in his anxiety, might have rattled out had not the Secretary interrupted with an indifferent "Exactly."

"Why was I not informed? Why am I never informed?"

"Immediate action was necessary and you were engaged. I substituted, therefore, to the best of my ability."

"Yes, you are careful about my engagements when you wish to do without me. Now, I'll not have it. I will not permit myself to be by-passed and sidetracked. I will not——"

"We delay," was the reply at ordinary speaking volume, and the High Minister's half shout faded. He coughed, hovered uncertainly at further speech, then said mildly:

"What are the details, Balkis?"

"Scarcely any. After two months of patient waiting, with nothing to show for it, this man Schwartz left—was followed—and was lost."

"How lost?"

"We are not sure, but there is a further fact. Our agent, Natter, missed three reporting periods last night. His alternates set out after him along the highway toward Chica and found him at dawn. He was in a ditch at the side of the highway—quite dead."

The High Minister paled. "The Outsider had killed him?"

"Presumably, though we cannot say certainly. There were

no visible signs of violence other than a look of agony on the dead face. There will be an autopsy, of course. He might have died of a stroke just at that inconvenient moment."

"That would be an incredible coincidence."

"So I think," was the cool response, "but if Schwartz killed him, it makes subsequent events puzzling. You see, Your Excellency, it seemed quite obvious from our previous analysis that Schwartz would make for Chica in order to see Shekt, and Natter was found dead on the highway between the Maren farm and Chica. We therefore sent out an alarm to that city three hours ago and the man was caught."

"Schwartz?" incredulously.

"Certainly."

"Why didn't you say that immediately?"

Balkis shrugged. "Your Excellency, there is more important work to be done. I said that Schwartz was in our hands. Well, he was caught quickly and easily, and that fact does not seem to me to jibe very well with the death of Natter. How could he be at once so clever as to detect and kill Natter—a most capable man—and so stupid as to enter Chica the very next morning and openly enter a factory, without disguise, to find a job?"

"Is that what he did?"

"That's what he did. . . . There are two possible thoughts that this gives rise to, therefore. Either he has already transmitted such information as he has to Shekt or Arvardan, and has now let himself be caught in order to divert our attention, or else other agents are involved, whom we have not detected and whom he is now covering. In either case, we must not be overconfident."

"I don't know," said the High Minister helplessly, his handsome face twisted into anxious lines. "It gets too deep for me."

Balkis smiled with more than a trace of contempt and volunteered a statement. "You have an appointment four hours from now with Professor Bel Arvardan."

"I have? Why? What am I to say to him? I don't want to see him."

"Relax. You must see him, Your Excellency. It seems

obvious to me that since the date of commencement of his fictitious expedition is approaching, he must play out the game by asking you for permission to investigate the Forbidden Areas. Ennius warned us he would, and Ennius must know exactly the details of this comedy. I suppose that you are able to return him froth for froth in this matter and to counter pretense with pretense."

The High Minister bowed his head. "Well, I shall try."

Bel Arvardan arrived in good time, and was able to look about him. To a man well acquainted with the architectural triumphs of all the Galaxy, the College of Ancients could scarcely seem more than a brooding block of steel-ribbed granite, fashioned in an archaic style. To one who was an archaeologist as well, it might signify, in its gloomy, nearly savage austerity, the proper home of a gloomy, nearly savage way of life. Its very primitiveness marked the turning back of eyes to the far past.

And Arvardan's thoughts slipped away once again. His two-month tour about Earth's western continents had proven not quite—amusing. That first day had ruined things. He found himself thinking back to that day at Chica.

He was instantly angry with himself for thinking about it again. She had been rude, egregiously ungrateful, a common Earthgirl. Why should he feel guilty? And yet . . .

Had he made allowances for her shock at discovering him to be an Outsider, like that officer who had insulted her and whose arrogant brutality he had repaid with a broken arm? After all, how could he know how much she had already suffered at the hands of Outsiders? And then to find out, like that, without any softening of the blow, that he was one.

If he had been more patient . . . Why had he broken it off so brutally? He didn't even remember her name. It was Pola something. Strange! His memory was ordinarily better than that. Was it an unconscious effort to forget?

Well, that made sense. Forget! What was there to remember, anyway? An Earthgirl. A common Earthgirl.

She was a nurse in a hospital. Suppose he tried to locate

the hospital. It had been just a vague blot in the night when he parted from her, but it must be in the neighborhood of that Foodomat.

He snatched at the thought and broke into a thousand angry fragments. Was he mad? What would he have gained? She was an Earthgirl. Pretty, sweet, somehow entic——

An Earthgirl!

The High Minister was entering, and Arvardan was glad. It meant relief from that day in Chica. But, deep in his mind, he knew that they would return. They—the thoughts, that is—always did.

As for the High Minister, his robe was new and glistening in its freshness. His forehead showed no trace of haste or doubt; perspiration might have been a stranger to it.

And the conversation was friendly, indeed. Arvardan was at pains to mention the well-wishings of some of the great men of the Empire to the people of Earth. The High Minister was as careful to express the thorough gratification that must be felt by all Earth at the generosity and enlightenment of the Imperial Government.

Arvardan expounded on the importance of archaeology to Imperial philosophy, on its contribution to the great conclusion that all humans of whatever world of the Galaxy were brothers—and the High Minister agreed blandly and pointed out that Earth had long held such to be the case and could only hope that the time would shortly come when the rest of the Galaxy might turn theory into practice.

Arvardan smiled very shortly at that and said, "It is for that very purpose, Your Excellency, that I have approached you. The differences between Earth and some of the Imperial Dominions neighboring it rest largely, perhaps, on differing ways of thinking. Still, a good deal of friction could be removed if it could be shown that Earthmen were not different, *racially*, from other Galactic citizens."

"And how would you propose to do that, sir?"

"That is not easy to explain in a word. As Your Excellency may know, the two main currents of archaeological thinking are commonly called the Merger Theory and the Radiation Theory."

"I am acquainted with a layman's view of both."

"Good. Now the Merger Theory, of course, involves the notion that the various types of humanity, evolving independently, have intermarried in the very early, scarcely documented days of primitive space travel. A conception like that is necessary to account for the fact that Humans are so alike one to the other now."

"Yes," commented the High Minister dryly, "and such a conception also involves the necessity of having several hundred, or thousand, separately evolved beings of a more or less human type so closely related chemically and biologically that intermarriage is possible."

"True," replied Arvardan with satisfaction. "You have put your finger on an impossibly weak point. Yet most archaeologists ignore it and adhere firmly to the Merger Theory, which would, of course, imply the possibility that in isolated portions of the Galaxy there might be subspecies of humanity who remained different, didn't intermarry——"

"You mean Earth," commented the High Minister.

"Earth *is* considered an example. The Radiation Theory, on the other hand——"

"Considers us all descendants of one planetary group of humans."

"Exactly."

"My people," said the High Minister, "because of the evidence of our own history, and of certain writings which are sacred to us and cannot be exposed to the view of Outsiders, are of the belief that Earth itself is the original home of humanity."

"And so I believe as well, and I ask your help to prove this point to all the Galaxy."

"You are optimistic. Just what is involved?"

"It is my conviction, Your Excellency, that many primitive artifacts and architectural remains may be located in those areas of your world which are now, unfortunately, masked by radioactivity. The age of the remains could be accurately calculated from the radioactive decay present and compared——"

But the High Minister was shaking his head. "That is out of the question."

"Why?" And Arvardan frowned in thorough amazement.

"For one thing," said the High Minister, reasoning mildly, "what do you expect to accomplish? If you prove your point, even to the satisfaction of all the worlds, what does it matter that a million years ago all of you were Earthmen? After all, twenty million years ago we were all apes, yet we do not admit present-day apes into the relationship."

"Come, Your Excellency, the analogy is unreasonable."

"Not at all, sir. Isn't it reasonable to assume that Earthmen, in their long isolation, have so changed from their emigrating cousins, especially under the influence of radioactivity, as now to form a different race?"

Arvardan bit at his lower lip and answered reluctantly, "You argue well on the side of your enemy."

"Because I ask myself what my enemy will say. So you will accomplish nothing, sir, except perhaps to further exacerbate the hatred against us."

"But," said Arvardan, "there is still the matter of the interests of pure science, the advantage of knowledge——"

The High Minister nodded gravely. "I am truly sorry to have to stand in the way of that. I speak now, sir, as one gentleman of the Empire to another. I myself would cheerfully help you, but my people are an obstinate and stiff-necked race, who over centuries have withdrawn into themselves because of the—uh—lamentable attitudes toward them in parts of the Galaxy. They have certain taboos, certain fixed Customs—which even I could not afford to violate."

"And the radioactive areas——"

"Are one of the most important taboos. Even if I were to grant you permission, and certainly my every impulse is to do so, it would merely provoke rioting and disturbances, which would not only endanger your life and those of the members of your expedition but would, in the long run, bring down upon Earth the disciplinary action of the Empire. I would betray my position and the trust of my people if I were to allow that."

"But I am willing to take all reasonable precautions. If you wish to send observers with me——Or, of course, I can offer to consult you before publishing any results obtained."

The High Minister said, "You tempt me, sir. It is an interesting project. But you overestimate my power, even if we leave the people themselves out of consideration. I am not an absolute ruler. In fact, my power is sharply limited—and all matters must be submitted to the consideration of the Society of Ancients before final decisions are possible."

Arvardan shook his head. "This is most unfortunate. The Procurator warned me of the difficulties, yet I was hoping that——When can you consult your legislature, Your Excellency?"

"The Presidium of the Society of Ancients will meet three days hence. It is beyond my power to alter the agenda, so it may be a few days more before the matter can be discussed. Say a week."

Arvardan nodded abstractedly. "Well, it will have to do.... By the way, Your Excellency——"

"Yes?"

"There is a scientist upon your planet whom I would like to meet. A Dr. Shekt at Chica. Now, I've been in Chica, but left before I could do much and would like to repair the omission. Since I am sure he is a busy man, I wonder if I could trouble you for a letter of introduction?"

The High Minister had stiffened visibly and for several moments said nothing. Then, "May I ask what it is you want to see him about?"

"Certainly. I have read of an instrument he has developed, which he calls a Synapsifier, I believe. It concerns the neuro-chemistry of the brain and could have something very interesting to do with another project of mine. I have been doing some work on the classification of humanity into encephalographic groups—brain-current types, you understand."

"Umm... I have heard vaguely about the device. I seem to recall that it was not a success."

"Well, maybe not, but he is an expert in the field and could probably be very helpful to me."

"I see. In that case a letter of introduction will be prepared immediately for you. Of course there must be no mention of your intentions with regard to the Forbidden Areas."

"That is understood, Your Excellency." He rose. "I thank you for your courtesy and your kind attitude and can only hope that the Council of Ancients will be liberal with respect to my project."

The Secretary entered after Arvardan left. His lips were spread in his characteristic cold, savage smile.

"Very good," he said. "You handled yourself well, Your Excellency."

The High Minister looked at him somberly and said, "What was that last about Shekt?"

"You are puzzled? Don't be. All things are working out well. You noticed his lack of heat when you vetoed his project. Was that the response of a scientist whose heart is set upon something withdrawn from his grasp for no apparent reason? Or is it the response of one who is playing a part and is relieved to be well rid of it?

"And again we have a queer coincidence. Schwartz escapes and makes his way to Chica. The very next day Arvardan appears here and, after a lukewarm rigmarole about his expedition, mentions casually that he is going to Chica to see Shekt."

"But why mention it, Balkis? It seems foolhardy."

"Because you are straightforward. Put yourself in his position. He imagines we suspect nothing. In such a case it is audacity that wins. He's going to see Shekt. Good! He mentions it frankly. He even asks for a letter of introduction. What better guarantee of honest and innocent intentions can he present? And that brings up another point. Schwartz may have discovered that he was being watched. He may have killed Natter. *But he has had no time to warn the others*, or this comedy could not have played itself out in just this fashion."

The Secretary's eyes were half lidded as he spun his

spider web. "There is no way of telling how long it will be before Schwartz's absence becomes suspicious for them, but it is at least safe to allow sufficient time for Arvardan to meet Shekt. We'll catch them together; there will be that much less they can deny."

"How much time do *we* have?" demanded the High Minister.

Balkis looked up thoughtfully. "The schedule is fluid, and ever since we uncovered Shekt's treason they've been on triple shift—and things are proceeding well. We await only the mathematical computations for the necessary orbits. What holds us up there is the inadequacy of our computers. Well . . . it may be only a matter of days now."

"Days!" It was said in a tone queerly compounded of triumph and horror.

"Days!" repeated the Secretary. "But remember—one bomb even two seconds before zero time will be enough to stop us. And even afterward there will be a period of from one to six months when reprisals can be taken. So we are not yet entirely safe."

Days! And then the most incredibly one-sided battle in the history of the Galaxy would be joined and Earth would attack all the Galaxy.

The High Minister's hands were trembling gently.

Arvardan was seated in a stratoplane again. His thoughts were savage ones. There seemed no reason to believe that the High Minister and his psychopathic subject population would allow an official invasion of the radioactive areas. He was prepared for that. Somehow he wasn't even sorry about it. He could have put up a better fight—if he had cared more.

As it was, by the Galaxy, there would be illegal entry. He would arm his ship and fight it out, if necessary. He would rather.

The bloody fools!

Who the devil did they think they were?

Yes, yes, he knew. They thought they were the original humans, the inhabitants of *the* planet——

The worse of it was he knew that they were right.

Well . . . The ship was taking off. He felt himself sinking back into the soft cushion of his seat and knew that within the hour he'd be seeing Chica.

Not that he was eager to see Chica, he told himself, but the Synapsifier thing could be important, and there was no use being on Earth if he didn't take advantage of it. He certainly never intended to return once he left.

Rathole!

Ennius was right.

This Dr. Shekt, however . . . He fingered his letter of introduction, heavy with official formality——

And then he sat bolt upright—or tried to, struggling bitterly against the forces of inertia that were compressing him down into his seat as the Earth still sank away and the blue of the sky was deepened into a rich purple.

He remembered the girl's name. It was Pola *Shekt*.

Now why had he forgotten? He felt angry and cheated. His mind was plotting against him, holding back the last name till it was too late.

But, deep underneath, *something* was rather glad of it.

partment on Science etc. when agents on observa-
They'd have just called me up and questioned me.
But his face wore a stubborn, set expression. "They

14. SECOND MEETING

In the two months that had elapsed from the day that Dr.
Shekt's Synapsifier had been used on Joseph Schwartz, the
physicist had changed completely. Physically not so much,
though perhaps he was a thought more stooped, a shade
thinner. It was his manner—abstracted, fearful. He lived
in an inner communion, withdrawn from even his closest
colleagues, and from which he emerged with a reluctance
that was plain to the blindest.

Only to Pola could he unburden himself, perhaps because
she, too, had been strangely withdrawn those two months.

"They're watching me," he would say. "I feel it somehow. Do you know what the feeling is like? . . . There's
been a turnover in the Institute in the last month or so, and
it's the ones I like and feel I can trust that go . . . I never
get a minute to myself. Always someone about. They won't
even let me write reports."

And Pola would alternately sympathize with him and
laugh at him, saying over and over again, "But what can
they possibly have against you to do all this? Even if you

did experiment on Schwartz, that's not such a terrible crime. They'd have just called you on the carpet for it."

But his face was yellow and thin as he muttered, "They won't let me live. My Sixty is coming and they won't let me live."

"After all you've done. Nonsense!"

"I know too much, Pola, and they don't trust me."

"Know too much about what?"

He was tired that night, aching to remove the load. He told her. At first she wouldn't believe him, and finally, when she did, she could only sit there, in cold horror.

Pola called up the State House the next day from a public Communi-wave at the other end of town. She spoke through a handkerchief and asked for Dr. Bel Arvardan.

He wasn't there. They thought he might be in Bonair, six thousand miles away, but he hadn't been following his scheduled itinerary very closely. Yes, they did expect him back in Chica eventually, but they didn't know exactly when. Would she leave her name? They would try to find out.

She broke connections at that and leaned her soft cheek against the glass enclosure, grateful for the coolness thereof. Her eyes were deep with unshed tears and liquid with disappointment.

Fool. *Fool!*

He had helped her and she had sent him away in bitterness. He had risked the neuronic whip and worse to save the dignity of a little Earthgirl against an Outsider and she had turned on him anyway.

The hundred credits she had sent to the State House the morning after that incident had been returned without comment. She had wanted then to reach him and apologize, but she had been afraid. The State House was for Outsiders only, and how could she invade it? She had never even seen it, except from a distance.

And now——She'd have gone to the palace of the Procurator himself to—to——

Only *he* could help them now. *He*, an Outsider who could talk with Earthmen on a basis of equality. *She* had never guessed him to be an Outsider until he had told her. He was so tall and self-confident. He would *know* what to do.

And someone *had* to know, or it would mean the ruin of all the Galaxy.

Of course so many Outsiders deserved it—but did all of them? The women and children and sick and old? The kind and the good? The Arvardans? The ones who had never heard of Earth? And they were humans, after all. Such a horrible revenge would for all time drown whatever justice might be—no, *was*—in Earth's cause in an endless sea of blood and rotting flesh.

And then, out of nowhere, came the call from Arvardan. Dr. Shekt shook his head. "I can't tell him."

"You must," said Pola savagely.

"Here? It is impossible—it would mean ruin for both."

"Then turn him away. *I'll* take care of it."

Her heart was singing wildly. It was only because of this chance to save so many countless myriads of humans, of course. She remembered his wide, white smile. She remembered how he had calmly forced a colonel of the Emperor's own forces to turn and bow his head to her in apology—to *her*, an Earthgirl, who could stand there and forgive him.

Bel Arvardan could do *anything*!

Arvardan could, of course, know nothing of all this. He merely took Shekt's attitude for what it seemed—an abrupt and odd rudeness, of a piece with everything else he had experienced on Earth.

He felt annoyed, there in the anteroom of the carefully lifeless office, quite obviously an unwelcome intruder.

He picked his words. "I would never have dreamed of imposing upon you to the extent of visiting you, Doctor, were it not that I was professionally interested in your Synapsifier. I have been informed that, unlike many Earthmen, you are not unfriendly to men of the Galaxy."

It was apparently an unfortunate phrase, for Dr. Shekt jumped at it. "Now, whoever your informant is, he does wrong to impute any especial friendliness to strangers as such. I have no likes and dislikes. I am an Earthman——"

Avradan's lips compressed and he half turned.

"You understand, Dr. Arvardan"—the words were hurried and whispered—"I am sorry if I seem rude, but I really cannot——"

"I quite understand," the archaeologist said coldly, though he did not understand at all. "Good day, sir."

Dr. Shekt smiled feebly. "The pressure of my work——"

"I am very busy too, Dr. Shekt."

He turned to the door, raging inwardly at all the tribe of Earthmen, feeling within him, involuntarily, some of the catchwords that were bandied so freely on his home world. The proverbs, for instance: "Politeness on Earth is like dryness in the ocean" or "An Earthman will give you anything as long as it costs nothing and is worth less."

His arm had already broken the photoelectric beam that opened the front door when he heard the flurry of quick steps behind him and a *hist* of warning in his ear. A piece of paper was thrust in his hand, and when he turned there was only a flash of red as a figure disappeared.

He was in his rented ground car before he unraveled the paper in his hand. Words were scrawled upon it:

"Ask your way to the Great Playhouse at eight this evening. Make sure you are not followed."

He frowned ferociously at it and read it over five times, then stared all over it, as though expecting invisible ink to bound into visibility. Involuntarily, he looked behind him. The street was empty. He half raised his hand to throw the silly scrap out of the window, hesitated, then stuffed it into his vest pocket.

Undoubtedly, if he had had one single thing to do that evening other than what the scrawl had suggested, that would have been the end of it, and, perhaps, of several trillions of people. But, as it turned out, he had nothing to do.

And, as it turned out, he wondered if the sender of the note had been——

* * *

At eight o'clock he was making his slow way as part of a long line of ground cars along the serpentine way that apparently led to the Great Playhouse. He had asked only once, and the passerby questioned had stared suspiciously at him (apparently no Earthman was ever free of that all-pervasive suspicion) and had said curtly, "You just follow all the rest of the cars."

It seemed that all the rest of the cars were indeed going to the Playhouse, for when he got there he found all being swallowed, one by one, into the gaping maw of the underground parking lot. He swung out of line and crawled past the Playhouse, waiting for he knew not what.

A slim figure dashed down from the pedestrian ramp and hung outside his window. He stared at it, startled, but it had the door open and was inside in a single gesture.

"Pardon me," he said, "but——"

"Ssh!" The figure was hunched down low in the seat. "Were you followed?"

"Should I have been?"

"Don't be funny. Go straight ahead. Turn when I tell you . . . My goodness, what are you waiting for?"

He knew the voice. A hood had shifted down to the shoulders, and light brown hair was showing. Dark eyes were gazing at him.

"You'd better move on," she said softly.

He did, and for fifteen minutes, except for an occasional muffled but curt direction, she said nothing. He stole glances at her and thought, with a sudden pleasure, that she was even prettier than he had remembered her. Strange that *now* he felt no resentment.

They stopped—or Arvardan did, at the girl's direction—at the corner of an unpeopled residential district. After a careful pause the girl motioned him ahead once more and they inched down a drive that ended in the gentle ramp of a private garage.

The door closed behind them and the light in the car was the only source of illumination.

And now Pola looked at him gravely and said, "Dr. Arvardan, I'm sorry that I had to do this in order to speak to you privately. I know that I have no standing in your good opinion to lose——"

"Don't think that," he said awkwardly.

"I must think that. I want you to believe that I fully realize how small and vicious I was that night. I don't have the proper words to apologize——"

"Please don't." He glanced away from her. "I might have been a little more diplomatic."

"Well . . ." Pola paused a few moments to regain a certain minimal composure. "It's not what I've brought you here for. You're the only Outsider I've ever met that could be kind and noble—and I need your help."

A cold pang shot through Avardan. Was this what it was all about? He packed that thought into a cold "Oh?"

And she cried, "No," in return. "It is not for me, Dr. Arvardan. It is for all the Galaxy. Nothing for myself. *Nothing!*"

"What is it?"

"First——I don't think anyone followed us, but if you hear any noise at all, would you—would you"—her eyes dropped—"put your arms about me, and—and—you know."

He nodded his head and said dryly, "I believe I can improvise without any trouble. Is it necessary to wait for noise?"

Pola reddened. "Please don't joke about it, or mistake my intentions. It would be the only way of avoiding suspicion of our real intentions. It is the one thing that would be convincing."

Arvardan said softly, "Are things that serious?"

He looked at her curiously. She seemed so young and so soft. In a way he felt it to be unfair. Never in his life did he act unreasoningly. He took pride in that. He was a man of strong emotions, but he fought them and beat them. And here, just because a girl seemed weak, he felt the unreasoning urge to protect her.

She said, "Things *are* that serious. I'm going to tell you something, and I know you won't believe it at first. But I want you to *try* to believe it. I want you to make up your mind that I'm sincere. And most of all I want you to decide that you will stick with us after I tell you and see it through. Will you try? I'll give you fifteen minutes, and if you think at the end of that time that I'm not worth trusting or bothering with, I'll leave, and that's the end of it."

"Fifteen minutes?" His lips quirked in an involuntary smile, and he removed his wrist watch and put it before him. "All right."

She clasped her hands in her lap and looked firmly ahead through the windshield that afforded a view only of the blank wall of the garage ahead.

He watched her thoughtfully—the smooth, soft line of her chin, belying the firmness into which she was attempting to force it, the straight and thinly drawn nose, the peculiarly rich overtone to the complexion, so characteristic of Earth.

He caught the corner of her eye upon him. It was hastily withdrawn.

"What's the matter?" he said.

She turned to him and caught her underlip in two teeth. "I was watching you."

"Yes, I could see that. Smudge on my nose?"

"No." She smiled tinily, the first since she had entered his car. He was becoming absurdly conscious of little things about her: the way her hair seemed to hover and float gently each time she shook her head. "It's just that I've been wondering ever since—that night—why you don't wear that lead clothing, if you're an Outsider. That's what fooled me. Outsiders generally look like sacks of potatoes."

"And I don't?"

"Oh no"—and there was a sudden tinge of enthusiasm in her voice—"you look—you look quite like an ancient marble statue, except that you're alive and warm. . . . I'm sorry. I'm being impertinent."

"You mean you think that it's my opinion you're an Earthgirl who doesn't know your place. You'll have to stop thinking that of me, or we can't be friendly. . . . I don't believe in the radioactivity superstition. I've measured the atmospheric radioactivity of Earth and I've conducted laboratory experiments on animals. I'm quite convinced that under ordinary circumstances the radiations won't hurt me. I've been here two months and I don't feel sick yet. My hair isn't falling out"—he pulled at it—"my stomach isn't in knots. And I doubt that my fertility is being endangered, though I will admit to taking slight precautions in that respect. But lead-impregnated shorts, you see, don't show."

He said that gravely, and she was smiling again. "You're slightly mad, I think," she said.

"Really? You'd be surprised how many very intelligent and famous archaeologists have said that—and in long speeches, too."

And she said suddenly, "Will you listen to me now? The fifteen minutes are up."

"What do you think?"

"Why, that you might be. If you weren't, you wouldn't still be sitting here. Not after what I've done."

He said softly, "Are you under the impression that I have to force myself very hard to sit here next to you? If you do, you're wrong. . . . Do you know, Pola, I've never seen, I really believe I've never seen, a girl quite as beautiful as yourself."

She looked up quickly, with fright in her eyes. "Please don't. I'm not trying for that. Don't you believe me?"

"Yes, I do, Pola. Tell me whatever it is you want to. I'll believe it and I'll help you." He believed himself, implicitly. At the moment Arvardan would cheerfully have undertaken to unseat the Emperor. He had never been in love before, and at that point he ground his thoughts to a halt. He had not used that word before.

Love? With an Earthgirl?

"You've seen my father, Dr. Arvardan?"

"Dr. Shekt is your father? . . . Please call me Bel. I'll call you Pola."

"If you want me to, I'll try. I suppose you were pretty angry with him."

"He wasn't very polite."

"He couldn't be. He's being watched. In fact, he and I arranged in advance that he was to get rid of you and I was to see you here. This is our house, you know. . . . You see"—her voice dropped to a tight whisper—"Earth is going to revolt."

Arvardan couldn't resist a moment of amusement.

"No!" he said, opening his eyes wide. "All of it?"

But Pola flared into instant fury. "Don't laugh at me. You said you would listen and believe me. Earth is going to revolt, and it is serious, because Earth can destroy all the Empire."

"Earth can do that?" Arvardan struggled successfully against a burst of laughter. He said gently, "Pola, how well do you know your Galactography?"

"As well as anybody, teacher, and what has that to do with it, anyway?"

"It has this to do with it. The Galaxy has a volume of several million cubic light-years. It contains two hundred million inhabited planets and an approximate population of five hundred quadrillion people. Right?"

"I suppose so, if you say so."

"It is, believe me. Now Earth is one planet, with a population of twenty millions, and no resources besides. In other words, there are twenty-five billion Galactic citizens for every single Earthman. Now what harm can Earth do against odds of twenty-five billion to one?"

For a moment the girl seemed to sink into doubt, then she emerged. "Bel," she said firmly, "I can't answer that, but my father can. He has not told me the crucial details, because he claims that that would endanger my life. But he will now, if you come with me. He's told me that Earth knows a way by which it can wipe out all life outside Earth, and he *must* be right. He's always been right before."

Her cheeks were pink with earnestness, and Arvardan longed to touch them. (Had he ever before touched her and felt horrified at it? What was happening to him?)

"Is it after ten?" asked Pola.

"Yes," he replied.

"Then he should be upstairs now—if they haven't caught him." She looked about with an involuntary shudder. "We can get into the house directly from the garage now, and if you'll come with me——"

She had her hand on the knob that controlled the car door, when she froze. Her voice was a husky whisper: "There's someone coming . . . Oh, quick——"

The rest was smothered. It was anything but difficult for Arvardan to remember her original injunction. His arms swept about her with an easy motion, and, in an instant, she was warm and soft against him. Her lips trembled upon his and were limitless seas of sweetness . . .

For about ten seconds he swiveled his eyes to their extremes in an effort to see that first crack of light or hear that first footstep, but then he was drowned and swept under by the excitement of it all. Blinded by stars, deafened by his own heartbeat.

Her lips left his, but he sought them again, frankly, and found them. His arms tightened, and she melted within them until her own heartbeat was shaking him in time to his own.

It was quite a while before they broke apart, and for a moment they rested, cheek against cheek.

Arvardan had never been in love before, and this time he did not start at the word.

What of it? Earthgirl or not, the Galaxy could not produce her equal.

He said, with a dreamy pleasure, "It must have been only a traffic noise."

"It wasn't," she whispered. "I didn't hear any noise."

He held her at arm's distance, but her eyes did not falter. "You devil. Are you serious?"

Her eyes sparkled. "I wanted you to kiss me. I'm not sorry."

"Do you think *I* am? Kiss me again, then, for no reason but that *I* want to this time."

Another long, long moment and she was suddenly away from him, arranging her hair and adjusting the collar of her dress with prim and precise gestures. "I think we had better go into the house now. Put out the car light. I've got a pencil flash."

He stepped out of the car after her, and in the new darkness she was the vaguest shadow in the little pockmark of light that came from her pencil flash.

She said, "You'd better hold my hand. There's a flight of stairs we must go up."

His voice was a whisper behind her. "I love you, Pola." It came out so easily—and it sounded so right. He said it again. "I love you, Pola."

She said softly, "You hardly know me."

"No. All my life. I swear! All my life. Pola, for two months I've been thinking and dreaming of you. I swear it."

"I am an Earthgirl, sir."

"Then I will be an Earthman. Try me."

He stopped her and bent her hand up gently until the pocket flash rested upon her flushed, tear-marked face. "Why are you crying?"

"Because when my fathers tells you what he knows, you'll know that you cannot love an Earthgirl."

"Try me on that too."

15. THE ODDS THAT VANISHED

Arvardan and Shekt met in a back room on the second story of the house, with the windows carefully polarized to complete opaqueness. Pola was downstairs, alert and sharp-eyed in the armchair from which she watched the dark and empty street.

Shekt's stooped figure wore somehow an air different from that which Arvardan had observed some ten hours previously. The physicist's face was still haggard, and infinitely weary, but where previously it had seemed uncertain and timorous, it now bore an almost desperate defiance.

"Dr. Arvardan," he said, and his voice was firm, "I must apologize for my treatment of you in the morning. I had hoped you would understand——"

"I must admit I didn't, sir, but I believe I do now."

Shekt seated himself at the table and gestured toward the bottle of wine. Arvardan waved his hand in a deprecating motion. "If you don't mind, I'll have some of the fruit instead . . . What is this? I don't think I've ever seen anything like it."

"It's a kind of orange," said Shekt. "I don't believe it grows outside Earth. The rind comes off easily." He demonstrated, and Arvardan, after sniffing at it curiously, sank his teeth into the winy pulp. He came up with an exclamation.

"Why, this is delightful, Dr. Shekt! Has Earth ever tried to export these objects?"

"The Ancients," said the biophysicist grimly, "are not fond of trading with the Outside. Nor are our neighbors in space fond of trading with us. It is but an aspect of our difficulties here."

Arvardan felt a sudden spasm of annoyance seize him. "That is the most stupid thing yet. I tell you that I could despair of human intelligence when I see what can exist in men's minds."

Shekt shrugged with the tolerance of lifelong use. "It is part of the nearly insoluble problem of anti-Terrestrianism, I fear."

"But what makes it so nearly insoluble," exclaimed the archaelogist, "is that no one seems to really want a solution! How many Earthmen respond to the situation by hating all Galactic citizens indiscriminately? It is an almost universal disease—hate for hate. Do your people really want equality, mutual tolerance? No! Most of them want only their own turn as top dog."

"Perhaps there is much in what you say," said Shekt sadly. "I cannot deny it. But that is not the whole story. Give us but the chance, and a new generation of Earthmen would grow to maturity, lacking insularity and believing wholeheartedly in the oneness of Man. The Assimilationists, with their tolerance and belief in wholesome compromise, have more than once been a power on Earth. I am one. Or, at least, I was one once. But the Zealots rule all Earth now. They are the extreme nationalists, with their dreams of past rule and future rule. It is against them that the Empire must be protected."

Arvardan frowned. "You refer to the revolt Pola spoke of?"

"Dr. Arvardan," Shekt said grimly, "it's not too easy a

job to convince anyone of such an apparently ridiculous possibility as Earth conquering the Galaxy, but it's true. I am not physically brave, and I am most anxious to live. You can imagine, then, the immense crisis that must now exist to force me to run the risk of committing treason with the eye of the local administration already upon me."

"Well," said Arvardan, "if it is that serious, I had better tell you one thing immediately. I will help you all I can, but only in my own capacity as a Galactic citizen. I have no official standing here, nor have I any particular influence at the Court or even at the Procurator's Palace. I am exactly what I seem to be—an archaeologist on a scientific expedition which involves only my own interests. Since you *are* prepared to risk treason, hadn't you better see the Procurator about this? He could *really* do something."

"That is exactly what I cannot do, Dr. Arvardan. It is that very contingency against which the Ancients guard me. When you came to my house this morning I even thought you might be a go-between. I thought that Ennius suspected."

"He may suspect—I cannot answer for that. But I am not a go-between. I'm sorry. If you insist on making me your confidant, I can promise to see him for you."

"Thank you. It is all I ask. That—and to use your good offices to intercede for Earth against too strong a reprisal."

"Of course." Arvardan was uneasy. At the moment he was convinced that he was dealing with an elderly and eccentric paranoiac, perhaps harmless, but thoroughly cracked. Yet he had no choice but to remain, to listen, and to try to smooth over the gentle insanity—for Pola's sake.

Shekt said, "Dr. Arvardan, you have heard of the Synapsifier? You said so this morning."

"Yes, I did. I read your original artical in *Physical Reviews*. I discussed the instrument with the Procurator and with the High Minister."

"With the High Minister?"

"Why, certainly. When I obtained the letter of introduction that you—uh—refused to see, I'm afraid."

"I'm sorry for that. But I wish you had not——What is the extent of your knowledge concerning the Synapsifier?"

"That it is an interesting failure. It is designed to improve learning capacity. It has succeeded to some extent on rats, but has failed on human beings."

Shekt was chagrined. "Yes, you could think nothing else from that article. It was publicized as a failure, and the eminently successful results have been suppressed, deliberately."

"Hmp. A rather unusual display of scientific ethics, Dr. Shekt."

"I admit it. But I am fifty-six, sir, and if you know anything of the customs of Earth, you know that I haven't long to live."

"The Sixty. Yes, I have heard of it—more than I would have liked, in fact." And he thought wryly of that first trip on a Terrestrian stratoliner. "Exceptions are made for noted scientists, among others, I have heard."

"Certainly. But it is the High Minister and the Council of Ancients who decide on that, and there is no appeal from their decisions, even to the Emperor. I was told that the price of life was secrecy concerning the Synapsifier and hard work for its improvement." The older man spread his hands helplessly. "Could I know then of the outcome, of the use to which the machine would be put?"

"And the use?" Arvardan extracted a cigarette from his shirt-pocket case and offered one to the other, which was refused.

"If you'll wait a moment——One by one, after my experiments had reached the point where I felt the instrument might be safely applied to human beings, certain of Earth's biologists were treated. In each case they were men I knew to be in sympathy with the Zealots—the extremists, that is. They all survived, though secondary effects made themselves shown after a time. One of them was brought back for treatment eventually. I could not save him. But, in his dying delirium, I found out."

It was close upon midnight. The day had been long and

much had happened. But now something stirred within Arvardan. He said tightly, "I wish you'd get to the point."

Shekt said, "I beg your patience. I must explain thoroughly, if you're to believe me. You, of course, know of Earth's peculiar environment—its radioactivity——"

"Yes, I have a fair knowledge of the matter."

"And of the effect of this radioactivity upon Earth and its economy?"

"Yes."

"Then I won't belabor the point. I need only say that the incidence of mutation on Earth is greater than in the rest of the Galaxy. The idea of our enemies that Earthmen are different thus has a certain basis of physical truth. To be sure, the mutations are minor, and most possess no survival value. If any permanent change has occurred in Earthmen, it is only in some aspects of their internal chemistry which enables them to display greater resistance to their own particular environment. Thus they show greater resistance to radiation effects, more rapid healing of burned tissues——"

"Dr. Shekt, I am acquainted with all you say."

"Then has it ever occurred to you that these mutational processes occur in living species on Earth other than human?"

There was a short silence, and then Arvardan said, "Why, no, it hasn't, though, of course, it is quite inevitable, now that you mention it."

"That is so. It happens. Our domestic animals exist in greater variety than on any other inhabited world. The orange you ate is a mutated variety, which exists nowhere else. It is this, among other things, which makes the orange so unacceptable for export. Outsiders suspect it as they suspect us—and we ourselves guard it as a valuable property peculiar to ourselves. And of course what applies to animals and plants applies also to microscopic life."

And now, indeed, Arvardan felt the thin pang of fear enter.

He said, "You mean—bacteria?"

"I mean the whole domain of primitive life. Protozoa,

bacteria, and the self-reproducing nucleoproteins that some people call viruses."

"And what are you getting at?"

"I think you have a notion of that, Dr. Arvardan. You seem suddenly interested. You see, there is a belief among your people that Earthmen are bringers of death, that to associate with an Earthman is to die, that Earthmen are the bearers of misfortune, possess a sort of evil eye——"

"I know all that. It is merely superstition."

"Not entirely. That is the dreadful part. Like all common beliefs, however superstitious, distorted, and perverted, it has a speck of truth at bottom. Sometimes, you see, an Earthman carries within his body some mutated form of microscopic parasite which is not quite like any known elsewhere, and to which, sometimes, Outsiders are not particularly resistant. What follows is simple biology, Dr. Arvardan."

Arvardan was silent.

Shekt went on, "We are caught sometimes, too, of course. A new species of germ will make its way out of the radioactive mists and an epidemic will sweep the planet, but by and large, Earthmen have kept pace. For each variety of germ and virus, we build our defense over the generations, and we survive. Outsiders don't have the opportunity."

"Do you mean," said Arvardan with a strangely faint sensation, "that contact with you now——" He pushed his chair back. He was thinking of the evening's kisses.

Shekt shook his head. "Of course not. We don't *create* the disease; we merely carry it. And even such carriage occurs very rarely. If I lived on your world, I would no more carry the germ than you would; I have no special *affinity* for it. Even here it is only one out of every quadrillion germs, or one out of every quadrillion of quadrillions, that is dangerous. The chances of your infection right now are less than that of a meteorite penetrating the roof of this house and hitting you. *Unless* the germs in question are deliberately searched for, isolated, and concentrated."

Again a silence, longer this time. Arvardan said in a queer, strangled voice, "Have Earthmen been doing that?"

He had stopped thinking in terms of paranoia. He was ready to believe.

"Yes. But for innocent reasons, at first. Our biologists are, of course, particularly interested in the peculiarities of Earth life, and, recently, isolated the virus of Common Fever."

"What is Common Fever?"

"A mild endemic disease on Earth. That is, it is always with us. Most Earthmen have it in their childhood, and its symptoms are not very severe. A mild fever, a transitory rash, and inflammation of the joints and of the lips, combined with an annoying thirst. It runs its course in four to six days, and the subject is thereafter immune. I've had it. Pola has had it. Occasionally there is a more virulent form of this same disease—a slightly different strain of virus is concerned, presumably—and then it is called Radiation Fever."

"Radiation Fever. I've heard of it," said Arvardan.

"Oh, really? It is called Radiation Fever because of the mistaken notion that it is caught after exposure to radioactive areas. Actually, exposure to radioactive areas is often followed by Radiation Fever, because it is in those areas that the virus is most apt to mutate to dangerous forms. But it is the virus and not the radiation which does it. In the case of Radiation Fever, symptoms develop in a matter of two hours. The lips are so badly affected that the subject can scarcely talk, and he may be dead in a matter of days.

"Now, Dr. Arvardan, this is the crucial point. The Earthman has adapted himself to Common Fever and the Outsider has not. Occasionally a member of the Imperial garrison is exposed to it, and, in that case, he reacts to it as an Earthman would to Radiation Fever. Usually he dies within twelve hours. He is then burned—by Earthmen—since any other soldier approaching also dies.

"The virus, as I say, was isolated ten years ago. It is a nucleoprotein, as are most filtrable viruses, which, however, possesses the remarkable property of containing an unusually high concentration of radioactive carbon, sulphur, and phosphorus. When I say unusually high I mean that fifty per cent of its carbon, sulphur, and phosphorus is radioactive. It is supposed that the effects of the organism on its host is largely that of its radiations, rather than of its toxins. Naturally it would seem logical that Earthmen, who are adapted to gamma radiations, are only slightly affected. Original research in the virus centered at first about the method whereby it concentrated its radioactive isotopes. As you know, no chemical means can separate isotopes except through very long and tedious procedures. Nor is any organism other than this virus known which can do so. But then the direction of research changed.

"I'll be short, Dr. Arvardan. I think you see the rest. Experiments might be conducted on animals from outside Earth, but not on Outsiders themselves. The numbers of Outsiders on Earth were too few to allow several to disappear without notice. Nor could premature discovery of their plans be allowed. So it was a group of bacteriologists that was sent to the Synapsifier, to return with insights enormously developed. It was they who developed a new mathematical attack on protein chemistry and on immunology, which enabled them finally to develop an artificial strain of virus that was designed to affect Galactic human beings—Outsiders—only. Tons of the crystallized virus now exist."

Arvardan was haggard. He felt the drops of perspiration glide sluggishly down his temple and cheek.

"Then you are telling me," he gasped, "that Earth intends to set loose this virus on the Galaxy; that they will initiate a gigantic bacteriological warfare——"

"Which we cannot lose and you cannot win. Exactly. Once the epidemic starts, millions will die each day, and nothing will stop it. Frightened refugees fleeing across space will carry the virus with them, and if you attempt to blow up entire planets, the disease can be started again in new centers. There will be no reason to connect the matter with Earth. By the time our own survival becomes suspicious, the ravages will have progressed so far, the despair of the Outsiders will be so deep, that nothing will matter to them."

"And all will die?" The appalling horror did not penetrate—could not.

"Perhaps not. Our new science of bacteriology works both ways. We have the antitoxin as well, and the means of production thereof. It might be used in case of early surrender. Then there *may* be some out-of-the-way eddies of the Galaxy that could escape, or even a few cases of natural immunity."

In the horrible blankness that followed—during which Arvardan never thought of doubting the truth of what he had heard, the horrible truth which at a stroke wiped out the odds of twenty-five billion to one—Shekt's voice was small and tired.

"It is not Earth that is doing this. A handful of leaders, perverted by the gigantic pressure that excluded them from the Galaxy, hating those who keep them outside, wanting to strike back at any cost, and with insane intensity——

"Once they have begun, the rest of Earth must follow. What can it do? In its tremendous guilt, it will have to finish what it started. Could it allow enough of the Galaxy to survive and thus risk a later punishment?

"Yet before I am an Earthman, I am a man. Must trillions die for the sake of millions? Must a civilization spreading over a Galaxy crumble for the sake of the resentment, however justified, of a single planet? And will we be better off for all that? The power in the Galaxy will reside still on those worlds with the necessary resources—and we have none. Earthmen may even rule at Trantor for a generation, but their children will become Trantorians, and in their turn will look down upon the remnant on Earth.

"And besides, is there an advantage to Humanity to exchange the tryanny of a Galaxy for the tyranny of Earth? No—no——There must be a way out for *all* men, a way to justice and freedom."

His hands stole to his face, and behind their gnarled fingers he rocked gently to and fro.

Arvardan had heard all this in a numbed haze. He mumbled, "There is no treason in what you have done, Dr. Shekt.

I will go to Everest immediately. The Procurator will believe me. He *must* believe me."

There was the sound of running footsteps, the flash of a frightened face into the room, the door left swinging open.

"Father——Men are coming up the walk."

Dr. Shekt went gray. "Quickly, Dr. Arvardan, through the garage." He was pushing violently. "Take Pola, and don't worry about me. I'll hold them back."

But a man in a green robe waited for them as they turned. He wore a thin smile and carried, with a casual ease, a neuronic whip. There was a thunder of fists at the main door, a crash, and the sound of pounding feet.

"Who are you?" demanded Arvardan in a feeble defiance of the armed green-robe. He had stepped before Pola.

"I?" said Green-robe harshly. "I am merely the humble Secretary of his Excellency, the High Minister." He advanced. "I almost waited too long. But not quite. Hmm, a girl, too. Injudicious——"

Arvardan said evenly, "I am a Galactic citizen, and I dispute your right to detain me—or, for that matter, to enter this house—without legal authority."

"I"—and the Secretary tapped his chest gently with his free hand—"am all the right and authority on this planet. Within a short time I will be all the right and authority on the Galaxy. We have all of you, you know—even Schwartz."

"Schwartz!" cried Dr. Shekt and Pola, nearly together.

"You are surprised? Come, I will bring you to him."

The last thing Arvardan was conscious of was that smile, expanding—and the flash of the whip. He toppled through a crimson sear of pain into unconsciousness.

16. CHOOSE YOUR SIDE!

For the moment Schwartz was resting uneasily on a hard bench in one of the small sub-basement rooms of the Chica "Hall of Correction."

The Hall, as it was commonly termed, was the great token of the local power of the High Minister and those surrounding him. It lifted its gloominess in a rocky, angular height that overshadowed the Imperial barracks beyond it, just as its shadow clutched at the Terrestrial malefactor far more than did the unexerted authority of the Empire.

Within its walls many an Earthman in past centuries had waited for the judgment that came to one who falsified or evaded the quotas of production, who lived past his time, or connived at another's such crime, or who was guilty of attempting subversion of the local government. Occasionally, when the petty prejudices of Terrestrial justice made particularly little sense to the sophisticated and usually blasé Imperial government of the time, a conviction might be set aside by the Procurator, but this meant insurrection, or, at the very least, wild riots.

Ordinarily, where the Council demanded death, the Procurator yielded. After all, it was only Earthmen who suffered——

Of all this, Joseph Schwartz, very naturally, knew nothing. To him, immediate optical awareness consisted of a small room, its walls transfused with but a dim light, its furniture consisting of two hard benches and a table, plus a small recess in the wall that served as washroom and sanitary convenience combined. There was no window for a glimpse of sky, and the drift of air into the room through the ventilating shaft was feeble.

He rubbed the hair that circled his bald spot and sat up ruefully. His attempt to escape to nowhere (for where on Earth was he safe?) had been short, not sweet, and had ended here.

At least there was the Mind Touch to play with.

But was that bad or good?

At the farm it had been a queer, disturbing gift, the nature of which he did not know, the possibilities of which he did not think of. Now it was a flexible gift to be investigated.

With nothing to do for twenty-four hours but brood on imprisonment, he could have been courting madness. As it was, he could Touch the jailers as they passed, reach out for guardsmen in the adjacent corridors, extend the furthest fibrils of his mind even to the Captain of the Hall in his distant office.

He turned the minds over delicately and probed them. They fell apart like so many walnuts—dry husks out of which emotions and notions fell in a sibilant rain.

He learned much in the process of Earth and Empire—more than he had, or could have, in all two months on the farm.

Of course one of the items that he learned, over and over again, beyond any chance of mistaking, was just this:

He was condemned to death!

There was no escape, no doubt, no reservation.

It might be today; it might be tomorrow. But he would die!

Somehow it sank in and he accepted it almost gratefully.

* * *

The door opened, and he was on his feet, in tense fear. One might accept death reasoningly, with every aspect of the conscious mind, but the body was a brute beast that knew nothing of reason. This was it!

No—it wasn't. The entering Mind Touch held nothing of death in it. It was a guard with a metal rod held ready in his hand. Schwartz knew what it was.

"Come with me," he said sharply.

Schwartz followed him, speculating on this odd power of his. Long before his guard could use his weapon, long before he could possibly know he should, he could be struck down without a sound, without a giveaway moment. His Mind was in Schwartz's mental hands. A slight squeeze and it would be over.

But why? There would be others. How many could he handle at once? How many pairs of hands were in his mind?

He followed, docilely.

It was a large, large room that he was brought into. Two men and a girl occupied it, stretched out corpsewise on high, high benches. Yet not corpses—since three active minds were much in evidence.

Paralyzed! Familiar?... Were they familiar?

He was stopping to look, but the guard's hard hand was on his shoulder. "Get on."

There was a fourth slab, empty. There was no death in the guard's mind, so Schwartz climbed on. He knew what was coming.

The guard's steely rod touched each of his limbs. They tingled and left him, so that he was nothing but a head, floating on nothingness.

He turned it.

"Pola," he cried. "You're Pola, aren't you? The girl who——"

She was nodding. He hadn't recognized her Touch as such. He had never been aware of it that time two months ago. At that time his mental progression had reached only the stage of sensitivity to "atmosphere." In the brilliance of hindsight, he remembered that well.

But from the contents he could still learn much. The one past the girl was Dr. Shekt; the one furthest of all was Dr. Bel Arvadan. He could filch their names, sense their despair, taste the last dregs of horror and fright in the young girl's mind.

For a moment he pitied them, and then he remembered who they were and what they were. And he hardened his heart.

Let them die!

The other three had been there for the better part of an hour. The room in which they were left was evidently one used for assemblies of several hundred. The prisoners were lost and lonely in its size. Nor was there anything to say. Arvardan's throat burned dryly and he turned his head from side to side with a futile restlessness. It was the only part of his body that he could move.

Shekt's eyes were closed and his lips were colorless and pinched.

Arvardan whispered fiercely, "Shekt. Shekt, I say!"

"What? . . . What?" A feeble whisper at best.

"What are you doing? Going to sleep? Think, man, think!"

"Why? What is there to think of?"

"Who is this Joseph Schwartz?"

Pola's voice sounded, thin and weary. "Don't you remember, Bel? That time in the department store, when I first met you—so long ago?"

Arvardan wrenched wildly and found he could lift his head two aching inches. A bit of Pola's face was just visible.

"Pola! Pola!" If he could have moved toward her—as for two months he might have and hadn't. She was looking at him, smiling so wanly that it might be a statue's smile, and he said, "We'll win out yet. You'll see."

But she was shaking her head—and his neck gave way, its tendons in panging agony.

"Shekt," he said again. "Listen to me. How did you meet this Schwartz? Why was he a patient of yours?"

"The Synapsifier. He came as a volunteer."

"And was treated?"

"Yes."

Arvardan revolved that in his mind. "What made him come to you?"

"I don't know."

"But then——Maybe he *is* an Imperial agent."

(Schwartz followed his thought well and smiled to himself. He said nothing, and he meant to keep on saying nothing.)

Shekt stirred his head. "An Imperial agent? You mean because the High Priest's Secretary says he is. Oh, nonsense. And what difference does it make? He's as helpless as we.... Listen, Arvardan, maybe, if we tell some sort of concerted story, they might wait. Eventually we might——"

The archaeologist laughed hollowly, and his throat burned at the friction. "We might live, you mean. With the Galaxy dead and civilization in ruins? Live? I might as well die!"

"I'm thinking of Pola," muttered Shekt.

"I am too," said the other. "Ask her.... Pola, shall we surrender? Shall we try to live?"

Pola's voice was firm. "I have chosen my side. I don't want to die, but if my side dies, I'll go with it."

Arvardan felt somehow triumphant. When he brought her to Sirius, they might call her an Earthgirl, but she was their equal, and he would, with a great and good pleasure, smash teeth into the throat of any——

And he remembered that he wasn't likely to bring her to Sirius—to bring anyone to Sirius. There wasn't likely to be a Sirius.

Then, as though to escape from the thought, to escape anywhere, he shouted, "You! Whatchername! Schwartz!"

Schwartz raised his head for a moment and allowed a glance to ooze out toward the other. He still said nothing.

"Who are you?" demanded Arvardan. "How did you get mixed up in this? What's your part in it?"

And at the question, all the injustice of everything descended on Schwartz. All the harmlessness of his past, all the infinite horror of the present burst in upon him, so that he said in a fury, "I? How did I get mixed up in it? Listen.

I was once a nobody. An honest man, a hard-working tailor. I hurt nobody, I bothered nobody, I took care of my family. And then, for no reason, for *no reason*—I came here."

"To Chica?" asked Arvardan, who did not quite follow.

"No, not to Chica!" shouted Schwartz in wild derision. "I came to this whole mad world....Oh, what do I care if you believe me or not? *My* world is in the past. My world had land and food and billions of people, and it was the *only* world."

Arvardan fell silent before the verbal assault. He turned to Shekt. "Can you understand him?"

"Do you realize," said Shekt in feeble wonder, "that he has a vermiform appendix, which is three and a half inches long? Do you remember, Pola? And wisdom teeth. And hair on his face."

"Yes, yes," shouted Schwartz defiantly. "And I wish I had a tail I could show you. *I'm from the past. I traveled through time.* Only I don't know how, and I don't know why. Now leave me alone." He added suddenly, "They will soon be here for us. This wait is just to break us."

Arvardan said suddenly, "Do you know that? Who told you?"

Schwartz did not answer.

"Was it the Secretary? Stocky man with a pug nose?"

Schwartz had no way of telling the physical appearance of those he Touched only by mind, but—secretary? There had been just a glimpse of a Touch, a powerful one of a man of power, and it seemed he had been a secretary.

"Balkis?" he asked in curiosity.

"What?" said Arvardan, but Shekt interrupted, "That's the name of the Secretary."

"Oh——What did he say?"

"He didn't say anything," said Schwartz. "I *know*. It's death for all of us, and there's no way out."

Arvardan lowered his voice. "He's mad, wouldn't you say?"

"I wonder....His skull sutures, now. They were primitive, very primitive."

Arvardan was amazed. "You mean——Oh, come, it's impossible."

"I've always supposed so." For the moment Shekt's voice was a feeble imitation of normality, as though the presence of a scientific problem had switched his mind to that detached and objective groove in which personal matters disappeared. "They've calculated the energy required to displace matter along the time axis and a value greater than infinity was arrived at, so the project has always been looked upon as impossible. But others *have* talked of the possibility of 'time faults,' analogous to geological faults, you know. Space ships *have* disappeared, for one thing, almost in full view. There's the famous case of Hor Devallow in ancient times, who stepped into his house one day and never came out, and wasn't inside either. . . . And then there's the planet, which you'll find in the Galactography books of the last century, which was visited by three expeditions that brought back full descriptions—and then was never seen again.

"Then there are certain developments in nuclear chemistry that seem to deny the law of conservation of massenergy. They've tried to explain that by postulating the escape of some mass along the time axis. Uranium nuclei, for instance, when mixed with copper and barium in minute but definite proportions, under the influence of light gamma irradiation, set up a resonating system——"

"Father," said Pola, "don't! There's no use——"

But Arvardan's interruption was peremptory. "Wait, now. Let me think. *I'm* the one who can settle this. Who better? Let me ask him a few questions. . . . Look, Schwartz."

Schwartz looked up again.

"Yours was the only inhabited world in the Galaxy?"

Schwartz nodded, then said dully, "Yes."

"But you only thought that. I mean you didn't have space travel, so you couldn't check up. There might have been many other inhabited worlds."

"I have no way of telling that."

"Yes, of course. A pity. What about atomic power?"

"We had an atomic bomb. Uranium—and plutonium—— I guess that's what made this world radioactive. There must have been another war after all—after I left.... Atomic bombs." Somehow Schwartz was back in Chicago, back in his old world, before the bombs. And he was sorry. Not for himself, but for that beautiful world....

But Arvardan was muttering to himself. Then, "All right. You had a language, of course."

"Earth? Lots of them."

"How about you?"

"English—after I was a grown man."

"Well, say something in it."

For two months or more Schwartz had said nothing in English. But now, with lovingness, he said slowly, "I want to go home and be with my own people."

Arvardan spoke to Shekt. "Is that the language he used when he was Synapsified, Shekt?"

"I can't tell," said Shekt, in mystification. "Queer sounds then and queer sounds now. How can I relate them?"

"Well, never mind.... What's your word for 'mother' in your language, Schwartz?"

Schwartz told him.

"Uh-*huh*. How about 'father'...'brother'...'one'—the numeral, that is...'two'...'three'...'house'...'man' ...'wife'..."

This went on and on, and when Arvardan paused for breath his expression was one of awed bewilderment.

"Shekt," he said, "either this man is genuine or I'm the victim of as wild a nightmare as can be conceived. He's speaking a language practically equivalent to the inscriptions found in the fifty-thousand-year-old strata on Sirius, Arcturus, Alpha Centauri, and twenty others. He *speaks* it. The language has only been deciphered in the last generation, and there aren't a dozen men in the Galaxy besides myself who can understand it."

"Are you sure of this?"

"Am I *sure*? Of course I'm sure. I'm an archaeologist. It's my business to know."

For an instant Schwartz felt his armor of aloofness cracking. For the first time he felt himself regaining the individuality he had lost. The secret was out; he was a man from the past, *and they accepted it*. It proved him sane, stilled forever that haunting doubt, and he was grateful. And yet he held aloof.

"I've got to have him." It was Arvardan again, burning in the holy flame of his profession. "Shekt, you have no idea what this means to archaeology. Shekt—it's a man from the past. Oh, Great Space!... Listen, we can make a deal. This is the proof Earth is looking for. They can have him. They can——"

Schwartz interrupted sardonically. "I know what you're thinking. You think that Earth will prove itself to be the source of civilization through me and that they will be grateful for it. I tell you, no! I've thought of it and I would have bartered for my own life. But they won't believe me—or you."

"There's absolute proof."

"They won't listen. Do you know why? Because they have certain fixed notions about the past. Any change would be blasphemy in their eyes, even if it were the truth. They don't want the truth; they want their traditions."

"Bel," said Pola, "I think he's right."

Arvardan ground his teeth. "We could try."

"We would fail," insisted Schwartz.

"How can you know?"

"I *know*!" And the words fell with such oracular insistence that Arvardan was silent before them.

It was Shekt who was looking at him now with a strange light in his tired eyes.

He asked softly, "Have you felt any bad effects as a result of the Synapsifier?"

Schwartz didn't know the word but caught the meaning. They *had* operated, and on his mind. How much he was learning!

He said, "No bad effects."

"But I see you learned our language rapidly. You speak it very well. In fact, you might be a native. Doesn't it surprise you?"

"I always had a very good memory," was the cold response.

"And so you feel no different now than before you were treated?"

"That's right."

Dr. Shekt's eyes were hard now, and he said, "Why do you bother? You know that I'm certain you know what I'm thinking."

Schwartz laughed shortly. "That I can read minds? Well, what of it?"

But Shekt had dropped him. He had turned his white, helpless face to Arvardan. "He can sense minds, Arvardan. How much I could do with him. And to be here—to be helpless . . ."

"What—what—what——" Arvardan popped wildly.

And even Pola's face somehow gained interest. "Can you really?" she asked Schwartz.

He nodded at her. She had taken care of him, and now they would kill her. Yet she was a traitor.

Shekt was saying. "Arvardan, you remember the bacteriologist I told you about, the one who died as a result of the effects of the Synapsifier? One of the first symptoms of mental breakdown was his claim that he could read minds. And he *could*. I found that out before he died, and it's been my secret. I've told no one—but it's possible, Arvardan, it's possible. You see, with the lowering of brain-cell resistance, the brain may be able to pick up the magnetic fields induced by the microcurrents of other's thoughts and reconvert it into similar vibrations in itself. It's the same principle as that of any ordinary recorder. It would be telepathy in every sense of the word——"

Schwartz maintained a stubborn and hostile silence as Arvardan turned slowly in his direction. "If this is so, Shekt, we might be able to use him." The archaeologist's mind was spinning wildly, working out impossibilities. "There may be a way out now. There *must* be a way out. For us and the Galaxy."

But Schwartz was cold to the tumult in the Mind Touch he sensed so clearly. He said, "You mean by my reading their minds? How would that help? Of course I can do more than read minds. How's that, for instance?"

It was a light push, but Arvardan yelped at the sudden pain of it.

"I did that," said Schwartz. "Want more?"

Arvardan gasped, "You can do that to the guards? To the Secretary? Why did you let them bring you here? Great Galaxy, Shekt, there'll be no trouble. Now, listen, Schwartz——"

"No," said Schwartz, "*you* listen. Why do *I* want to get out? Where will I be? Still on this dead world. I want to go home, and I *can't* go home. I want my people and my world, and I can't have them. And I *want* to die."

"But it's a question of all the Galaxy, Schwartz. You can't think of yourself."

"Can't I? Why not? Must I worry about your Galaxy now? I hope your Galaxy rots and dies. I know what Earth is planning to do, and I am glad. The young lady said before she had chosen her side. Well, I've chosen my side, and my side is Earth."

"What?"

"Why not? I'm an Earthman!"

17. CHANGE YOUR SIDE!

An hour had passed since Arvardan had first waded thickly out of unconsciousness to find himself slabbed like a side of beef awaiting the cleaver. And nothing had happened. Nothing but this feverish, inconclusive talk that unbearably passed the unbearable time.

None of it lacked purpose. He knew that much. To lie prone, helpless, without even the dignity of a guard, without even that much concession to a conceivable danger, was to become conscious of overwhelming weakness. A stubborn spirit could not survive it, and when the inquisitor *did* arrive there would be little defiance, or none, for him to be presented with.

Arvardan needed a break in the silence. He said, "I suppose this place is Spy-waved. We should have talked less."

"It isn't," came Schwartz's voice flatly. "There's nobody listening."

The archaeologist was ready with an automatic "How do *you* know?" but never said it.

For a power like that to exist! And not for him, but for

a man of the past who called himself an Earthman and wanted to die!

Within optical sweep was only a patch of ceiling. Turning, he could see Shekt's angular profile; the other way, a blank wall. If he lifted his head he could make out, for a moment, Pola's pale, worn expression.

Occasionally there was the burning thought that he was a man of the Empire—of the *Empire*, by the Stars; a Galactic citizen—and that there was a particularly vile injustice in *his* imprisonment, a particularly deep impurity in the fact that he had allowed *Earthmen* to do this to him.

And that faded too.

They might have put him next to Pola . . . No, it was better this way. He was not an inspiring sight.

"Bel?" The word trembled into sound and was strangely sweet to Arvardan, coming as it did in this vortex of coming death.

"Yes, Pola?"

"Do you think they'll be much longer?"

"Maybe not, darling. . . . It's too bad. We wasted two months, didn't we?"

"My fault," she whispered. "My fault. We might have had these last few minutes, though. It's so—unnecessary."

Arvardan could not answer. His mind whirred in circles of thought, lost on a greased wheel. Was it his imagination, or did he feel the hard plastic on which he was so stiffly laid? How long would the paralysis last?

Schwartz *must* be made to help. He tried guarding his thoughts—knew it to be ineffective.

He said, "Schwartz——"

Schwartz lay there as helpless, and with an added, uncalculated refinement to his suffering. He was four minds in one.

By himself he might have maintained his own shrinking eagerness for the infinite peace and quiet of death, fought down the last remnants of that love of life which even as recently as two days previously—three?—had sent him reeling away from the farm. But how could he? With the poor, weak horror of death that hung like a pall over Shekt; with the strong chagrin and rebellion of Arvardan's hard, vital mind; with the deep and pathetic disappointment of the young girl.

He should have closed his own mind. What did he need to know of the sufferings of others? He had his own life to live, his own death to die.

But they battered at him softly, incessantly—probing and sifting through the crannies.

And Arvardan said, "Schwartz," then, and Schwartz knew that they wanted him to save them. Why should he? Why should he?

"Schwartz," repeated Arvardan insinuatingly, "you can live a hero. You have nothing to die for here—not for those men out there."

But Schwartz was gathering the memories of his own youth, clutching them desperately to his wavering mind. It was a queer amalgamation of past and present that finally brought forth his indignation.

But he spoke calmly, restrainedly. "Yes, I can live a hero—and a traitor. They want to kill me, those *men* out there. You call them men, but that was with your tongue; your mind called them something I didn't get, but it was vile. And not because they were vile, but because they were Earthmen."

"That's a lie," hotly.

"That is *not* a lie," as hotly, "and everyone here knows that. They want to kill me, yes—but that is because they think I'm one of your kind of people, who can condemn an entire planet at a stroke and drench it with your contempt, choke it slowly with your insufferable superiority. Well, protect yourself against these worms and vermin who are somehow managing to threaten their Godlike overlords. Don't ask for the help of one of them."

"You talk like a Zealot," said Arvardan with amazement. "Why? Have *you* suffered? You were a member of a large and independent planet, you say. You were an Earthman when Earth was the sole repository of life. You're one of *us*, man; one of the rulers. Why associate yourself with a desperate remnant? This is not the planet you remember. My planet is more like the old Earth than is this diseased world."

Schwartz laughed. "I'm one of the rulers, you say? Well, we won't go into that. It isn't worth explaining. Let's take you instead. You're a fine sample of the product sent us by the Galaxy. You are tolerant and wonderfully bighearted, and admire yourself because you treat Dr. Shekt as an equal. But underneath—yet not so far underneath that I can't see it plainly in your mind—you are uncomfortable with him. You don't like the way he talks or the way he looks. In fact, you don't like him, even though he is offering to betray Earth. . . . Yes, and you kissed a girl of Earth recently and look back upon it as a weakness. You're ashamed of it——"

"By the Stars, I'm not. . . . Pola," desperately, "don't believe him. Don't listen to him."

Pola spoke quietly. "Don't deny it, or make yourself unhappy about it, Bel. He's looking below the surface to the residue of your childhood. He would see the same if he looked into mine. He would see things similar if he could look into his own in as ungentlemanly a fashion as he probes ours."

Schwartz felt himself reddening.

Pola's voice did not rise in pitch or intensity as she addressed him directly. "Schwartz, if you can sense minds, investigate mine. Tell me if I intend treason. Look at my father. See if it is not true that he could have avoided the Sixty easily enough if he had co-operated with the madmen who will ruin the Galaxy. What has he gained by his treason? . . . And look again, see if any of us wish to harm Earth or Earthmen.

"You say you have caught a glimpse of Balkis's mind. I don't know what chance you have had to poke through its dregs. But when he's back, when it's too late, sift it, strain his thoughts. Find out that he's a madman——Then, die!"

Schwartz was silent.

Arvardan broke in hurriedly, "All right, Schwartz, tackle my mind now. Go as deep as you want. I was born on

Baronn in the Sirius Sector. I lived my life in an atmosphere of anti-Terrestrianism in the formative years, so I can't help what flaws and follies lie at the roots of my subconscious. But look on the surface and tell me if, in my adult years, I have not fought bigotry in myself. Not in others; that would be easy. But in myself, and as hard as I could.

"Schwartz, you don't know our history! You don't know of the thousands and tens of thousands of years in which Man spread through the Galaxy—of the wars and misery. You don't know of the first centuries of the Empire, when still there was merely a confusion of alternating despotism and chaos. It is only in the last two hundred years, now, that our Galactic government has become a representative one. Under it the various worlds are allowed their cultural autonomy—have been allowed to govern themselves—have been allowed voices in the common rule of all.

"At no time in history has Humanity been as free from war and poverty as now; at no time has Galactic economy been so wisely adjusted; at no time have prospects for the future been as bright. Would you destroy it and begin all over? And with what? A despotic theocracy with only the unhealthy elements of suspicion and hatred in it.

"Earth's grievance is legitimate and will be solved some-day, if the Galaxy lives. But what *they* will do is no solution. Do you *know* what they intend doing?"

If Arvardan had had the ability that had come to Schwartz, he would have detected the struggle in Schwartz's mind. Intuitively, however, he knew the time had come to halt for a moment.

Schwartz was moved. All those worlds to die—to fester and dissolve in horrible disease... Was he an Earthman after all? Simply an Earthman? In his youth he had left Europe and gone to America, but was he not the same man despite that? And if after him men had left a torn and wounded earth for the worlds beyond the sky, were they less Earthmen? Was not all the Galaxy his? Were not they all—all—descended from himself and his brothers?

He said heavily, "All right, I'm with you. How can I help?"

"How far out can you reach for minds?" asked Arvardan eagerly, with a hastening quickness as though afraid still of a last change of mind.

"I don't know. There are minds outside. Guards, I suppose. I think I can reach out into the street even, but the further I go, the less sharp it becomes."

"Naturally," said Arvardan. "But how about the Secretary? Could you identify his mind?"

"I don't know," mumbled Schwartz.

A pause . . . The minutes stretched by unbearably.

Schwartz said, "Your minds are in the way. Don't watch me. Think of something else."

They tried to. Another pause. Then, "No—I can't—I can't."

Arvardan said with a sudden intensity, "I can move a bit—Great Galaxy, I can wiggle my feet. . . . Ouch!" Each motion was a savage twinge.

He said, "How hard can you hurt someone, Schwartz? Can you do it harder than the way you hurt me a while back I mean?"

"I've killed a man."

"You have? How did you do that?"

"I don't know. It just gets done. It's—it's——" Schwartz looked almost comically helpless in his effort to put the wordless into words.

"Well, can you handle more than one at a time?"

"I've never tried, but I don't think so. I can't read two minds at one time."

Pola interrupted. "You can't have him kill the Secretary, Bel. It won't work."

"Why not?"

"How will we get out? Even if we caught the Secretary alone and killed him, there would be hundreds waiting for us outside. Don't you see that?"

But Schwartz broke in, huskily, "I've got him."

"Whom?" It came from all three. Even Shekt was staring wildly at him.

"The Secretary. I think it's his Mind Touch."

"Don't let him go." Arvardan almost rolled over in his

attempts at exhortation, and tumbled off the slab, thumping to the floor with one half-paralyzed leg working futilely to wedge underneath his body and lift.

Pola cried. "You're hurt!" and suddenly found the hinges of her arm uncreaking as she tried to lift her elbow.

"No, it's all right. Suck him dry, Schwartz. Get all the information you can."

Schwartz reached out until his head ached. He clutched and clawed with the tendrils of his own mind, blindly, clumsily—like an infant thrusting out fingers it can't quite handle for an object it can't quite reach. Until now he had taken whatever he could find, but now he was looking—looking——

Painfully, he caught wisps, "Triumph! He's sure of the results.... Something about space bullets. He's started them.... No, not started. Something else.... He's going to start them."

Shekt groaned. "They're automatically guided missiles to carry the virus, Arvardan. Aimed at the various planets."

"But where are they kept, Schwartz?" insisted Arvardan. "Look, man, look——"

"There's a building I—can't—quite—see.... Five points—a star—a name; Sloo, maybe——"

Shekt broke in again. "That's it. By all the stars in the Galaxy, that's it. The Temple of Senloo. It's surrounded by radioactive pockets on all sides. No one would ever go there but the Ancients. Is it near the meeting of two large rivers, Schwartz?"

"I can't——Yes—yes—yes."

"When, Schwartz, when? When will they be set off?"

"I can't see the day, but soon—soon. His mind is bursting with that——It will be very soon." His own head seemed bursting with the effort.

Arvardan was dry and feverish as he raised himself finally to his hands and knees, though they wobbled and gave under him. "Is he coming?"

"Yes. He's at the door."

His voice sank and stopped as the door opened.

Balkis's voice was one of cold derision as he filled the

room with success and triumph. "Dr. Arvardan! Had you not better return to your seat?"

Arvardan looked up at him, conscious of the cruel indignity of his own position, but there was no answer to make, and he made none. Slowly he allowed his aching limbs to lower him to the ground. He waited there, breathing heavily. If his limbs could return a bit more, if he could make a last lunge, if he could somehow seize the other's weapons——

That was no neuronic whip that dangled so gently from the smoothly gleaming Flexiplast belt that held the Secretary's robe in place. It was a full-size blaster that could shred a man to atoms in an instantaneous point of time.

The Secretary watched the four before him with a savage sense of satisfaction. The girl he tended to ignore, but otherwise it was a clean sweep. There was the Earthman traitor; there the Imperial agent; and there the mysterious creature they had been watching for two months. Were there any others?

To be sure, there was still Ennius, and the Empire. Their arms, in the person of these spies and traitors, were pinioned, but there remained an active brain somewhere—perhaps to send out other arms.

The Secretary stood easily, hands clasped in contemptuous disregard of any possible necessity of quickly reaching his weapon. He spoke quietly and gently. "Now it is necessary to make things absolutely clear. There is war between Earth and the Galaxy—undeclared as yet, but, nevertheless, war. You are our prisoners and will be treated as will be necessary under the circumstances. Naturally the recognized punishment for spies and traitors is death——"

"Only in the case of legal and declared war," broke in Arvardan fiercely.

"Legal war?" questioned the Secretary with more than a trace of a sneer. "What is *legal* war? Earth has *always* been at war with the Galaxy, whether we made polite mention of the fact or not."

"Don't bother with him," said Pola to Arvardan softly. "Let him have his say and finish with it."

Arvardan smiled in her direction. A queer, spasmodic smile, for it was with a vast strain that he staggered to his feet and remained there, gasping.

Balkis laughed softly. With unhurried steps he shortened the distance between himself and the Sirian archaeologist to nothing. With an equally unhurried gesture he rested a soft hand upon the broad chest of the other and shoved.

With splintering arms that would not respond to Arvardan's demand for a warding motion, with stagnant trunk muscles that could not adjust the body's balance at more than snail speed, Arvardan toppled.

Pola gasped. Lashing her own rebellious flesh and bone, she descended from her particular bench slowly—so slowly.

Balkis let her crawl toward Arvardan.

"Your lover," he said. "Your strong Outside lover. Run to him, girl! Why do you wait? Clasp your hero tightly and forget in his arms that he steams in the sweat and blood of a billion martyred Earthmen. And there he lies, bold and valiant—brought to Earth by the gentle push of an Earthman's hand."

Pola was on her knees beside him now, her fingers probing beneath the hair for blood or the deadly softness of crushed bone. Arvardan's eyes opened slowly and his lips formed a "Never mind!"

"He's a coward," said Pola, "who would fight a paralyzed man and boast his victory. Believe me, darling, few Earthmen are like that."

"I know it, or you would not be an Earthwoman."

The Secretary stiffened. "As I said, all lives here are forfeit, but, nevertheless, can be bought. Are you interested in the price?"

Pola said proudly, "In our case, you would be. That I know."

"Ssh, Pola." Arvardan had not yet recovered his breath entirely. "What are you proposing?"

"Oh," said Balkis, "you are willing to sell yourself? As I would be, for instance? I, a vile Earthman?"

"You know best what you are," retorted Arvardan. "As for the rest, I am not selling myself; I am buying her."

"I refuse to be bought," said Pola.

"Touching," grated the Secretary. "He stoops to our females, our Earth-squaws—and can still play-act at sacrifice."

"What are you proposing?" demanded Arvardan.

"This. Obviously, word of our plans has leaked out. How it got to Dr. Shekt is not difficult to see, but how it got to the Empire is puzzling. We would like to know, therefore, just what the Empire does know. Not what you have learned, Arvardan, but what the Empire now knows."

"I am an archaeologist and not a spy," bit out Arvardan. "I don't know anything at all about what the Empire knows—but I hope they know a damned lot."

"So I imagine. Well, you may change your mind. Think, all of you."

Throughout, Schwartz had contributed nothing; nor had he raised his eyes.

The Secretary waited, then said, perhaps a trifle savagely, "Then I'll outline the price to you of your non-cooperation. It will not be simply death, since I am quite certain that all of you are prepared for that unpleasant and inevitable eventuality. Dr. Shekt and the girl, his daughter, who, unfortunately for herself, is implicated to a deadly extent, are citizens of Earth. Under the circumstances, it will be most appropriate to have both subjected to the Synapsifier. You understand, Dr. Shekt?"

The physicist's eyes were pools of pure horror.

"Yes, I see you do," said Balkis. "It is, of course, possible to allow the Synapsifier to damage brain tissue just sufficiently to allow the production of an acerebral imbecile. It is a most disgusting state: one in which you will have to be fed, or starve: be cleaned, or live in dung: be shut up, or remain a study in horror to all who see. It may be a lesson to others in the great day that is coming.

"As for you"—and the Secretary turned to Arvardan—"and your friend Schwartz, you are Imperial citizens, and therefore suitable for an interesting experiment. We have never tried our concentrated fever virus on you Galactic dogs. It would be interesting to show our calculations correct. A small dose, you see, so that death is not quick. The disease might work its way to the inevitable over a period of a week, if we dilute the injection sufficiently. It will be very painful."

And now he paused and watched them through slitted eyes. "All that," he said, "is the alternative to a few well-chosen words at the present time. How much does the Empire know? Have they other agents active at the present moment? What are their plans, if any, for counteraction?"

Dr. Shekt muttered, "How do we know that you won't have us killed anyway, once you have what you want of us?"

"You have my assurance that you will die horribly if you refuse. You will have to gamble on the alternative. What do you say?"

"Can't we have time?"

"Isn't that what I'm giving you now? Ten minutes have passed since I entered, and I am still listening. . . . Well, have you anything to say? What, nothing? Time will not endure forever, you must realize. Arvardan, you still knot your muscles. You think perhaps you can reach me before I can draw my blaster. Well, what if you can? There are hundreds outside, and my plans will continue without me. Even your separate modes of punishment will continue without me.

"Or perhaps you, Schwartz. You killed our agent. It was you, was it not? Perhaps you think you can kill me?"

For the first time Schwartz looked at Balkis. He said coldly, "I can, but I won't."

"That is kind of you."

"Not at all. It is very cruel of me. You say yourself that there are things worse than simple death."

Arvardan found himself suddenly staring at Schwartz in a vast hope.

18. DUEL!

Schwartz's mind was whirling. In a queer, hectic way he felt at ease. There was a piece of him that seemed in absolute control of the situation, and more of him that could not believe that. Paralysis had been applied later to him than to the others. Even Dr. Shekt was sitting up, while he himself could just budge an arm and little more.

And, staring up at the leering mind of the Secretary, infinitely foul and infinitely evil, he began his duel.

He said, "I was on your side originally, for all that you were preparing to kill me. I thought I understood your feelings and your intentions... But the minds of these others here are relatively innocent and pure, and yours is past description. It is not even for the Earthman you fight, but for your own personal power. I see in you not a vision of a free Earth, but of a re-enslaved Earth. I see in you not the disruption of the Imperial power, but its replacement by a personal dictatorship."

"You see all that, do you?" said Balkis. "Well, see what you wish. I don't need your information after all, you know—

187

not so badly that I must endure insolence. We have advanced
the hour of striking, it seems. Had you expected *that*?
Amazing what pressure will do, even on those who swear
that more speed is impossible. Did you see that, my dramatic
mind reader?"

Schwartz said, "I didn't. I wasn't looking for it, and
it passed my notice.... But I can look for it now. Two
days——Less——Let's see——Tuesday—six in the
morning— Chica time."

The blaster was in the Secretary's hand, finally. He advanced in abrupt strides and towered over Schwartz's drooping figure.

"How did you know that?"

Schwartz stiffened; somewhere mental tendrils bunched
and grasped. Physically his jaw muscles clamped rigorously
shut and his eyebrows curled low, but these were purely
irrelevant—involuntary accompaniments to the real effort.
Within his brain there was that which reached out and seized
hard upon the Mind Touch of the other.

To Arvardan, for precious, wasting seconds, the scene
was meaningless; the Secretary's sudden motionless silence
was not significant.

Schwartz muttered gaspingly, "I've got him.... Take
away his gun. I can't hold on——" It died away in a gurgle.

And then Arvardan understood. With a lurch he was on
all fours. Then slowly, grindingly, he lifted himself once
more, by main force, to an unsteady erectness. Pola tried
to rise with him, could not quite make it. Shekt edged off
his slab, sinking to his knees. Only Schwartz lay there, his
face working.

The Secretary might have been struck by the Medusa
sight. On his smooth and unfurrowed forehead perspiration
gathered slowly, and his expressionless face hinted of no
emotion. Only that right hand, holding the blaster, showed
any signs of life. Watch closely, and you might see it jerk
ever so gently; note the curious flexing pressure of it upon
the contact button: a gentle pressure, not enough to do harm,
but returning, and returning——

"Hold him tight," gasped Arvardan with a ferocious joy. He steadied himself on the back of a chair and tried to gain his breath. "Let me get to him."

His feet dragged. He was in a nightmare, wading through molasses, swimming through tar; pulling with torn muscles, so slowly—so slowly.

He was not—could not be—conscious of the terrific duel that proceeded before him.

The Secretary had only one aim, and that was to put just the tiniest force into his thumb—three ounces, to be exact, since that was the contact pressure required for the blaster's operation. To do so his mind had only to instruct a quiveringly balanced tendon, already half contracted, to—to——

Schwartz had only one aim, and that was to restrain that pressure—but in all the inchoate mass of sensation presented to him by the other's Mind Touch, he could not know which particular area was alone concerned with that thumb. So it was that he bent his efforts to produce a stasis, a complete stasis——

The Secretary's Mind Touch heaved and billowed against restraint. It was a quick and fearfully intelligent mind that confronted Schwartz's untried control. For seconds it remained quiescent, waiting—then, in a terrific, tearing attempt, it would tug wildly at this muscle or that——

To Schwartz it was as if he had seized a wrestling hold which he must maintain at all costs, though his opponent threw him about in frenzies.

But none of this showed. Only the nervous clenching and unclenching of Schwartz's jaw; the quivering lips, bloodied by the biting teeth—and that occasional soft movement on the part of the Secretary's thumb, straining—straining.

Arvardan paused to rest. He did not want to. He had to. His outstretched finger just touched the fabric of the Secretary's tunic and he felt he could move no more. His agonized lungs could not pump the breath his dead limbs required. His eyes were blurred with the tears of effort, his mind with the the haze of pain.

He gasped, "Just a few more minutes, Schwartz. Hold him, hold him——"

Slowly, slowly, Schwartz shook his head. "I can't—I can't——"

And indeed, to Schwartz all the world was slipping away into dull, unfocused chaos. The tendrils of his mind were becoming stiff and nonresilient.

The Secretary's thumb pressed once again upon the contact. It did not relax. The pressure grew by tiny stages.

Schwartz could feel the bulging of his own eyeballs, the writhing expansion of the veins in his forehead. He could sense the awful triumph that gathered in the mind of the other——

Then Arvardan lunged. His stiff and rebellious body toppled forward, hands outstretched and clawing.

The yielding, mind-held Secretary toppled with him. The blaster flew sideways, clanging along the hard floor.

The Secretary's mind wrenched free almost simultaneously, and Schwartz fell back, his own skull a tangled jungle of confusion.

Balkis struggled wildly beneath the clinging dead weight of Arvardon's body. He jerked a knee into the other's groin with a vicious strength while his clenched fist came down sideways on Arvardan's cheekbone. He lifted and thrust—and Arvardan rolled off in huddled agony.

The Secretary staggered to his feet, panting and disheveled, and stopped again.

Facing him was Shekt, half reclining. His right hand, shakingly supported by the left, was holding the blaster, and although it quivered, the business end pointed at the Secretary.

"You pack of fools," shrilled the Secretary, passion-choked, "what do you expect to gain? I have only to raise my voice——"

"And you, at least," responded Shekt weakly, "will die."

"You will accomplish nothing by killing me," said the Secretary bitterly, "and you know it. You will not save the Empire you would betray us to—and you would not save even yourselves. Give me that gun and you will go free."

He extended a hand, but Shekt laughed wistfully. "I am not mad enough to believe that."

"Perhaps not, but you are half paralyzed." And the Secretary broke sharply to the right, far faster than the physicist's feeble wrist could veer the blaster.

But now Balkis's mind, as he tensed for the final jump, was utterly and entirely on the blaster he was avoiding. Schwartz extended his mind once again in a final jab, and the Secretary tripped and slammed downward as if he had been clubbed.

Arvardan had risen painfully to his feet. His cheek was red and swollen and he hobbled when he walked. He said, "Can you move, Schwartz?"

"A little," came the tired response. Schwartz slid out of his seat.

"Anyone else coming this way, maybe?"

"Not that I can detect."

Arvardan smiled grimly down at Pola. His hand was resting on her soft brown hair and she was looking up at him with brimming eyes. Several times in the last two hours he had been sure that never, never would he feel her hair or see her eyes again.

"Maybe there will be a later after all, Pola?"

And she could only shake her head and say, "There's not enough time. We only have till six o'clock Tuesday."

"Not enough time? Well, let's see." Arvardan bent over the prone Ancient and pulled his head back, none too gently.

"Is he alive?" He felt futilely for a pulse with his still-numb finger tips and then placed a palm beneath the green robe. He said, "His heart's beating, anyway. . . . You've a dangerous power there, Schwartz. Why didn't you do this in the first place?"

"Because I wanted to see him held static." Schwartz clearly showed the effects of his ordeal. "I thought that if I could hold him, we could lead him out before; use him as decoy; hide behind his skirts."

Shekt said, in sudden animation, "We might. There's the Imperial garrison in Fort Dibburn not half a mile away. Once there, we're safe and can get word to Ennius."

"Once there! There must be a hundred guards outside, with hundreds more between here and there——And what can we do with a stiff green-robe? Carry him? Shove him along on little wheels?" Arvardan laughed humorlessly.

"Besides," said Schwartz gloomily, "I couldn't hold him very long. You saw——I failed."

Shekt said earnestly, "Because you're not used to it. Now listen, Schwartz, I've got a notion as to what it is you do with your mind. It's a receiving station for the electromagnetic fields of the brain. I think you can transmit also. Do you understand?"

Schwartz seemed painfully uncertain.

"You must understand," insisted Shekt. "You'll have to concentrate on what you want him to do—and first we're going to give him his blaster back."

"What!" The outraged exclamation was neatly triple.

Shekt raised his voice. "He's got to lead us out of here. We can't get out otherwise, can we? And how can it look less suspicious than to allow him to be obviously armed?"

"But I couldn't hold him. I tell you I couldn't." Schwartz was flexing his arms, slapping them, trying to get back into the feel of normality. "I don't care what your theories are, Dr. Shekt. You don't know what goes on. It's a slippery, painful thing, and it's not easy."

"I know, but it's the chance we take. Try it now, Schwartz. Have him move his arm when he comes to." Shekt's voice was pleading.

The Secretary moaned as he lay there, and Schwartz felt the reviving Mind Touch. Silently, almost fearfully, he let it gather strength—then spoke to it. It was a speech that included no words; it was the silent speech you send to your arm when you want it to move, a speech so silent you are not yourself aware of it.

And Schwartz's arm did not move; it was the Secretary's that did. The Earthman from the past looked up with a wild smile, but the others had eyes only for Balkis—Balkis, that recumbent figure, with a lifting head, with eyes from which the glaze of unconsciousness was vanishing, and an arm which peculiarly and incongruously jerked outward at a ninety-degree angle.

Schwartz bent to his task.

The Secretary lifted himself up in angular fashion; nearly, but not quite, overbalancing himself. And then, in a queer and involuntary way, he danced.

It lacked rhythm; it lacked beauty; but to the three who watched the body, and to Schwartz, who watched body and mind, it was a thing of indescribable awe. For in those moments the Secretary's body was under the control of a mind not materially connected with it.

Slowly, cautiously, Shekt approached the robotlike Secretary and, not without a qualm, extended his hand. In the open palm thereof lay the blaster, butt first.

"Let him take it, Schwartz," said Shekt.

Balkis's hand reached out and grasped the weapon clumsily. For a moment there was a sharp, devouring glitter in his eyes, and then it all faded. Slowly, slowly, the blaster was put into its place in the belt, and the hand fell away.

Schwartz's laugh was high-pitched. "He almost got away, there." But his face was white as he spoke.

"Well? Can you hold him?"

"He's fighting like the devil. But it's not as bad as before."

"That's because you know what you're doing," said Shekt, with an encouragement he did not entirely feel. "Transmit, now. Don't try to hold him; just pretend you're doing it yourself."

Arvardan broke in. "Can you make him talk?"

There was a pause, then a low, rasping growl from the Secretary. Another pause; another rasp.

"That's all," panted Schwartz.

"But why won't it work?" asked Pola. She looked worried.

Shekt shrugged. "Some pretty delicate and complicated muscles are involved. It's not like yanking at the long limb muscles. Never mind, Schwartz. We may get by without."

The memory of the next two hours was something no

two of those that took part in the queer odyssey could duplicate. Dr. Shekt, for instance, had acquired a queer rigidity
in which all his fears were drowned in one breathless and
helpless sympathy with the inwardly struggling Schwartz.
Throughout he had eyes only for that round face as it slowly
furrowed and twisted with effort. For the others he had
hardly time for more than a moment's glance.

The guards immediately outside the door saluted sharply
at the appearance of the Secretary, his green robe redolent
of officialdom and power. The Secretary returned the salute
in a fumbling, flat manner. They passed, unmolested.

It was only when they had left the great Hall that Arvardan became conscious of the madness of it all. The great,
unimaginable danger to the Galaxy and the flimsy reed of
safety that bridged, perhaps, the abyss. Yet even then, *even
then*, Arvardan felt himself drowning in Pola's eyes. Whether
it was the life that was being snatched from him, the future
that was being destroyed about him, the eternal unavailabil-
ity of the sweetness he had tasted—whatever it was, no
one had ever seemed to him to be so completely and dev-
astatingly desirable.

In aftertime she was the sum of his memories. Only the
girl——

And upon Pola the sunny brightness of the morning burned
down so that Arvardan's downturned face blurred before
her. She smiled up at him and was conscious of that strong,
hard arm on which her own rested so lightly. That was the
memory that lingered afterward. Flat, firm muscle lightly
covered by glossy-textured plastic cloth, smooth and cool
under her wrist——

Schwartz was in a sweating agony. The curving drive
that led away from the side entrance from which they had
emerged was largely empty. For that he was hugely thankful.

Schwartz alone knew the full cost of failure. In the enemy
Mind that he controlled he could sense the unbearable hu-
miliation, the surpassing hatred, the utterly horrible re-
solves. He had to search that Mind for the information that
guided him—the position of the official ground car, the

proper route to take——And, in searching, he also experienced the galling bitterness of the determined revenge that would lash out should his control waver for but the tenth part of the second.

The secret fastnesses of the Mind in which he was forced to rummage remained his personal possession forever. In aftertimes there came the pale gray hours of many an innocent dawn during which once again he had guided the steps of a madman down the dangerous walks of an enemy stronghold.

Schwartz gasped at the words when they reached the ground car. He no longer dared relax sufficiently to utter connected sentences. He choked out quick phrases: "Can't—drive car—can't make—him—make drive—complicated—can't——"

Shekt soothed him with a soft, clucking sound. He dared not touch him, dared not speak in an ordinary way, dared not distract Schwartz's mind for a second.

He whispered, "Just get him into the back seat, Schwartz. I'll drive. I know how. From now on just keep him still, and I'll take the blaster away."

The Secretary's ground car was a special model. Because it was special, it was different. It attracted attention. Its green headlight turned to the right and left in rhythmic swings as the light dimmed and brightened in emerald flashes. Men paused to watch. Ground cars advancing in the opposite direction moved to the side in a respectful hurry.

Had the car been less noticed, had it been less obtrusive, the occasional passer-by might have had time to note the pale, unmoving Ancient in the back seat—might have wondered—might have scented danger——

But they noticed only the car, so that time passed. . . .

A soldier blocked the way at the gleaming chromium gates that rose sheerly in the expansive, overwhelming way that marked all Imperial structures in sharp contrast to the squatly massive and brooding architecture of Earth. His huge force gun shot out horizontally in a barring gesture, and the car halted.

Arvardan leaned out. "I'm a citizen of the Empire, soldier. I'd like to see your commanding officer."

"I'll have to see your identification, sir."

"That's been taken from me. I am Bel Arvardan of Baronn, Sirius. I am on the Procurator's business and I'm in a hurry."

The soldier lifted a wrist to his mouth and spoke softly into the transmitter. There was a pause while he waited for an answer, and then he lowered his rifle and stepped aside. Slowly the gate swung open.

19. THE DEADLINE THAT APPROACHED

The hours that followed saw turmoil within and without Fort Dibburn. More so, perhaps, in Chica itself.

It was at noon that the High Minister at Washenn inquired via Communi-wave after his Secretary, and a search for the latter failed. The High Minister was displeased; the minor officials at the Hall of Correction were perturbed.

Questioning followed, and the guards outside the assembly room were definite that the Secretary had left with the prisoners at ten-thirty in the morning . . . No, he had left no instructions. They could not say where he was going; it was, of course, not their place to ask.

Another set of guards was equally uninformed and uninformative. A general air of anxiety mounted and swirled.

At 2 P.M. the first report arrived that the Secretary's ground car had been seen that morning—no one had seen if the Secretary was within—some thought he had been driving, but had only asssumed it, it turned out——

By two-thirty it had been ascertained that the car had entered Fort Dibburn.

At not quite three, it was finally decided to put in a call to the commander of the fort. A lieutenant had answered.

It was impossible at that time, they learned, for information on the subject to be given. However, His Imperial Majesty's officers requested that order be maintained for the present. It was further requested that news of the absence of a member of the Society of Ancients be not generally distributed until further notice.

But that was enough to achieve the direct opposite of the Imperial desires.

Men engaged in treason cannot take chances when one of the prime members of a conspiracy is in the hands of the enemy forty-eight hours before trigger time. It can mean only discovery or betrayal, and these are but the reverse sides of a single coin. Either alternative would mean death.

So word went out——

And the population of Chica stirred——

The professional demagogues were on the street corners. The secret arsenals were broken open and the hands that reached withdrew with weapons. There was a twisting drift toward the fort, and at 6 P.M. a new message was sent to the commandant, this time by personal envoy.

Meanwhile, this activity was matched in a smaller way by events within the fort. It had begun dramatically when the young officer meeting the entering ground car reached out a hand for the Secretary's blaster.

"I'll take that," he said curtly.

Shekt said, "Let him take it, Schwartz."

The Secretary's hand lifted the blaster and stretched out; the blaster left it, was carried away—and Schwartz, with a heaving sob of breaking tension, let go.

Arvardan was ready. When the Secretary lashed out like an insane steel coil released from compression, the archaeologist pounced upon him, fists pumping down hard.

The officer snapped out orders. Soldiers were running up. When rough hands laid hold of Arvardan's shirt collar and dragged him up, the Secretary was limp upon the seat. Dark blood was flowing feebly from the corner of his mouth. Arvardan's own already bruised cheek was open and bleeding.

He straightened his hair shakily. Then, pointing a rigid finger, said firmly, "I accuse that man of conspiring to overthrow the Imperial Government. I must have an immediate interview with the commanding officer."

"We'll have to see about that, sir," said the officer civilly. "If you don't mind, you will have to follow me—all of you."

And there, for hours, it rested. Their quarters were private, and reasonably clean. For the first time in twelve hours they had a chance to eat, which they did, despite considerations, with dispatch and efficiency. They even had the opportunity of that further necessity of civilization, a bath.

Yet the room was guarded, and as the hours passed, Arvardan finally lost his temper and cried, "But we've simply exchanged prisons."

The dull, meaningless routine of an army camp drifted about them, ignoring them. Schwartz was sleeping and Arvardan's eyes went to him. Shekt shook his head.

"We can't," he said. "It's humanly impossible. The man is exhausted. Let him sleep."

"But there are only thirty-nine hours left."

"I know—but wait."

A cool and faintly sardonic voice sounded. "Which of you claims to be a citizen of the Empire?"

Arvardan sprang forward. "I am. I——"

And his voice failed as he recognized the speaker. The latter smiled rigidly. His left arm he held a bit stiffly as a remaining memento of their last meeting.

Pola's voice was faint behind him. "Bel, it's the officer— the one of the department store."

"The one whose arm he broke," came the sharp addition. "My name is Lieutenant Claudy and yes, you are the same man. So you are a member of the Sirian worlds, are you? And yet you consort with these. Galaxy, the depths a man can sink to! And you've still got the girl with you." He waited and then said slowly and deliberately, "The Ear-thiesquaw!"

Arvardan bristled, then subsided. He couldn't—not yet——

He forced humbleness into his voice. "May I see the colonel, Lieutenant?"

"The colonel, I am afraid, is not on duty now."

"You mean he's not in the city?"

"I didn't say that. He can be reached—if the matter is sufficiently urgent."

"It is. . . . May I see the officer of the day?"

"At the moment I am the officer of the day."

"Then call the colonel."

And slowly the lieutenant shook his head. "I could scarcely do so without being convinced of the gravity of the situation."

Arvardan was shaking with impatience. "By the Galaxy, stop fencing with me! It's life and death."

"Really?" Lieutenant Claudy swung a little swagger stick with an air of affected dandyism. "You might crave an audience with me."

"All right. . . . Well, I'm waiting."

"I said—you might *crave* one."

"May I have an audience, Lieutenant?"

But there was no smile on the lieutenant's face. "I said, *crave* one—before the girl. Humbly."

Arvardan swallowed and drew back. Pola's hand was on his sleeve. "Please, Bel. You mustn't get him angry."

The archaeologist growled huskily, "Bel Arvardan of Sirius humbly craves audience with the officer of the day."

Lieutenant Claudy said, "That depends."

He took a step toward Arvardan and quickly and viciously brought the flat of his palm down hard upon the bandage that dressed Arvardan's open cheek.

Arvardan gasped and stifled a shriek.

The lieutenant said, "You resented that once. Don't you this time?"

Arvardan said nothing.

The lieutenant said, "Audience granted."

Four soldiers fell in before and behind Arvardan. Lieutenant Claudy led the way.

Shekt and Pola were alone with the sleeping Schwartz, and Shekt said, "I don't hear *him* any more, do you?"

Pola shook her head. "I haven't either, for quite a while. But, Father, do you suppose he'll do anything to Bel?"

"How can he?" said the old man gently. "You forget that he's not really one of us. He's a citizen of the Empire and cannot be easily molested. . . . You *are* in love with him, I suppose?"

"Oh, terribly, Father. It's silly, I know."

"Of course it is." Shekt smiled bitterly. "He is honest. I do not say he isn't. But what can he do? Can he live here with us on *this* world? Can he take you home? Introduce an Earthgirl to his friends? His family?"

She was crying. "I know. But maybe there won't be any afterwards."

And Shekt was on his feet again, as though the last phrase had reminded him. He said again, "I don't hear him."

It was the Secretary he did not hear. Balkis had been placed in an adjoining room, where his caged-lion steps had been clearly and ominously audible. Except that now they weren't.

It was a little point, but in the single mind and body of the Secretary there had somehow become centered and symboled all the sinister force of disease and destruction that were being loosed on the giant network of living stars. Shekt jarred Schwartz gently. "Wake up," he said.

Schwartz stirred. "What is it?" He felt scarcely rested. His tiredness went in and in, so deep as to come out at the other side, projecting in jagged streaks.

"Where's Balkis?" urged Shekt.

"Oh—oh yes." Schwartz looked about wildly, then remembered that it was not with his eyes that he looked and saw most clearly. He sent out the tendrils of his mind and they circled, sensing tensely for the Mind they knew so well.

He found it, and avoided touching it. His long immersion

in it had not increased his fondness for the clinging of its diseased wretchedness.

Schwartz muttered, "He's on another floor. He's talking to someone."

"To whom?"

"No one whose mind I've ever Touched before. Wait— let me listen. Maybe the Secretary will——Yes, he calls him Colonel."

Shekt and Pola looked quickly at one another.

"It can't be treason, can it?" whispered Pola. "I mean, surely an officer of the Empire wouldn't deal with an Earth-man against the Emperor, would he?"

"I don't know," said Shekt miserably. "I am ready to believe anything."

Lieutenant Claudy was smiling. He was behind a desk, with a blaster at his finger tips and the four soldiers behind him. He spoke with the authority that such a situation would lend one.

"I don't like Earthies," he said. "I never liked them. They're the scum of the Galaxy. They're diseased, super-stitious, and lazy. They're degenerate and stupid. But, by the Stars, most of them know their place.

"In a way, I can understand them. That's the way they were born, and they can't help it. Of course I wouldn't endure what the Emperor endures from them—I mean their blasted customs and traditions—if *I* were the Emperor. But that's all right. Someday we'll learn——"

Arvardan exploded. "Now look here. I didn't come to listen——"

"You'll listen, because I'm not finished. I was about to say that what I *can't* understand is the workings of the mind of an Earthie-lover. When a man—a *real* man, suppos-edly—can get so low in filth as to crawl in among them and go nosing after their womenfolk, I have no respect for him. He's worse than they are——"

"Then to Space with you and your poor filthy excuse of a mind!" fiercely. "Do you know that there's treason against the Empire afoot? Do you know just how dangerous the

situation is? Every minute you delay endangers every one
of the quadrillions in the Galaxy——"

"Oh, I don't know, Dr. Arvardan. It *is* Dr., isn't it? I
mustn't forget your honors. You see, I've got a theory of
my own. You're one of them. Maybe you were born in
Sirius, but you've got a black Earthman's heart, and you're
using your Galactic citizenship to advance their cause. You've
kidnaped this official of theirs, this Ancient. (A good thing,
by the way, in itself, and I wouldn't mind rattling his throat
for him.) *But* the Earthmen are looking for him already.
They've sent a message to the fort."

"They have? Already? Then why are we talking here? I
must see the colonel if I have to——"

"You expect a riot, trouble of any sort? Perhaps you even
planned one as the first step in an arranged revolt, eh?"

"Are you mad? Why would I want to do that?"

"Well, then, you wouldn't mind if we released the Ancient?"

"You cannot." Arvardan rose to his feet, and for a moment it looked as though he might hurl himself across the
desk at the other.

But the blaster was in Lieutenant Claudy's hand. "Oh,
can't we? Look here, now. I've gotten a little of my own
back. I've slapped you and made you crawl before your
Earthie pals. I've made you sit here while I told you to your
face what a low worm you are. And now I would love an
excuse to blast your arm off in exchange for what you did
to mine. Now make another move."

Arvardan froze.

Lieutenant Claudy laughed and put his blaster away. "It's
too bad I have to save you for the colonel. He's to see you
at five-fifteen."

"You knew that—you knew that all the time." Frustration tore his throat into hoarse sandpaper.

"Certainly."

"If the time we have lost, Lieutenant Claudy, means that
the issue is lost, then neither of us will have much time to
live." He spoke with an iciness that distorted his voice into
something horrible. "But you will die first, because I shall

spend my last minutes smashing your face into splintered bone and mashed brain."

"I'll be waiting for you, Earthie-lover. Any time!"

The commanding officer of Fort Dibburn had grown stiff in the service of the Empire. In the profound peace of the last generations there was little in the way of "glory" that any army officer could earn, and the colonel, in common with others, earned none. But in the long, slow rise from military cadet he had seen service in every part of the Galaxy—so that even a garrison on the neurotic world of Earth was to him but an additional chore. He wanted only the peaceful routine of normal occupation. He asked nothing beyond this, and for it was willing to humble himself— even, when it was necessary, to apologize to an Earthgirl.

He seemed tired when Arvardan entered. His shirt collar was open and his tunic, with its blazing yellow "Spaceship and Sun" of Empire, hung loosely over the back of his chair. He cracked the knuckles of his right hand with an abstracted air as he stared solemnly at Arvardan.

"A very confusing story, all this," he said, "very. I recall you well, young man. You are Bel Arvardan of Baronn, and the principal of a previous moment of considerable embarrassment. Can't you keep out of trouble?"

"It is not only myself that is in trouble, Colonel, but all the rest of the Galaxy as well."

"Yes, I know," somewhat impatiently. "Or at least I know that that is what you claim. I am told that you no longer have papers of identification."

"They were taken from me, but I am known at Everest. The Procurator himself can identify me, and will, I hope, before evening falls."

"We'll see about that." The colonel crossed his arms and teetered backward on his chair. "Suppose you give me your side of the story."

"I have been made aware of a dangerous conspiracy on the part of a small group of Earthmen to overthrow the Imperial Government by force, which, if not made known at once to the proper authorities, may well succeed in destroying both the Government and much of the Empire itself."

"You go too far, young man, in this very rash and farfetched statement. That the men of Earth could stage annoying riots, lay siege to this fort, do considerable damage, I am quite prepared to admit—but I do not for a moment conceive them capable of as much as driving the Imperial forces from his planet, let alone destroying the Imperial Government. Yet I will listen to the details of this—uh—plot."

"Unfortunately, the seriousness of the matter is such that I feel it vital that the details be told to the Procurator himself in person. I request, therefore, to be put into communication with him now, if you don't mind."

"Ummm. . . . Let us not act too hurriedly. Are you aware that the man you have brought in is Secretary to the High Minister of Earth, one of their Ancients and a very important man to them?"

"Perfectly!"

"And yet you say that he is a prime mover in this conspiracy you mention."

"He is."

"Your evidence?"

"You will understand me, I am sure, when I say that I cannot discuss that with anyone but the Procurator."

The colonel frowned and regarded his fingernails. "Do you doubt my competency in the case?"

"Not at all, sir. It is simply that only the Procurator has the authority to take the decisive action required in this case."

"What decisive action do you refer to?"

"A certain building on Earth must be bombed and totally destroyed within thirty hours, or the lives of most, or all, of the inhabitants of the Empire will be lost."

"What building?" asked the colonel wearily.

Arvardan snapped back, "May I be connected with the Procurator, please?"

There was a pause of deadlock. The colonel said stiffly, "You realize that in forcibly kidnaping an Earthman you have rendered yourself liable to trial and punishment by the Terrestrial authorities? Ordinarily the government will protect its citizens as a matter of principle and insist upon a Galactic trial. However, affairs on Earth are delicate and I have strict instructions to risk no avoidable clash. Therefore, unless you answer my questions fully, I will be forced to turn you and your companions over to the local police."

"But that would be a death sentence. For yourself too! . . . Colonel, I am a citizen of the Empire, and I demand an audience with the Pro——"

A buzzer on the colonel's desk interrupted him. The colonel turned to it, closing a contact. "Yes?"

"Sir," came the clear voice, "a body of natives have encircled the fort. It is believed they are armed."

"Has there been any violence?"

"No, sir."

There was no sign of emotion on the colonel's face. This, at least, was what he was trained for. "Artillery and aircraft are to be made ready—all men to battle stations. Withhold all fire except in self-defense. Understood?"

"Yes, sir. An Earthman under flag of truce wishes audience."

"Send him in. Also send the High Minister's Secretary here again."

And now the colonel glared coldly at the archaeologist. "I trust you are aware of the appalling nature of what you have caused."

"I demand to be present at the interview," cried Arvardan, nearly incoherent with fury, "and I further demand the reason for your allowing me to rot under guard here for hours while you closet yourself with a native traitor. I tell you that I am not ignorant that you interviewed him before speaking with me."

"Are you making any accusations, sir?" demanded the colonel, his own voice ascending the scale. "If so, make them plainly."

"I make no accusations. But I will remind you that you will be accountable for your actions hereafter, and that you

may well be known in the future, if you have a future, as
the destroyer, by your stubbornness, of your people."

"Silence! I am not accountable to you, at any rate. We
will conduct affairs, henceforward, as *I* choose. Do you
understand?"

20. THE DEADLINE THAT WAS REACHED

The Secretary passed through the door held open by a soldier. On his purpling, swollen lips there was a brief, cold smile. He bowed to the colonel and remained completely unaware, to all appearances, of the presence of Arvardan.

"Sir," said the colonel to the Earthman, "I have communicated to the High Minister the details of your presence here and the manner in which it came about. Your detention here is, of course, entirely—uh—unorthodox, and it is my purpose to set you free as soon as I can. However, I have here a gentleman who, as you probably know, has lodged against you a very serious accusation; one which, under the circumstances, we must investigate——"

"I understand, Colonel," said the Secretary calmly. "However, as I have already explained to you, this man has been on Earth, I believe, only a matter of two months or so, so that his knowledge of our internal politics is nonexistent. This is a flimsy basis, indeed, for any accusation."

Arvardan retorted in anger, "I am an archaeologist by profession, and one who has specialized of late on Earth and its customs. My knowledge of its politics is far from nonexistent. And in any case, I am not the only one who makes the accusation."

The Secretary did not look at the archaeologist either now or later. He spoke exclusively to the colonel. He said, "One of our local scientists is involved in this; one who, approaching the end of his normal sixty years, is suffering from delusions of persecution. Then, in addition, there is another man, one of unknown antecedents and a history of idiocy. All three could not raise a respectable accusation among them."

Arvardan jumped to his feet. "I demand to be heard——"

"Sit down," said the colonel coldly and unsympathetically. "You have refused to discuss the matter with me. Let the refusal stand. Bring in the man with the flag of truce."

It was another member of the Society of Ancients. Scarcely a flicker of the eyelid betrayed any emotion on his part at the sight of the Secretary. The colonel rose from his chair and said, "Do you speak for the men outside?"

"I do, sir."

"I assume, then, that this riotous and illegal assembly is based upon a demand for the return of your fellow countryman here?"

"Yes, sir. He must be immediately freed."

"Indeed! Nevertheless, the interest of law and order and the respect due His Imperial Majesty's representatives on this world require that the matter cannot possibly be discussed while men are gathered in armed rebellion against us. You must have your men disperse."

The Secretary spoke up pleasantly. "The colonel is perfectly correct, Brother Cori. Please calm the situation. I am perfectly safe here, and there is no danger—for anybody. Do you understand? For anybody. It is my word as an Ancient."

"Very well, Brother. I am thankful you are safe."

He was ushered out.

The colonel said curtly, "We will see that you leave here

safely as soon as matters in the city have returned to normal. Thank you for your co-operation in this matter just concluded."

Arvardan was again on his feet. "I forbid it. You will let loose this would-be murderer of the human race while forbidding me an interview with the Procurator when that would be simply in accord with my rights as a Galactic citizen." Then, in a paroxysm of frustration, "Will you show more consideration to an Earthman dog than you will to me?"

The Secretary's voice sounded over that last near-incoherent rage. "Colonel, I will gladly remain until such time as my case is heard by the Procurator, if that is what this man wants. An accusation of treason is serious, and the suspicion of it—however farfetched—may be sufficient to ruin my usefulness to my people. I would really appreciate the opportunity to prove to the Procurator that none is more loyal to the Empire than myself."

The colonel said stiffly, "I admire your feelings, sir, and freely admit that were I in your place my attitude would be quite different. You are a credit to your race, sir. I will attempt contact with the Procurator."

Arvardan said nothing more until led back to his cell.

He avoided the glance of the others. For a long time he sat motionless, with a knuckle pinched between gnawing teeth.

Until Shekt said, "Well?"

Arvardan shook his head. "I just about ruined everything."

"What did you do?"

"Lost my temper; offended the colonel; got nowhere——I'm no diplomat, Shekt."

He felt riven with the sudden urge for self-defense. "What could I do?" he cried. "Balkis had already been to the colonel, so that I couldn't trust him. What if he'd been offered his life? What if he's been in on the plot all along? I know it's a wild thought, but I couldn't take the chance. It was too suspicious. I wanted to see Ennius himself."

The physicist was on his feet, withered hands clasped behind his back. "Well, then—is Ennius coming?"

"I suppose so. But it is only at Balkis's own request, and that I don't understand."

"Balkis's own request? Then Schwartz must be right."

"Yes? What has Schwartz been saying?"

The plump Earthman was sitting on his cot. He shrugged his shoulders when the eyes turned to him and spread out his hands in a helpless gesture. "I caught the Secretary's Mind Touch when they took him past our room just now. He's definitely had a long talk with this officer you talked to."

"I know."

"But there's no treason in that officer's mind."

"Well," miserably, "then I guessed wrong. I'll eat worms when Ennius comes. What about Balkis?"

"There's no worry or fear in his mind; only hate. And now it's mostly hate for us, for capturing him, for dragging him here. We've wounded his vanity horribly, and he intends to square it with us. I saw little daydream pictures in his mind. Of himself, singlehanded, preventing the entire Galaxy from doing anything to stop him even while we, with our knowledge, work against him. He's giving us the odds, the trumps, and then he'll smash us anyway and triumph over us."

"You mean that he will risk his plans, his dreams of Empire, just to vent a little spite at us? That's mad."

"I know," said Schwartz with finality. "*He* is mad."

"And he thinks he'll succeed?"

"That's right."

"Then we must have you, Schwartz. We'll need your mind. Listen to me——"

But Shekt was shaking his head. "No, Arvardan, we couldn't work that. I woke Schwartz when you left and we discussed the matter. His mental powers, which he can describe only dimly, are obviously not under perfect control. He can stun a man, or paralyze him, or even kill him. Better than that, he can control the larger voluntary muscles even against the subject's will, but no more than that. In the case of the Secretary, he couldn't make the man talk, the small muscles about the vocal cords being beyond him. He couldn't co-ordinate motion well enough to have the Secretary drive a car; he even balanced him while walking only with difficulty. Obviously, then, we couldn't control Ennius, for instance, to the point of having him issue an order, or write one. I've thought of that, you see . . ." Shekt shook his head as his voice trailed away.

Arvardan felt the desolation of futility descend upon him. Then, with a sudden pang of anxiety, "Where's Pola?"

"She's sleeping in the alcove."

He would have longed to wake her—longed——Oh, longed a lot of things.

Arvardan looked at his watch. It was almost midnight, and there were only thirty hours left.

He slept for a while after that, then woke for a while, as it grew light again. No one approached, and a man's very soul grew haggard and pale.

Arvardan looked at his watch. It was almost midnight, and there were only six hours left.

He looked about him now in a dazed and hopeless way. They were all here now—even the Procurator, at last. Pola was next to him, her warm little fingers on his wrist and that look of fear and exhaustion on her face that more than anything else infuriated him against all the Galaxy.

Maybe they all deserved to die, the stupid, stupid— stupid——

He scarcely saw Shekt and Schwartz. They sat on his left. And there was Balkis, the damnable Balkis, with his lips still swollen, one cheek green, so that it must hurt like the devil to talk—and Arvardan's own lips stretched into a furious, aching smile at the thought and his fists clenched and writhed. His own bandaged cheek ached less at the thought.

Facing all of them was Ennius, frowning, uncertain, almost ridiculous, dressed as he was in those heavy, shapeless, lead-impregnated clothes.

And he was stupid, too. Arvardan felt a thrill of hatred

shoot through him at the thought of these Galactic trimmers who wanted only peace and ease. Where were the conquerors of three centuries back? Where? . . .

Six hours left——

Ennius had received the call from the Chica garrison some eighteen hours before and he had streaked half around the planet at the summons. The motives that led him to that were obscure but nonetheless forceful. Essentially, he told himself, there was nothing to the matter but a regrettable kidnaping of one of those green-robed curiosities of superstitious, hagridden Earth. That, and these wild and undocumented accusations. Nothing, certainly, that the colonel on the spot could not have handled.

And yet there was Shekt—Shekt was in this——And not as the accused, but as an accuser. It was confusing.

He sat now facing them, thinking, quite conscious that his decision in this case might hasten a rebellion, perhaps weaken his own position at court, ruin his chances at advancement—— As for Arvardan's long speech just now about virus strains and unbridled epidemics, how seriously could he take it? After all, if he took action on the basis of it, how credible would the matter sound to his superiors?

And yet Arvardan was an archaeologist of note.

So he postponed the matter in his mind by saying to the Secretary, "Surely you have something to say in this matter?"

"Surprisingly little," said the Secretary with easy confidence. "I would like to ask what evidence exists for supporting the accusation?"

"Your Excellency," said Arvardan with snapping patience, "I have already told you that the man admitted it in every detail at the time of our imprisonment day before yesterday."

"Perhaps," said the Secretary, "you choose to credit that, Your Excellency, but it is simply an additional unsupported statement. Actually the only facts to which outsiders can bear witness to are that *I* was the one violently taken prisoner, not they; that it was *my* life that was in peril, not theirs. Now I would like my accuser to explain how he could find all this out in the nine weeks that he has been on the planet, when you, the Procurator, in years of service here, have found nothing to my disadvantage?"

"There is reason in what the Brother says," admitted Ennius heavily. "How *do* you know?"

Arvardan replied stiffly, "Prior to the accused's confession I was informed of the conspiracy by Dr. Shekt."

"Is that so, Dr. Shekt?" The Procurator's glance shifted to the physicist.

"That is so, Your Excellency."

"And how did you find out?"

Shekt said, "Dr. Arvardan was admirably thorough and accurate in his description of the use to which the Synapsifier was put and in his remarks concerning the dying statements of the bacteriologist, F. Smitko. This Smitko was a member of the conspiracy. His remarks were recorded and the recording is available."

"But, Dr. Shekt, the dying statements of a man known to be in delirium—if what Dr. Arvardan said is true—cannot be of very great weight. You have nothing else?"

Arvardan interrupted by striking his fist on the arm of his chair and roaring, "Is this a law court? Has someone been guilty of violating a traffic ordinance? We have no time to weigh evidence on an analytical balance or measure it with micrometers. I tell you we have till six in the morning, five and a half hours, in other words, to wipe out this enormous threat. . . . You knew Dr. Shekt previous to this time, Your Excellency. Have you known him to be a liar?"

The Secretary interposed instantly. "No one accused Dr. Shekt of deliberately lying, Your Excellency. It is only that the good doctor is aging and has, of late, been greatly concerned over his approaching sixtieth birthday. I am afraid that a combination of age and fear have induced slight paranoiac tendencies, common enough here on Earth. . . . Look at him! Does he seem to you quite normal?"

He did not, of course. He was drawn and tense, shattered by what had passed and what was to come.

Yet Shekt forced his voice into normal tones, even into calmness. He said, "I might say that for the last two months

I have been under the continual watch of the Ancients; that my letters have been opened and my answers censored. But it is obvious that all such complaints would be attributed to the paranoia spoken of. However, I have here Joseph Schwartz, the man who volunteered as a subject for the Synapsifier one day when you were visiting me at the Institute."

"I remember." There was a feeble gratitude in Ennius's mind that the subject had, for the moment, veered. "Is that the man?"

"Yes."

"He looks none the worse for the experience."

"He is far the better. The exposure to the Synapsifier was uncommonly successful, since he had a photographic memory to begin with, a fact I did not know at the time. At any rate, he now has a mind which is sensitive to the thoughts of others."

Ennius leaned far forward in his chair and cried in a shocked amazement, "What? Are you telling me he reads minds?"

"That can be demonstrated, Your Excellency. But I think the Brother will confirm the statement."

The Secretary darted a quick look of hatred at Schwartz, boiling in its intensity and lightninglike in its passage across his face. He said, with but the most imperceptible quiver in his voice, "It is quite true, Your Excellency. This man they have here has certain hypnotic faculties, though whether that is due to the Synapsifier or not I don't know. I might add that this man's subjection to the Synapsifier was not recorded, a matter which you'll agree is highly suspicious."

"It was not recorded," said Shekt quietly, "in accordance with my standing orders from the High Minister." But the Secretary merely shrugged his shoulders at that.

Ennius said peremptorily, "Let us get on with the matter and avoid this petty bickering. . . . What about this Schwartz? What have his mind-reading powers, or hypnotic talents, or whatever they are, to do with the case?"

"Shekt intends to say," put in the Secretary, "that Schwartz can read my mind."

"Is that it? Well, and what is he thinking?" asked the Procurator, speaking to Schwartz for the first time.

"He's thinking," said Schwartz, "that we have no way of convincing you of the truth of our side of what you call the case."

"Quite true," scoffed the Secretary, "though that deduction scarcely calls for much mental power."

"And also," Schwartz went on, "that you are a poor fool, afraid to act, desiring only peace, hoping by your justice and impartiality to win over the men of Earth, and all the more a fool for so hoping."

The Secretary reddened. "I deny all that. It is an obvious attempt to prejudice you, Your Excellency."

But Ennius said, "I am not so easily prejudiced." And then, to Schwartz, "And what am *I* thinking?"

Schwartz replied, "That even if I could see clearly within a man's skull, I need not necessarily tell the truth about what I see."

The Procurator's eyebrows lifted in surprise. "You are correct, quite correct. Do you maintain the truth of the claims put forward by Drs. Arvardan and Shekt?"

"Every word of it."

"So! Yet unless a second such as you can be found, one who is not involved in the matter, your evidence would not be valid in law even if we could obtain general belief in you as a telepath."

"But it is not a question of the law," cried Arvardan, "but of the safety of the Galaxy."

"Your Excellency"—the Secretary rose in his seat—"I have a request to make. I would like to have this Joseph Schwartz removed from the room."

"Why so?"

"This man, in addition to reading minds, has certain powers of mental force. I was captured by means of a paralysis induced by this Schwartz. It is my fear that he may attempt something of the sort now against me, or even against you, Your Excellency, that forces me to the request."

Arvardan rose to his feet, but the Secretary overshouted him to say, "No hearing can be fair if a man is present who might subtly influence the mind of the judge by means of admitted mental gifts."

Ennius made his decision quickly. An orderly entered, and Joseph Schwartz, offering no resistance, nor showing the slightest sign of perturbation on his moonlike face, was led away.

To Arvardan it was the final blow.

As for the Secretary, he rose now and for the moment stood there—a squat, grim figure in green; strong in his self-confidence.

He began, in serious, formal style, "Your Excellency, all of Dr. Arvardan's beliefs and statements rest upon the testimony of Dr. Shekt. In turn, Dr. Shekt's beliefs rest upon the dying delirium of one man. And all this, Your Excellency, *all this*, somehow never reached the surface until after Joseph Schwartz was submitted to the Synapsifier.

"Who, then, is Joseph Schwartz? Until Joseph Schwartz appeared on the scene, Dr. Shekt was a normal, untroubled man. You yourself, Your Excellency, spent an afternoon with him the day Schwartz was brought in for treatment. Was he abnormal then? Did he inform you of treason against the Empire? Of certain babblings on the part of a dying biochemist? Did he seem even troubled? Or suspicious? He says now that he was instructed by the High Minister to falsify the results of the Synapsifier tests, not to record the names of those treated. Did he tell you that then? Or only now, *after* that day on which Schwartz appeared?

"Again, who is Joseph Schwartz? He spoke no known language at the time he was brought in. So much we found out for ourselves later, when we first began to suspect the stability of Dr. Shekt's reason. He was brought in by a farmer who knew nothing of his identity, or, indeed, any facts about him at all. Nor have any since been discovered.

"Yet this man has strange mental powers. He can stun at a hundred yards by thought alone—kill at closer range. I myself have been paralyzed by him; my arms and legs were manipulated by him; my mind might have been manipulated by him if he had wished.

"I believe, certainly, that Schwartz did manipulate the

minds of these others. They say I captured them, that I threatened them with death, that I confessed to treason and to aspiring to Empire——Yet ask of them one question, Your Excellency. Have they not been thoroughly exposed to the influence of Schwartz, that is, of a man capable of controlling their minds?

"Is not perhaps Schwartz a traitor? If not, who *is* Schwartz?"

The Secretary seated himself, calm, almost genial.

Arvardan felt as though his brain had mounted a cyclotron and was spinning outward now in faster and faster revolutions.

What answer could one make? That Schwartz was from the past? What evidence was there for that? That the man spoke a genuinely primitive speech? But only he himself— Arvardan—could testify to that. And he, Arvardan, might well have a manipulated mind. After all, how could he tell his mind had not been manipulated? Who *was* Schwartz? What had so convinced him of this great plan of Galactic conquest?

He thought again. From where came his conviction of the truth of the conspiracy? He was an archaeologist, given to doubting, but now——Had it been one man's word? One girl's kiss? Or Joseph Schwartz?

He couldn't think! *He couldn't think!*

"Well?" Ennius sounded impatient. "Have you anything to say, Dr. Shekt? Or you, Dr. Arvardan?"

But Pola's voice suddenly pierced the silence. "Why do you ask them? Can't you see that it's all a lie? Don't you see that he's tying us all up with his false tongue? Oh, we're all going to die, and I don't care any more—but we could stop it, we could stop it——And instead we just sit here and—and—*talk*——" She burst into wild sobs.

The Secretary said, "So we are reduced to the screams of a hysterical girl. . . . Your Excellency, I have this proposition. My accusers say that all this, the alleged virus and whatever else they have in mind, is scheduled for a definite time—six in the morning, I believe. I offer to remain in your custody for a week. If what they say is true, word of an epidemic in the Galaxy ought to reach Earth within a few days. If such occurs, Imperial forces will still control Earth——"

"Earth is a fine exchange, indeed, for a Galaxy of humans," mumbled the white-faced Shekt.

"I value my own life, and that of my people. We are hostages for our innocence, and I am prepared at this instant to inform the Society of Ancients that I will remain here for a week of my own free will and prevent any disturbances that might otherwise occur."

He folded his arms.

Ennius looked up, his face troubled. "I find no fault in this man——"

Arvardan could stand it no more. With a quiet and deadly ferocity, he arose and strode quickly toward the Procurator. What he meditated was never known. Afterward he himself could not remember. At any rate, it made no difference. Ennius had a neuronic whip and used it.

For the third time since landing on Earth everything about Arvardan flamed up into pain, spun about, and vanished.

In the hours during which Arvardan was unconscious the six o'clock deadline was reached——

21. THE DEADLINE THAT PASSED

And passed!

Light——
Blurring light and misty shadows—melting and twisting, and then coming into focus.
A face——Eyes upon his——
"Pola!" Things were sharp and clear to Arvardan in a single, leaping bound. "What time is it?"
His fingers were hard upon her wrist, so that she winced involuntarily.
"It's past seven," she whispered. "Past the deadline."
He looked about wildly, starting from the cot on which he lay, disregarding the burning in his joints. Shekt, his lean figure huddled in a chair, raised his head to nod in brief mournfulness.
"It's all over, Arvardan."
"Then Ennius——"
"Ennius," said Shekt, "would not take the chance. Isn't that strange?" He laughed a queer, cracked rasping laugh.

"The three of us singlehandedly discover a vast plot against humanity, singlehandedly we capture the ringleader and bring him to justice. It's like a visicast, isn't it, with the great all-conquering heroes zooming to victory in the nick of time? That's where they usually end it. Only in our case the visicast went on and we found that nobody believed us. That doesn't happen in visicasts, does it? Things end happily there, don't they? It's funny——" The words turned into rough, dry sobs.

Arvardan looked away, sick. Pola's eyes were dark universes, moist and tear-filled. Somehow, for an instant, he was lost in them—they *were* universes, star filled. And toward those stars little gleaming metallic cases were streaking, devouring the light-years as they penetrated hyperspace in calculated, deadly paths. Soon—perhaps already—they would approach, pierce atmospheres, fall apart into unseen deadly rains of virus——

Well, it was over.

It could no longer be stopped.

"Where is Schwartz?" he asked weakly.

But Pola only shook her head. "They never brought him back."

The door opened, and Arvardan was not so far gone in the acceptance of death as to fail to look up with a momentary wash of hope upon his face.

But it was Ennius, and Arvardan's face hardened and turned away.

Ennius approached and looked momentarily at the father and daughter. But even now Shekt and Pola were primarily Earth creatures and could say nothing to the Procurator, even though they knew that short and violent as their future lives were to be, that of the Procurator would be even shorter and more violent.

Ennius tapped Arvardan on the shoulder. "Dr. Arvardan?"

"Your Excellency?" said Arvardan in a raw and bitter imitation of the other's intonation.

"It is after six o'clock." Ennius had not slept that night.

With his official absolution of Balkis had come no absolute assurance that the accusers were completely mad—or under mental control. He had watched the soulless chronometer tick away the life of the Galaxy.

"Yes," said Arvardan. "It is after six and the stars still shine."

"But you still think you were right?"

"Your Excellency," said Arvardan, "in a matter of hours the first victim will die. They won't be noticed. Human beings die every day. In a week hundreds of thousands will have died. The percentage of recovery will be close to zero. No known remedies will be available. Several planets will send out emergency calls for epidemic relief. In two weeks scores of planets will have joined the call and States of Emergency will be declared in the nearer sectors. In a month the Galaxy will be a writhing mass of disease. In two months not twenty planets will remain untouched. In six months the Galaxy will be dead.... And what will *you* do when those first reports come in?

"Let me predict that as well. You will send out reports that the epidemics may have started on Earth. This will save no lives. You will declare war on the Ancients of Earth. This will save no lives. You will wipe the Earthman from the face of his planet. This will save no lives.... Or else you will act as go-between for your friend Balkis and the Galactic Council, or the survivors thereof. You may then have the honor of handing the wretched remnants of the crumbs of the Empire to Balkis in return for antitoxin, which may or may not reach sufficient worlds in sufficient quantities in sufficient time to save a single human being."

Ennius smiled without conviction. "Don't you think you're being ridiculously overdramatic?"

"Oh yes. I'm a dead man and you're a corpse. But let's be devilishly cool and Imperial about it, don't y'know?"

"If you resent the use of the neuronic whip——"

"Not at all," ironically. "I'm used to it. I hardly feel it any more."

"Then I am putting it to you as logically as I can. This has been a nasty mess. It would be difficult to report sensibly, yet as difficult to suppress without reason. Now the other accusers involved are Earthmen; your voice is the only one which would carry weight. Suppose you sign a statement to the effect that the accusation was made at a time when you were not in your——Well, we'll think of some phrase that will cover it without bringing in the notion of mental control."

"That would be simple. Say I was crazy, drunk, hypnotized, or drugged. Anything goes."

"Will you be reasonable? Now look, I tell you that you *have* been tampered with." He was whispering tensely. "You're a man of Sirius. Why have you fallen in love with an Earthgirl?"

"What?"

"Don't shout. I say—in your normal state, could you ever have gone native? Could you have considered that sort of thing?" He nodded his head just perceptibly in the direction of Pola.

For an instant Arvardan stared at him in surprise. Then, quickly, his hand shot out and seized the highest Imperial authority on Earth by the throat. Ennius's hands wrenched wildly and futilely at the other's grip.

Arvardan said, "That sort of thing, eh? Do you mean Miss Shekt? If you do, I want to hear the proper respect, eh? Ah, go away. You're dead anyway."

Ennius said gaspingly, "Dr. Arvardan, you will consider yourself under ar——"

The door opened again, and the colonel was upon them.

"Your Excellency, the Earth rabble has returned."

"What? Hasn't this Balkis spoken to his officials? He was going to arrange for a week's stay."

"He has spoken and he's still here. But so is the mob. We are ready to fire upon them, and it is my adivce as military commander that we proceed to do that. Have you any suggestions, Your Excellency?"

"Hold your fire until I see Balkis. Have him sent in here." He turned. "Dr. Arvardan, I will deal with you later."

* * *

Balkis was brought in, smiling. He bowed formally to Ennius, who yielded him the barest nod in return.

"See here," said the Procurator brusquely, "I am informed your men are packing the approaches to Fort Dibburn. This was not part of our agreement. . . . Now, we do not wish to cause bloodshed, but our patience is not inexhaustible. Can you disperse them peaceably?"

"If I choose, Your Excellency."

"If you choose? You had better choose. And at once."

"Not at all, Your Excellency!" And now the Secretary smiled and flung out an arm. His voice was a wild taunt, too long withheld, now gladly released. "Fool! You waited too long and can die for that! Or live a slave, if you prefer—but remember that it will not be an easy life."

The wildness and fervor of the statement produced no shattering effect on Ennius. Even here, at what was undoubtedly the profoundest blow of Ennius's career, the stolidity of the Imperial career diplomat did not desert him. It was only that the grayness and deep-eyed weariness about him deepened.

"Then I lost so much in my caution? The story of the virus—was true?" There was almost an abstract, indifferent wonder in his voice. "But Earth, yourself—you are all my hostages."

"Not at all," came the instant, victorious cry. "It is you and yours that are *my* hostages. The virus that now is spreading through the Universe has not left Earth immune. Enough already saturates the atmosphere of every garrison on the planet, including Everest itself. We of Earth are immune, but how do you feel, Procurator? Weak? Is your throat dry? Your head feverish? It will not be long, you know. And it is only from us that you can obtain the antidote."

For a long moment Ennius said nothing, his face thin and suddenly incredibly haughty.

Then he turned to Arvardan and in cool, cultured tones said, "Dr. Arvardan, I find I must beg your pardon for having doubted your word. Dr. Shekt, Miss Shekt—my apologies."

Arvardan bared his teeth. "Thank you for your apologies. They will be of great help to everybody."

"Your sarcasm is deserved," said the Procurator. "If you will excuse me, I will return to Everest to die with my family. Any question of compromise with this—man is, of course, out of the question. My soldiers of the Imperial Procuracy of Earth will, I am sure, acquit themselves properly before their death, and not a few Earthmen will undoubtedly have time to light the way for us through the passages of death. . . . Good-by."

"Hold on. Hold on. Don't go." Slowly, slowly, Ennius looked up to the new voice.

Slowly, slowly, Joseph Schwartz, frowning a bit, swaying a bit with weariness, stepped across the threshold.

The Secretary tensed and sprang backward. With a sudden, wary suspicion, he faced the man from the past.

"No," he gritted, "you can't get the secret of the antidote out of me. Only certain men have it, and only certain others are trained to use it properly. All these are safely out of your reach for the time it takes the toxin to do its work."

"They are out of reach now," admitted Schwartz, "but not for the time it would take the toxin to do its work. You see, there is no toxin, and no virus to stamp out."

The statement did not quite penetrate. Arvardan felt a sudden choking thought enter his mind. *Had* he been tampered with? *Had* all this been a gigantic hoax, one that had taken in the Secretary as well as himself? If so, why?

But Ennius spoke. "Quickly, man. Your meaning."

"It's not complicated," said Schwartz. "When we were here last night I knew I could do nothing by simply sitting and listening. So I worked carefully on the Secretary's mind for a long time. . . . I dared not be detected. And then, finally, he asked that I be ordered out of the room. This was what I wanted, of course, and the rest was easy.

"I stunned my guard and left for the airstrip. The fort was on a twenty-four-hour alert. The aircraft were fueled, armed, and ready for flight. The pilots were waiting. I picked one out—and we flew to Senloo."

The Secretary might have wished to say something. His jaws writhed soundlessly.

It was Shekt who spoke. "But you could force no one to fly a plane, Schwartz. It was all you could do to make a man walk."

"Yes, when it's against his will. But from Dr. Arvardan's mind I knew how Sirians hated Earthmen—so I looked for a pilot who was born in the Sirius Sector and found Lieutenant Claudy."

"Lieutenant Claudy?" cried Arvardan.

"Yes——Oh, you know him. Yes, I see. It's quite clear in your mind."

"I'll bet. . . . Go ahead, Schwartz."

"This officer *hated* Earthmen with a hate that's difficult to understand, even for me, and I was inside his mind. He *wanted* to bomb them. He *wanted* to destroy them. It was only discipline that tied him fast and kept him from taking out his plane then and there.

"That kind of a mind is different. Just a little suggestion, a little push, and discipline was not enough to hold him. I don't even think he realized that I climbed into the plane with him."

"How did you find Senloo?" whispered Shekt.

"In my time," said Schwartz, "there was a city called St. Louis. It was at the junction of two great rivers. . . . We found Senloo. It was night, but there was a dark patch in a sea of radioactivity—and Dr. Shekt had said the Temple was an isolated oasis of normal soil. We dropped a flare— at least it was my mental suggestion—and there was a five-pointed building below us. It jibed with the picture I had received in the Secretary's mind. . . . Now there's only a hole, a hundred feet deep, where that building was. That happened at three in the morning. No virus was sent out and the universe is free."

It was an animal-like howl that emerged from the Secretary's lips— the unearthly screech of a demon. He seemed to gather for a leap, and then—collapsed.

A thin froth of saliva trickled slowly down his lower lip.

"I never touched him," said Schwartz softly. Then, staring thoughtfully at the fallen figure, "I was back before six, but I knew I would have to wait for the deadline to pass. Balkis would *have* to crow. I knew that from his mind, and it was from his own mouth, only, that I could convict him. . . . Now there he lies."

22: THE BEST IS YET TO BE

Thirty days had passed since Joseph Schwartz had lifted off an airport runway on a night dedicated to Galactic destruction, with alarm bells shrilling madly behind him and orders to return burning the ether toward him.

He had not returned; not, at least, until he had destroyed the Temple of Senloo.

The heroism was finally made official now. In his pocket he had the ribbon of the Order of the Spaceship and Sun, First Class. Only two others in all the Galaxy had ever gotten it nonposthumously.

That was something for a retired tailor.

No one, of course, outside the most official of officialdom, knew exactly what he had done, but that didn't matter. Someday, in the history books, it would all become part of a bright and indelible record.

He was walking through the quiet night now toward Dr. Shekt's house. The city was peaceful, as peaceful as the starry glitter above. In isolated places on Earth bands of Zealots still made trouble, but their leaders were dead or

228

captive and the moderate Earthmen, themselves, could take care of the rest.

The first huge convoys of normal soil were already on their way. Ennius had again made his original proposal that Earth's population be moved to another planet, but that was out. Charity was not wanted. Let Earthmen have a chance to remake their own planet. Let them build once again the home of their father's, the native world of man. Let them labor with their hands, removing the diseased soil and replacing it with healthy, seeing the green grow where all had been dead and making the desert bloom in beauty once again.

It was an enormous job; it could take a century—but what of that? Let the Galaxy lend machinery; let the Galaxy ship food; let the Galaxy supply soil. Of their incalculable resources, it would be a trifle—and it would be repaid.

And someday, once again, the Earthman would be a people among peoples, inhabiting a planet among planets, looking all humanity in the eye in dignity and equality.

Schwartz's heart pounded at the wonder of it all as he walked up the steps to the front door. Next week he left with Arvardan for the great central worlds of the Galaxy. Who else of his generation had ever left Earth?

And momentarily he thought of the old Earth, *his* Earth. So long dead. So long dead.

And yet but three and a half months had passed...

He paused, his hand on the point of signaling at the door, as the words from within sounded in his mind. How clearly he heard thoughts now, like tiny bells.

It was Arvardan, of course, with more in his mind than words alone could ever handle. "Pola, I've waited and thought, and thought and waited. I won't any more. You're coming with me."

And Pola, with a mind as eager as his, yet with words of the purest reluctance, said, "I couldn't, Bel. It's quite impossible. My backwoods manners and bearing... I'd feel *silly* in those big worlds out there. And, besides, I'm only an Ear——"

"Don't say it. You're my wife, that's all. If anyone asks

what and who you are, you're a native of Earth and a citizen of the Empire. If they want further details, you're my wife."

"Well, and after you make this address at Trantor to your archaeological society, what next?"

"What next? Well, first we take a year off and see every major world in the Galaxy. We won't skip one, even if we have to get on and off it by mail ship. You'll get yourself an eyeful of the Galaxy and the best honeymoon that government money can buy."

"And then . . ."

"And then it's back to Earth, and we'll volunteer for the labor battalions and spend the next forty years of our lives lugging dirt to replace the radioactive areas."

"Now why are you going to do that?"

"Because"—there was the suspicion of a deep breath at this point in Arvardan's Mind Touch—"I love you and it's what you want, and because I'm a patriotic Earthman and have the honorary naturalization papers to prove it."

"All right . . ."

And at this point the conversation stopped.

But, of course, the Mind Touches did not, and Schwartz, in full satisfaction, and a little embarrassment, backed away. He could wait. Time enough to disturb them when things had settled down further.

He waited in the street, with the cold stars burning down— a whole Galaxy of them, seen and unseen.

And for himself, and the new Earth, and all those millions of planets far beyond, he repeated softly once more that ancient poem that he alone now, of so many quadrillions, knew:

> "Grow old along with me!
> The best is yet to be,
> The last of life, for which the first was made . . ."

whit and wnen you are either a native of Earth and a citizen
of the Empire. If not, you are either outside, you're my wife."
"Well, and when do we make the galleys at Trantor whaor

AFTERWORD

Pebble in the Sky was written in 1949 and first published
in 1950. At that time, only four years after Hiroshima, I
(and the world, generally, I believe) underestimated the
effects on living tissue of low-level radioactivity. I thought
it, at the time, to be a legitimate speculation that Earth
might be generally radioactive and that human life could
nevertheless survive.

I no longer think so, but it is impossible to change the
book since the radioactivity of Earth is essential to the plot.
I can only ask you to continue to suspend your disbelief in
that respect and enjoy the book (assuming you do) on its
own terms.

Isaac Asimov
November, 1982

ABOUT THE AUTHOR

Isaac Asimov was born in the Soviet Union to his great surprise. He moved quickly to correct the situation. When his parents emigrated to the United States, Isaac (three years old at the time) stowed away in their baggage. He has been an American citizen since the age of eight.

Brought up in Brooklyn, and educated in its public schools, he eventually found his way to Columbia University and, over the protests of the school administration, managed to annex a series of degrees in chemistry, up to and including a Ph.D. He then infiltrated Boston University and climbed the academic ladder, ignoring all cries of outrage, until he found himself Professor of Biochemistry.

Meanwhile, at the age of nine, he found the love of his life (in the inanimate sense) when he discovered his first science-fiction magazine. By the time he was eleven, he began to write stories, and at eighteen, he actually worked up the nerve to submit one. It was rejected. After four long months of tribulation and suffering, he sold his first story and, thereafter, he never looked back.

In 1941, when he was twenty-one years old, he wrote the classic short story "Nightfall" and his future was assured. Shortly before that he had begun writing his robot stories, and shortly after that he had begun his Foundation series.

What was left except quantity? At the present time, he has published over 340 books, distributed through every major division of the Dewey system of library classification, and shows no signs of slowing up. He remains as youthful, as lively, and as lovable as ever, and grows more handsome with each year. You can be sure that this is so since he has written this little essay himself and his devotion to absolute objectivity is notorious.

He is married to Janet Jeppson, psychiatrist and writer, has two children by a previous marriage, and lives in New York City.